D0829591

"What do you want, Jessie Dee McVey?"

What did she want? The question whirled nonsensically, darting numbly into little-used corners of her brain and blurring into indistinct, unfamiliar patterns. What did she want? Not this. Not this quiet place and this gentle man....

He lifted her lifeless fingers between his and brought them slowly to his shoulder, to his collar. Warm textured flesh fell against the coolness of her fingertips, his breath was slow and deep as he brought his face to rest against hers. His beard was like silk against her cheek. Her fingers moved against the skin of his neck experimentally, an almost imperceptible caress.

Her breath quavered in her throat as she moved her hand slowly around his neck, beneath the thick curl of silky hair, and cupped it there. What did she want? Maybe no more than this moment....

ABOUT THE AUTHOR

Rebecca Flanders is a native of Georgia who began her writing career at age nine. She completed her first novel by the time she was nineteen and sold her first book in 1979. Rebecca's hobbies are oil- and waterpainting and both composing and listening to music.

Books by Rebecca Flanders

HARLEQUIN AMERICAN ROMANCES
  6-A MATTER OF TRUST
24-BEST OF FRIENDS
41-SUDDENLY LOVE
51-GILDED HEART

HARLEQUIN PRESENTS
632-MORNING SONG
666-FALKONE'S PROMISE

These books may be available at your local bookseller.

For a free catalog listing all titles currently available, send your name and address to:

Harlequin Reader Service
P.O. Box 52040, Phoenix, AZ 85072-2040
Canadian address: Stratford, Ontario N5A 6W2

Gilded Heart

REBECCA FLANDERS

Harlequin Books

TORONTO • NEW YORK • LONDON
AMSTERDAM • PARIS • SYDNEY • HAMBURG
STOCKHOLM • ATHENS • TOKYO • MILAN

Published April 1984

ISBN 0-373-16051-8

Copyright © 1984 by Rebecca Flanders. All rights reserved.
Philippine copyright 1984. Australian copyright 1984.
Except for use in any review, the reproduction or utilization of
this work in whole or in part in any form by any electronic,
mechanical or other means, now known or hereafter invented,
including xerography, photocopying and recording, or in any
information storage or retrieval system, is forbidden without
the permission of the publisher, Harlequin Enterprises Limited,
225 Duncan Mill Road, Don Mills, Ontario, Canada M3B 3K9.

All the characters in this book have no existence outside the
imagination of the author and have no relation whatsoever to
anyone bearing the same name or names. They are not even
distantly inspired by any individual known or unknown to the
author, and all the incidents are pure invention.

The Harlequin trademarks, consisting of the words
HARLEQUIN AMERICAN ROMANCE, HARLEQUIN
AMERICAN ROMANCES, and the portrayal of a Harlequin,
are trademarks of Harlequin Enterprises Limited; the portrayal
of a Harlequin is registered in the United States Patent and
Trademark Office and in the Canada Trade Marks Office.

Printed in U.S.A.

WINTER 1979

Chapter One

The man who came to repair Jessie McVey's telephone had long hair, a beard, and brown eyes. He wore an often-washed and well-worn flannel shirt in an orange and brown plaid, and a leather belt laden with tools hugged the top of low-slung, ill-fitting faded jeans. His hair was dark, and the cut—or rather lack of one—was shaggy, curling upward toward the back and waving in at the collarbone, feathering forward near the temples and cheeks. The beard was full but not as long as his hair. In the driveway behind him the yellow parking lights of the official telephone company service truck barely pierced the drizzly fog of the dull gray day. It took Jessie's swiftly observant artistic eye about five seconds to catalog these impressions, and then she burst into irate speech before he could say a word.

"Well, it's about damn time!" The misty chill of a February morning curled about her ankles through the scant protection of the screen door, but Jessie hardly felt it. The room temperature was comfortably maintained by an oil-burning space heater, and Jessie was steaming. "Five days—*five days* ago I reported my telephone was out of order. But let me be five days late paying my bill, and you'll disconnect my service without blinking an eye. Twice a day, every day, I've called from the pay phone three miles down the road and been assured someone would be out before five o'clock. Five days I've waited faithfully for someone to come—five days I've stayed home from work...."

That was not strictly true. Two of those days had been a weekend, two of them she had spent fighting off the flu, and today was the first day she had really felt like getting up. But what idea could the omniscient Bell Telephone System have of how helpless it felt to be sick and alone and totally cut off from civilization by the malfunction of one small black plastic box? What did they care? The very thought started her seething all over again. "And do you know what excuse I finally got? Can you just guess? They *misplaced* the work order! This, from the largest communications operation in the world! You employ millions of people and handle billions of calls a day, you can press a button and talk to a satellite hundreds of miles above the earth, but you can't find one lousy work order? For this you just got a three million dollar rate hike? What are you staring at?"

He still stood at the door, his lips parted, his breath indrawn for his first official greeting, and his eyes had taken on an unmistakable twinkle as he politely endured her tirade. He said simply, "Good morning, ma'am, I'm with Southern Bell, and I believe you're having trouble with your telephone?"

She glared at him, her cheeks reddening with the sudden realization of the childishness of her outburst, and she unlocked the screen with an abrupt motion. "Come in," she mumbled.

He wiped his feet on the mat before entering, then proceeded to check the work order in a very business-like way. "One black rotary dial and a bedroom extension?"

"That's right," she said ungraciously, and started to lead the way.

But he needed no guidance. He found the plain, utilitarian telephone on the corner table that divided the small living room from the kitchen, turned it over, checked the wiring, then proceeded without invitation down the short hallway that led to the bedroom. Jessie started to follow him, then scowled and shrugged and turned back to the kitchen, where she took out the rest of her frustration on a mound of bread dough she had been kneading.

She knew she should be ashamed of herself. She was usually a very mild-tempered person and was not the type to take out her frustration on sales clerks or secretaries or the man at the refund desk in a department store. If she received an undercooked meal in a restaurant she would eat it rather than send it back and still leave a generous tip. But her private war with Southern Bell was of long-standing duration, beginning when she had had to wait three weeks for installation of service and to pay a seventy-five dollar deposit despite the fact that she had an excellent credit rating, moving on to a misprint in the telephone directory that had resulted in her receiving after-midnight calls from drunks trying to reach Bob's Liquor Store, and culminating in her withholding payment of her bill in protest. This noble attempt to fight city hall had resulted in disconnection of her service and a demand that she pay another fifty dollar deposit before service would be reestablished. After that Jessie was convinced that she had become number one on the telephone company's hit list. Mysterious long-distance charges began to appear on her bill and trying to get them removed was like pulling teeth. Her telephone would ring at all hours of the day and night with no one on the other end. She got more than her share of wrong numbers. About once every three months she would pick up the receiver and hear nothing but static, and the most recent episode was typical of the struggle she had to put forth to obtain repair service. It was a vendetta, pure and simple. After all, next to the IRS, the Bell Telephone System was the most powerful corporation in the United States, and they had their ways.

The repairman returned from the bedroom and set to work at the telephone in the living room. Jessie folded the bread dough and gave it one more enthusiastic punch, glancing at him. She grudgingly had to admit some sort of apology was due. "I'm sorry I yelled at you before," she mumbled, not looking at him. "I know it's not your fault and you're not paid to deal with irate customers, but I just want to go on record as saying that I consider this a perfect example of gross inefficiency and bureaucratic waste—"

"You might be interested," he interrupted cheerfully, "in a special we're running this month. For just three dollars and forty cents a month, plus a nominal installation fee, you can change to touch-tone service in color-coordinated wall or desk princess units, and for an additional one-fifty a month you can add a third extension. I think you'll find the package price much more economical than what you're paying now."

She stared at him. Just as she had always suspected, employees of Southern Bell were brainwashed with a stock vocabulary consisting of fifty phrases or less. Among the most popular were, "Your number please" and "I'm sorry for the inconvenience, ma'am, we'll

have someone out by five o'clock this afternoon."
Even repairmen, with their nonregulation haircuts and
scrap-bag uniforms, were apparently not immune to
the telephone company's computerized version of customer relations. "A third extension?" she demanded
impatiently. "I have enough trouble with the two I've
got! Where would I put another one? In the bathroom?"

There was a very uncomputerized twinkle in his eye,
but he kept his face sober. "You'd be surprised how
many people enjoy the convenience of a bathroom extension," he assured her. But then, after a moment of
thoughtfulness, he decided, "Forget the extension.
Waste of money. What you really need is touch-tone
dialing. It's the way of the future," he explained to her.
"Within ten years—twenty at the outside—you won't
be able to function without it. The push-buttons on
your phone will be the console of your own personal
computer. You'll use it to hook into your television set
for video communication and direct-line buying. You'll
be able to punch out a code and pay all your bills, shop
for groceries, make bank deposits, file your tax return...even leave pre-recorded coded messages when
you're away from home. You really can't afford to be
without it. Fortunately, I have a couple in the truck—
the dark blue would look good in here, and forest green
for the bedroom."

Jessie watched him go in amazement. She had no
intention of ordering new telephones—the last thing
she wanted to do was give Southern Bell more of her
money. But when he returned with the two slimline
models, her sales resistance had magically melted
away. She could not help but admire his technique, for
she would be looking at those telephones for months

and wondering whatever had possessed her to buy them.

He had the most beautiful hands Jessie had ever seen on a man, and watching him work fascinated her. The sound of his voice startled her into a guilty blush, and she turned away quickly as he said, "Your wiring is shot. It's no wonder you've had so much trouble."

"Well, for goodness' sake," she exclaimed in exasperation, "why didn't anyone ever fix it before?"

"Electricity is a fascinating thing," he continued, his attention focused on the delicate maneuvers he was making with small tools at the wall connection. Jessie broke off a piece of the sweet dough and popped it into her mouth before turning the mound into a warm bowl to rise. "It exists in a static state all around us but only makes itself known under a very narrow set of carefully-timed conditions. It's powerful enough to keep an object weighing six sextillion tons rotating in an almost invariable pattern about the sun, but can be filtered down to perform such a delicate task as ringing a door bell or activating an electric light filament. It can turn light patterns through a cathode tube into something the human mind perceives as television pictures or magnify sound impulses into something the brain perceives as a human voice over the telephone. Of course you realize you don't really see television pictures or hear telephone communications; it's all just a trick the mind plays to make the impossible more palatable."

She watched him curiously as she mixed sugar and cinnamon for the sweet rolls she intended to make with the bread dough. This did not sound like any of the telephone company's prepackaged speeches she was used to. She wondered if he was doing it deliberately to catch her off-guard.

"By the same token," he continued without looking up, "electrical activity—sun spots—ninety-three million miles away can interrupt television and radio signals and even cause geological and meteorological changes on earth. Even our own bodies are walking electromagnets, which can't help but make one wonder about the truth behind the theory of personal charisma and sexual chemistry. After all, each of us is sending out and assimilating thousands of electrical impulses every minute of every day, and the nervous system is essentially no more than an electrical conductor with the brain as its center. Is it unreasonable to assume that instant subconscious impressions—love at first sight, inexplicable animosities, and even immediate sexual attraction—are nothing more than the interaction of one person's electrical impulses with another's?"

Jessie could not contain her curiosity another moment. "You sound like a physics professor," she suggested, wondering what in the world a man like this was doing working for the telephone company. He didn't fit into any mold she had ever encountered.

He grinned, and for one brief moment she knew all about electrical impulses and sexual chemistry. For one brief moment he was a living advertisement for his own theories, and then she quickly repressed the instinctive reaction she felt as absurd. "College dropout," he informed her.

"Oh?" She turned away, nervously licking a bit of cinnamon-sugar mixture from her index finger. It was stupid. There was no such thing as sexual chemistry, and even if there was, she certainly wouldn't feel it for him. There was nothing sexy about him at all. "What did you major in? While you were there, I mean?"

"Fast cars and loose women," he replied immediately. "I have to check out the wiring under the house. Don't lock me out."

Jessie found herself struggling with a smile as she watched him go. Interesting character. He could go a long way toward restoring her faith in the impersonal computerized conglomerate of red tape that was the telephone company.

By the time he returned she had spread the bread dough with butter and cinnamon-sugar and put it away for its second rising, made herself a snack of peanut-butter crackers, and eaten a jelly and cream-cheese sandwich on rye bread. Two days of near fasting had left her craving some very strange things, and Jessie always ate when she was nervous. Though she could not consciously admit being anxious now, she did find herself repeatedly listening for signs of his return and peeking out the doors and windows at regular intervals. It was just that she was glad for the distraction on this dreary winter day after being confined indoors, and he was...interesting.

She was finishing off a Snickers bar and boiling water for tea when he came back in, announcing, "That should do it." Drops of moisture clung to his satiny black hair and glistened on his beard, and his face was chapped with cold. He went directly to the telephone and dialed a number, then spoke into it cheerfully. "Hey, sweetheart, I'm all done here.... Nope, I don't want to hear it. I'm on lunch break. I'll check in with you later."

Jessie hesitated for just a moment as she poured the boiling water over the tea mixture in her cup. He looked so cold. And he *had* said he was on lunch break. She offered, "Would you like some Russian tea? It's very good."

He did not hesitate at all. "Sounds great. Maybe it will thaw me out."

Now, that was really stupid, she scolded herself as she took out another cup. Since when did you start fraternizing with repairmen? You've practically invited him to spend his lunch break with you, and what will you talk about? First thing you know he'll be thinking you're coming on to him, if he doesn't already. Stupid. Really stupid.

She placed the two cups on the kitchen table with a little smile, and he sat across from her, his eyes assessing her in a friendly, mildly interested way as he warmed his hands about the cup. She couldn't think of a single thing to say. Then he saved her the trouble. "So, Jessie," he inquired pleasantly, "how long have you been divorced?"

Of all the things in the world she might have been prepared for, this was not one of them. She stared at him in astonishment, a strange sensation of curiosity mixed with something like déjà vu creeping over her, and underlying it all was a sharp edge of uneasy suspicion. "How did you know my first name?" she demanded. Alarm quickened. "How did you know I was divorced?"

He grinned, and she was too disturbed to notice the twinkle in his eye that belied any malicious intent. "Why darlin'," he drawled in what seemed to her a very menacing tone, "didn't you know that there are no secrets from the most powerful communications network in the world? All we have to do is punch a few buttons on a computer, and we can know everything about you from your credit rating to the day you lost your virginity—and to whom. Big Brother is truly watching."

Her cup rattled in the saucer as she gulped down a

burning sip of tea. That was definitely a nonregulation-type comment. Alarm coiled within her as an awful suspicion grew. He was either playing very cleverly on her telephone-company paranoia, or... or she had invited some sort of weird pervert into her home. Come to think of it, everything he had said since entering her house—or almost everything—had had very definite sexual undertones, and the way he looked at her.... She clenched her hands in her lap and demanded somewhat hoarsely, "Let me see some identification."

He seemed to be vastly amused by her discomfiture, and she got the fleeting impression that he had read every thought she had had since he came in. His eyes twinkled merrily as he reached into his pocket and politely presented her with a laminated I.D. card.

She took it cautiously between thumb and forefinger, darting her wary gaze from the photo on the card to him and back again. It was him all right. Keith Michaelson, a certified employee of Southern Bell. Age twenty-eight, hair black, eyes brown, six feet one inch tall, one hundred sixty-five pounds. She glanced at him again suspiciously. What did that prove? That if he raped her she could complain to Southern Bell?

She continued to hold on to the card as though it were her last defense against a fate worse than death, and he explained patiently, "The work order read 'Mrs. Jessie McVey,' but your telephone is listed under 'J. D. McVey'... a pretty common practice of women living alone. Also, you're not wearing a wedding ring, and there are no signs of male occupancy in the house, and your bed—" again that unnerving little twinkle in his eye "—which you forgot to make, by the way, is only rumpled on one side. Through some very high-caliber processes of deductive reasoning, I therefore concluded that you were once married but are no longer. No help needed from Big Brother this time.''

It all made perfect sense. She was overreacting again, flinging up those automatic defenses that were always at the ready whenever a man came into sight.... He was probably just a nice fellow in search of nothing more than tea and conversation to break up the boredom of the day. Nevertheless, she pointed out with a trace of suspicion in her voice, ''I could have been a widow.''

He shook his head firmly and sipped from the cup. ''Widows keep pictures of the dear departed around.''

She returned the card to him, trying to disguise the rather reluctant admiration in her eyes. ''Quite a detective, aren't you?''

''I missed my calling, all right.'' He tucked the card back into his pocket and added, ''This tea is very good. What's in it?''

''Orange breakfast drink, lemonade mix, cinnamon, and cloves,'' she replied, pleased to have the conversation on neutral ground. But her relief was a little premature.

''What happened?'' he inquired, still fixing her with that lively, interested gaze. What nice eyes he had. They looked as though they had never encountered a secret or a hardship and were at any given moment only a blink away from dancing with laughter. ''To your marriage, I mean.''

She lowered her eyes quickly and found herself looking instead at his hands. She made herself look into the steaming brown contents of her cup and countered pleasantly, ''How long have you been working for the telephone company?''

His easy chuckle acknowledged her desire for privacy

but did not consent to it. "All right then, we'll try something easier. What does the D in J.D. stand for?"

She could not prevent a dimpling smile as she glanced back at him. "I'm not going to tell you that, either." This was really ridiculous. Just because a man had beautiful hands and friendly eyes was no justification for the sudden sense of excitement she felt at sitting across the table from him over a cup of tea. She wasn't interested, and even if she was, it certainly wouldn't be in a man with shoulder-length hair and a beard. It had just been too long since she had allowed herself the luxury of male companionship, that was all. She was getting soft in her old age and, she realized for the very first time, dangerously vulnerable.

And that, of course, was no explanation at all for the sudden compulsion she felt to turn the tables on him by inquiring, "Are you married?"

She could have bitten her tongue the minute the words were out. What did she care whether he was married or not? Painful embarrassment was in her eyes as they grazed quickly across his twinkling ones, and she took a hasty sip of tea as he replied, "You answer mine first."

"Dee," she said unaccountably. Why was she encouraging him when it would really be better if he just finished his tea and left? She didn't have time to sit here flirting with a perfect stranger, and she simply wasn't interested.... "Jessie Dee. That's all there is."

He nodded, and his eyes crinkled at the corners as he sipped again from his cup. "I'm not married." And then, thankfully, the phone rang.

It had been so long since Jessie had heard that sound that she did not react to it immediately. Or maybe it had something to do with the unaccustomed male pres-

ence crowding her small table and her intense awareness of the fact, or perhaps it was the sudden fascination she had discovered for the way his long forefinger
absently caressed the rim of his cup, just where his lips
had touched. He, however, seemed to be operating
under no such handicap, and in the middle of the second ring he reached his long arm over to the telephone
stand and answered it.

"It's for you," he informed her mildly, and there
was an amused little gleam in his eye that made her
blush. She had the feeling he knew exactly what effect
his presence was having on her, and that irritated her.

Jessie took the receiver from him impatiently as she
stood. "Who did you think it was for?" she retorted,
and walked the extension of the cord into the living
area for privacy.

It was Sammy, one of her two employers, and he
demanded, "Who the hell was that?" But he wasn't
interested in an answer. "It's about damn time you got
your phone fixed; I've been calling you all morning.
Listen, I'm going crazy down here; do you think you
could put in a couple of hours this afternoon? I've got a
rush order for two hundred shirts, and if I don't get the
design laid in by tonight, I'll never make it."

"What is it?" she inquired.

"Nothing fancy, just graphic lettering and a line
sketch. It's for the Boar's Tavern promotion."

"Hey, congratulations!" Sammy had been after that
account for weeks. "And just to show you how much
confidence I had in you, I've got the sketches all ready.
I'll bring them down this afternoon and even help you
set up, how's that?"

She could almost see his relieved grin over the telephone. "Hey, I love you, you know that?"

"You just want my body," she teased back, and he laughed. Sammy was twenty years old and at one time he might have fancied himself in love with her. Basically he was too mature to confuse an adolescent crush with the real thing—but not too mature to deny himself the ego boost of being seen in the company of an older woman. They had developed a friendly, easy-going relationship during the year Jessie had been supplying him with designs for his screen-printed T-shirt business, and it was the only kind of man-woman relationship Jessie was interested in—a safe one.

"I have to stop by the store first," she added, glancing at the sunflower clock over the stove, "and see how things have been going down there. I've been out for two days, you know."

"Yeah, I know." There was belated concern in his voice. "Are you feeling better?"

"As if you cared," she returned dryly. "I'll see you about three, okay?"

"Thanks, Jess. You're really terrific."

"I know, I know, Get back to work; time is money."

"Sounds like a great slogan for a T-shirt. Bye, babe."

When she turned away from the telephone she was relieved to notice that her guest had not been eavesdropping on her conversation—but she was also a little apprehensive, because he had wandered over to the small desk and work area opposite the kitchen table and was examining the corkboard wall that displayed her sketches. Jessie's cartoons were her one indulgence, her secret pride, her treasured children. She was always a little nervous when they were subjected to outside scrutiny. She watched the changing expressions on his face with mounting tension as he examined each of the dozens of political drawings that plastered her wall with separate and careful assessment. Some made him smile, some made him thoughtful, some produced an ironic quirk of the brow that was exactly the reaction she had wanted to provoke.

"These are very good," he said at last, turning back to her. "Do you do this professionally?"

She felt an overwhelming sense of pride and relief at the compliment of a stranger who was, after all, hardly qualified to judge. But a flush of pleasure warmed her cheeks as she gathered up the cups and took them to the sink. "No. It's just a hobby."

He looked back at the corkboard thoughtfully, and then at her. "You're too good for that, and I think you know it. Why don't you do it professionally?"

She shrugged, afraid to look at him lest he see how pleased she was. He had unknowingly touched on a very secret daydream, one that she had never shared with anyone, and she felt her ego blossom under his gentle stroking in the same way a flower unfolds to the morning sun. But she only answered casually, "There are approximately seven hundred and fifty markets for political cartoonists, and almost three times that many aspiring cartoonists. In other words, artistic satisfaction may help you sleep better at night, but it doesn't pay the rent."

"Aha." There was a teasing light in his eye. "Another artist bites the dust beneath the bonds of the free enterprise system."

She pretended to consider this. "If you mean I had rather be rich than famous, I suppose you're right. Rich *and* famous would be nice, too, but you can't have it all."

"A slave to the almighty dollar?"

She matched his bantering tone. "Isn't everyone?"

"No qualms about selling out to commercial success when you could be making a meaningful statement on the condition of the world?"

She rinsed the cups and stacked them in the drainer. "It helps if you remember the Sistine Chapel was just a fancy billboard painted with sixteenth century oils. Of course," she added thoughtfully, "if I could be rich and famous *and* make a meaningful statement on the condition of the world, I wouldn't fight it."

He laughed. He had a nice laugh, rich and rolling, and his eyes crinkled like shiny cellophane with the pleasure of it. She got the impression that everything this man did was carried out with the same enthusiasm, the single-minded absorption with present pleasures that is generally found only in the very young and the very old. It was impossible not to respond to laughter like that, and Jessie felt the response begin in the center of her stomach and spread warmly outward.

He glanced again at the display. "You've obviously had some high-class training."

"New York," she admitted. "Commercial art and marketing. I even worked in an ad agency for a little while."

She could not tell whether or not he was impressed, and she was irritated with herself because she thought she was trying to impress him. He inquired only, "So how did you end up in Tennessee?"

She shrugged and preheated the oven for the cinnamon rolls. "How does any woman end up anywhere? My husband got transferred."

She knew immediately she had paved the way for more prying questions, and she was enormously grateful at that moment for the ringing of the telephone. She answered it quickly.

It was Anna, and she sounded awful. "Thank heavens I reached you. I hope you're over whatever you had because now I've got it. You are feeling better, aren't you? I know this is your regular day off, but could you please come down and work out the afternoon? If I don't get out of here within the next ten minutes, you're going to end up carrying me out in a paper bag. Please say you will."

Jessie looked hesitantly at the kitchen clock. "I don't know, Anna, I promised Sammy—"

"Please." The voice was hoarse and desperate. "You can close up at four. I'm dying, Jess."

Jessie's smile revealed sympathy mixed with remembered misery. "Yeah, I know the feeling. I'll be there as soon as I can. Just hang on."

"I'm doing my best."

As soon as she hung up she dialed Sammy's number and explained the situation to him. "I'll drop the sketches off on my way to work and then I'll stop by this evening to help you set up."

"Aw, Jessie, I was counting on you for the whole afternoon...."

"I'm doing the best I can, hon. I've only got two hands."

"Damn it, Jessie, why do you have to work two jobs anyway?"

"Because neither one of you pays me enough to keep my creditors happy," she retorted. "Now stop pouting and get busy holding down the fort until I get there."

"Sometimes I wonder who's the boss around here anyway," Sammy muttered just before he hung up.

"You're a popular lady," commented her guest as she turned away from the telephone.

Jessie made a wry face as she put the cinnamon rolls into the oven. They could bake while she changed her clothes. "Just indispensable," she replied, and quickly wiped her hands on her flour-dusted jeans. She glanced at him a little nervously. "Well...I guess you heard, I have to go. Thanks for fixing my telephone."

He smiled lazily and saluted her with two fingers near his temple. "We aim to please."

Her laugh was a little false as she looked up into his very masculine face. He suddenly seemed to be standing very close. "Yeah, well, that must be a recently acquired motto. Up to this point you sure could have fooled me."

He was looking at her very strangely. There was an absent half-smile on his lips, and his eyes were lazily bright, focused with unnerving absorption on her face...her lips. She brought her hand to her throat as though to prevent his gaze from travelling any farther, and the room was suddenly charged with—yes, electricity. Well, could she blame him? She had done nothing to discourage him, and inviting him to stay and have a cup of tea surely could not have been construed as a neutral gesture by a healthy young man who was probably used to taking his opportunities where he found them. It was just that she was not used to fending off passes, and the prospect made her extremely nervous. Besides, there was an unmistakable masculine vitality about him that seemed to vibrate across the short distance that separated them, and she suddenly realized he was quite good-looking...despite the beard.

It was quite ridiculous, of course, but as he stood there looking her over in a very leisurely, almost predatory way, the tension grew to an almost audible buzz in her ears. She really didn't need this. She was usually so careful not to get herself into awkward situations with men.... And even though Jessie knew the answer before she asked the question, she demanded in a voice made tight with annoyance and nervousness, "What are you staring at?"

"Your lips," he answered casually, and she thought, Oh, no. A pulse jumped in her temples, and she turned quickly away as schoolgirlish color flooded her face. I really don't need this, she thought, but a wave of silly anticipatory excitement flooded her as she heard him take a step behind her.

And the disappointment she felt was just as acute when she at last ventured a glance at him and saw he had only moved toward the door. "If you have any more problems, be sure to give us a call," he said pleasantly. "Have a good day, now."

She stood there for perhaps ten seconds after he was gone, berating herself for her childish and extremely irrational reaction to the entire episode. There was no excuse for it, none at all. She had set herself up for that one, and she was usually so much more careful.... With a scowl and a shrug of pure annoyance she removed the rolls from the oven before hurrying to change her clothes.

As she locked up the house and began the drive through the cold mist she found it was rather easy to put the entire morning out of her mind. She was a busy woman, after all, and she really didn't have time for any of it.

Chapter Two

When Frank had been transferred to Nashville, Jessie had decided to stop working. The friends she left behind in New York had been appalled—sharing a husband's glory was neither smart nor fashionable in the circles in which they had traveled. Perhaps Jessie had convinced herself it would be enough, perhaps her sudden decision to be a devoted executive wife was no more than a last-ditch attempt to save a marriage that she had known after the first week was in big trouble. At any rate, there were no jobs in Nashville to compete with the one she had had in New York. When she found herself an abandoned wife little more than a year after the move, she had taken the first job that came along—sales clerk in a small boutique called Designs on You. She had been inundated with calls from friends in New York begging her to come back; even her old boss had made it clear he would welcome her back to the firm at any time. She had stayed in Nashville, and after a time felt confident enough with Anna to suggest a few changes in advertising policy. She drew up compelling sketches for inexpensive circulars and designed small newspaper ads, and profits increased. She re-evaluated their store-front and point-of-sale advertising methods and even began to experiment with radio. Anna was thrilled, and the past two years had shown an almost fifty per cent increase in sales. It had been a way for Jessie to get her feet wet without really committing herself.

Jessie put in long hours at the boutique, for she and Anna divided managerial and sales duties, and after the shop closed Jessie often stayed to set the ads or work on new layouts for local newspapers and radio. In her spare moments she drew up designs for Sammy. His business, too, had shown a marked increase in profits since the day she had walked into his shop to browse and ended up tossing off a few ideas for original T-shirt designs. Sammy had once told her she had the Midas touch, and that made her smile rather dryly. There had been a time when she had been convinced of that herself, when her fiercest ambition had been to make it to the top at the fastest rate possible, when she had pictured herself living on caviar and Champagne forever after. Deep down Jessie knew she still had a hunger for all she'd left behind, but it was something she tried not to think about.

It was pitch dark when Jessie got home that evening, rainy, cold, and windy. She shivered as she turned on the lamps and turned up the thermostat; then she hung her wet coat on the rack by the door and snatched up a cinnamon roll before going to change into dry clothes. The unmade bed stared at her reproachfully, and she felt a tingle of color warm her cold cheeks as she remembered the deductive reasoning employed by the repairman this afternoon. Automatically she started to toss the coverlet over the rumpled bedclothes, then scowled at her own foolishness and went to run a steamy bath.

Jessie's house was thirty years old, and it was really more of a bungalow than a house. There was one bedroom and one old-fashioned bath, a square living room with mismatched windows, and a country kitchen. The plumbing was temperamental and the insulation nonexistent; in heavy storms the roof leaked, and in the summer she fought a constant battle against the insects who thought the cracks and crevices beneath her doors and windows were a standing invitation to a free meal. After the divorce it had been all she could afford, and she'd been lucky to find it. Over the years she had turned an architect's nightmare into a charming home with casual country furnishings—most of them bought at auctions or rescued from friends' attics—original artwork, handmade cushions, and afghans and hooked rugs. The walls were decorated with lengths of fabric in interesting prints that had cost twelve cents a yard at a mill warehouse and with coordinating paint in bold colors, rather than wallpaper. It wasn't a Park Avenue penthouse, but all in all Jessie was satisfied with her surroundings.

Tingling from the hot bath and a brisk drying with a coarse towel, Jessie rubbed the steam off the bathroom mirror and grimaced at her reflection. As usual she looked a mess. Her face was perfectly square, forehead broad and chin stubborn, her eyes an uncompromising green. Her figure was good enough for a size ten dress, but soft, not firm. Her thighs were a little heavy. Her hair was her worst feature. It was a nondescript beige color with natural streaks of silver-blond that some people found interesting; to Jessie's eye the streaks were in the wrong places, and they looked more like premature gray than blond. Thick and coarse, her hair was blunt-cut just below the shoulders and completely unmanageable in wet weather. Tonight she simply caught the frizzy mess back with a rubber band, and as she pulled on a warm terry houserobe it occurred to her to wonder what in the world that telephone repairman had seen in her this afternoon...if anything at all.

The storm was really increasing in ferocity, and the rain that was pounding against her kitchen windowpane sounded as though it were beginning to turn to ice. She shivered elaborately as she drew the kitchen curtains over the black night and turned to put on a pot of coffee.

She was opening a can of tuna when an indistinct noise at the back door caught her attention. She listened, and what began as a faint whining or mewing between onslaughts of winter wind gradually grew more demanding until it reached the proportions of a howl—the definite sounds of an animal in distress.

She opened the door a crack against a blast of cold wind and rain and looked down cautiously. At her feet was one of the most pitiful sights she had ever seen. Hardly bigger than a good-sized domestic rat, the kitten could have been described as no more than a scrap of fur had not every scrap of fur he possessed been plastered to his violently shivering body. Jessie's eyes widened in amused incredulity as she exclaimed, "Was that *you* making all that noise?" Then her amusement quickly changed to despair as the next sound the animal uttered came out as no more than a shaky croak, and she looked down at it with dry resignation. "Well," she said, "you sure knew which house to pick, didn't you?" A cat. That was all she needed. "Good old Jessie with the heart of gold, never known to turn away a stranded traveler, always ready to make room for one more...." With a sigh she bent to scoop up the shivering handful of wet fur. "Well, you may as well come in. No sense in both of us catching pneumonia."

She turned back inside, and then from out of the dark a voice said, "Do you have room for one more stray?"

Jessie gasped. He was wearing a black slicker, and with the icy rain glistening in drops on his dark hair and beard he looked very much like a specter rising up out of the night—despite the pleasant smile on his face and the soft brown eyes that were illuminated by her kitchen light. For a long time she could only stare, and when at last she found her voice it sounded strange, almost choked. "Mister..." She stumbled over the name, although she knew it as well as she did her own. "Michaelson."

"Ms McVey," he returned politely.

The kitten dug its tiny claws into her shoulder, seeking more warmth, and she shifted its weight as she shivered in the draft of the door. "What—what are you doing here?"

"Freezing," he answered, and she recovered herself.

"Oh! Well, of course..." She pushed the door open wider. "Come in. I just wasn't expecting..." Once again she got a firm grip on herself and, trying not to sound rude, inquired, "What...do you want?"

His grin was completely disarming. "We're not allowed to proposition customers while on duty." He closed the door behind him, adding, "Furthermore, I should think I would be at least as welcome as your other little guest there, because unless he came crawling to the door dragging a bottle of milk, I at least—" with a flourish, he produced a bottle of wine and set it on the counter "—brought my own refreshments."

Jessie giggled in spite of herself. Her other little

guest was now crawling up her shoulder and nuzzling its cold, wet body behind her ear, and she plucked him off, saying, "Well, I think you're big enough to take care of yourself, but this little fellow seems to need some immediate attention. Excuse me a minute."

She took a towel from the mini-dryer in the corner and began to rub down the cat while he removed his raincoat and hung it on the rack beside hers. He asked for a corkscrew, and she directed him to a drawer. By the time she had placed the open can of tuna on the floor and watched her miniscule visitor dive into it as though it were his last meal, he was pouring the wine. For a moment she stood there watching him, and a wave of tingling nervousness brought heat to her face and a patch of dampness to the back of her knees. This she had certainly not expected. What was he doing here? She did not want him here. Her eyes fell upon those beautifully shaped artistic hands, one steadying the glass as the other poured the crystal liquid, and she was acutely aware of her floor-length terry housecoat with its worn cuffs and raveling sash—and of the fact that she was absolutely naked underneath.

"Liebfraumilch," Keith informed her with a smile as he handed her a glass. "Have you ever had it?"

"No, I haven't." Jessie returned his smile a little uncertainly as she tasted the light, musty-scented liquid. She did like his smile. When he smiled something about his eyes reminded her of a child—sweet, unaffected, capable of giving and receiving utter frankness in the simplicity of innocence. "It's very good."

His hand brushed across her shoulder lightly, guiding her to the living room, and she cast about frantically in her mind for something to say while she wondered how she had gotten herself into this. Once again he saved her the trouble. "Do you mind," he inquired, "if we get something out of the way first?"

Jessie looked up at him with a smile and a question on her lips just as he stepped gracefully in front of her, and then he was kissing her. Like a ray of sunshine on a spring morning his lips fell upon hers, amazingly soft, electrically warm. It was not a long kiss nor particularly passionate, as each of them still held a glass of wine in one hand, but the stinging flare of awareness that surged through her caught her off-guard. It was like a sudden intravenous injection of a potent drug; it flamed through her veins and weakened her limbs, and even her skin seemed to come alive, every inch of it tingling and vibrating in an effort to absorb the unexpected onslaught of sensations. It was surely an overreaction to a kiss that was, by force of circumstances, not very intimate, but it was just that it was so unexpected... it was just that it had been so long since...

Keith lifted his face, and Jessie found herself staring into a pair of eyes that looked like melted chocolate. There was soft appreciation in those eyes, a sort of gentle wonder, the frank delight of one who has just experienced an unexpected pleasure and has no qualms about showing it. There was also a definite intent to prolong that pleasure.

Abruptly she said, "Excuse me, please." She deposited her glass on the counter and made her way with as much dignity as possible to her bedroom.

Once there she leaned against the closed door, and then, on second thought, she locked it. Her heart was pounding and her cheeks were hot. She thought it was from anger. What had gotten into her? She was acting like it was the first time she had been kissed.

It was like the first time. It was better than the first time.

And anyway, what kind of line was that—"Do you mind if we get something out of the way first"? What did he mean by that? Get something out of the way.... What was next on his checklist?

Jessie threw off the robe and the cool air was a welcome relief to her overheated body. She stepped into her underwear and jerked a pair of jeans over her hips. She supposed in the sophisticated world of modern man-woman relationships it was perfectly acceptable for a man to expect a kiss within five minutes after walking in the door... it saved time all around, didn't it? It left the rest of the evening free for the real purpose of his visit, a tussle between the sheets. And all for the price of a bottle of wine. Deliberately she pulled an unattractive gray sweat shirt over her head and even donned a pair of heavy wool socks. With every part of her now decently covered, she started to unbind and brush her hair, but instinct rebelled. She stared at her reflection in the mirror, the mutinous set of her jaw, the overly bright emerald eyes, the pinkish tint to her complexion that lingered like recent exposure to a hot oven. The only thing that disturbed her was that she was no longer certain the color was due to anger.

Jessie still felt a certain amount of righteous indignation. She had done nothing to give him the impression that she would welcome his advances, that he could just stroll into her house and start leading her toward the bedroom. All she had done was be polite to a nameless repairman, and he had definitely taken advantage of the situation. She was not the type of girl who picked up any stranger who happened to come to her door—insurance salesmen, plumbers, the Fuller

Brush man.... This was beginning to sound like something out of a B-rated movie. The best thing to do was march right out there and give him a piece of her mind, then escort him firmly to the door.

The only thing was... she had enjoyed it. Enjoyed it? She had practically *melted*. Her hormones must be a wreck. She had not been with a man in two years, and she hadn't missed it. She had not needed it. There was no room for any of that in her life, and she simply wasn't interested. Then why did one very harmless little kiss turn her into some sort of mindless center of sexual response and leave her entire body nothing more than a quivering jumble of nerves even now? There must be a medical explanation, she thought.

What was it he had said about electricity?

Jessie smoothed slightly damp palms on her jeans and went back out into the living room, firm in her resolve. With each step her determination waned. A person who has a hard time sending back an inedible meal is not going to find it easy to order a man who has just kissed her out into the cold night. Then again, she hadn't seemed to have too much trouble telling him off this morning. She hadn't worried about hurting anyone's feelings *then*. What she really needed was more backbone.

Jessie paused at the entrance to the living room, looking at him. He was wearing a black turtleneck sweater and jeans that were not nearly as faded or worn as the ones he had worn this morning. In the subdued light of the single lamp, with his hair waving below his collar and shadowing his face, he looked like a romantic hero from one of those seventeenth-century swashbuckling novels. He was half-turned from her, examining her record collection, and he did not notice her immediately. She wondered unaccountably what kind of music he liked, and then dismissed the thought quickly. This was really ridiculous. She cleared her throat, grappling again for determination and common sense, and he looked up.

Nothing in his expression revealed any recollection whatsoever of their last encounter. He did not comment on her change of clothes or acknowledge with his eyes that he even recognized it. He simply said, lifting his wineglass a little to indicate his surroundings, "You have a really nice house, Jessie." There was something about the way he said that, or perhaps something about his expression when he said it, that let her know instinctively this was no idle compliment. "I can see your touch in every inch of it."

Firm resolve melted like half-chilled gelatin in a pan of warm water. He had the most unusual way of speaking, expressing his thoughts with carefully chosen words and succinct phrases. And when he looked as he did now, thoughtful and assessive, his careful gaze drinking in every detail of a new experience, no emotion was hidden by his face. One got the impression that this was a man incapable of telling a lie or issuing a false platitude, and that he would not recognize one if he saw it.

Jessie's murmured "Thank you" sounded woefully inadequate, and then Keith smiled at her and she almost forgot why she had returned. Almost. He gestured her toward the sofa, where he had placed her glass of wine on the coffee table. "Finish your wine," he invited.

She was suddenly disoriented. Keith was acting as though he were the host and she the nervous guest. He was perfectly at ease and at home, and she was not used to masterful men. She was not used to any kind of men. She must have hesitated for a moment, but before she knew it she was sinking down onto the chintz-covered sofa and taking up her wineglass. After all, what harm could it do to share a glass of wine and a few minutes' conversation with a man? Maybe it was about time she started easing back into the social stream.

When he sat down beside her, she knew what harm it could do. She took a quick sip of the refreshing wine and glanced at him out of the corner of her eye. He was sitting much too close, his elbow crooked along the back of the couch very near her shoulder, one leg bent at a comfortable angle upon the cushions as he sat half-turned toward her. The tight-fitting black sweater outlined the firm, lean muscles of his arms and hugged his chest. He was not a broadly built man—in fact, he was just this side of skinny—but what there was of him was not wasted. It was all sculpted into one long, lean form of unmistakable masculinity, and it made her very nervous.

Keith did not say anything, but Jessie could feel his eyes upon her. She could see his graceful hand resting so near her shoulder, and she leaned forward abruptly, replacing her glass on the table and fumbling for a pack of cigarettes she had, thankfully, left there this morning. She was surprised to see that delicate, long-fingered hand fall lightly over hers. "Don't do that," he requested gently.

"Oh—I'm sorry." She straightened up slowly. What was she apologizing for? It was her house, and she could smoke if she wanted to. "Does cigarette smoke bother you?"

"Yes," he admitted. "It spoils the taste of your mouth."

Jessie was prepared for it that time. She'd had plenty of fair warning and she could have done something about it if she'd wanted to. But she seemed to be paralyzed as he set his glass deliberately beside hers and straightened up to bring that slender, beautifully formed hand to cup her cheek. His fingers were splayed from her temple to the curve of her skull, and his thumb caressed her jawline. The other hand slid around her and rested lightly against her hip as he shifted his weight so that their thighs touched. Good Lord, Jessie thought somewhat incoherently, whatever happened to the art of courtship? Go directly to bed, do not pass go.... This man was the utter limit. She had gotten herself into a real mess this time, and she knew she had to do something to get out, but all she could do was sit there and look into those soft brown eyes and let her heart leap to a crazy two-four time in the back of her mouth.

Just at the last minute, just as his warm breath fanned across her face, Jessie broke away, ducking under his arm and leaning forward to scoop up a handful of candy from the dish on the table. "Do you mind telling me," she demanded, and was surprised to find her voice was a little breathless, "exactly what you think you're doing?" Her glare was severe, but the color in her cheeks was not from anger. She was trying to stay calm, and she really did not want to make a scene, so rather than jumping to her feet and demanding that he leave her house, she scooted over to the corner of the sofa and faced him with what she hoped was a cool conversational demeanor. She could be just as sophisticated as the next person, given half a chance.

He settled back, his long arm resting along the back of the sofa, absolutely unruffled. He was smiling pleasantly. "I'm trying to let you know that I find you attractive and that I would like to get to know you better."

"Oh!" It came out like a bark of laughter. She popped a candy into her mouth and swallowed without tasting it, fixing him with a cynically amused gaze. "And of course the quickest way to get to know a woman is to take her to bed, right?"

"In a word, yes." His eyes were twinkling. He was enjoying this thoroughly. "However," he pointed out, "I don't recall issuing that particular invitation to you—yet."

"Oh, no?" she replied archly. "Then what do you call that—" she gestured abruptly toward the kitchen area, where their last encounter had taken place "—that *line* you used on me the minute you walked in the door: 'Let's get something out of the way....' Is it your custom to—to *attack* women you don't even know within three minutes after saying *hello*?" Jessie was not succeeding too well in staying calm. Her voice was rising. She ate another piece of candy.

"I did not attack you," Keith replied smoothly, watching her in a very unhurried, almost friendly way. "And I don't use lines; I always say exactly what I mean. You know as well as I do," he pointed out reasonably, "that if I hadn't kissed you when I did we both would have been waiting for it all evening, wondering about it, building it up all out of proportion. It was better to get it out of the way so that we could concentrate on more important things."

She was absolutely flabbergasted. She did not know what to say. She popped another piece of candy into her mouth, growing increasingly uncomfortable under his mild, perfectly confident gaze, but she refused to shift her eyes.

"Also," he added as an afterthought, "people who are attracted to each other should be honest about it. They shouldn't waste time playing games. Getting tangled up in all those archaic courtship rituals is self-destructive, and that's a bad way to begin any relationship." He smiled, and his eyes were drinking in her face inch by inch, layer by layer. Brows, lips, nose, cheeks, all painstakingly, patiently examined one by one. Pretty soon he would be effortlessly stripping away each mask, each defense that protected a vulnerable soul from a harsh world, and the prospect filled Jessie with terror. He said very gently, "I'm attracted to you."

She had to break the gaze. "Well," she replied sharply, "that's just fine. But you might be interested to know I'm *not* attracted to you."

"You're not?" There was a definite trace of amusement in his tone.

"No," Jessie said firmly, and popped a chocolate into her mouth. She glared at him, even though the rise and fall of her chest was still somewhat uneven and the room was definitely too warm for the heavy sweat shirt and wool socks. How dare he make her so uncomfortable in her own home. She hadn't even invited him, he had just assumed.... She would take great pleasure in proving his assumptions wrong and putting this conceited creature with his over-confident come-ons distinctly in his place. "I don't like beards," she told him darkly. "And your hair is much too long. I don't find anything about you attractive at all."

An eyebrow lifted in a manner that seemed to be more amused than insulted. "Nothing at all?"

"Nothing," she responded flatly. As her confidence returned in slow, tentative waves, she felt relaxed enough to sit back. She stiffened when she felt her head rest against the curve of his arm. But before she could move away his finger was absently stroking the side of her neck, just beneath the earlobe and down to the collarbone. She placed another chocolate in her mouth and chewed determinedly, trying to ignore him.

"You don't feel anything?" he insisted. She refused to look at him because she was sure his eyes were laughing. Why should he laugh when she had just done her best to massacre his ego? "No magic?"

All right, if he insisted upon going the sophisticated route. "No," she answered, and ate another chocolate.

"No chemistry? No electrical sparks?"

"None."

"Then why are you sweating?"

The chocolate went gummy in her mouth. She swallowed hard. "Women do not sweat," she informed him, trying not to squirm away from the finger that was now making a lazy pattern within the valley of her collarbone. "They perspire."

"Maybe so," he conceded. "But that—" he traced a light finger across her faintly damp forehead "—is sweat."

Her eyes flew to his amused ones just briefly, and then uncomfortably away. She refused to let him get the better of her. Obviously he had the most experience in this sort of verbal and sexual intimidation and she had apparently become some sort of challenge, but she would not let him win hands down. "Maybe," she replied acidly, forcing another chocolate past her lips, "I'm just warm."

"Oh, I have no doubt that you're very warm." His voice was silky smooth. His hand moved down to caress her shoulder, and he shifted his body slightly so that his lean chest was in her direct line of vision, and when she lifted her eyes she would be forced to look into his. She did so bravely.

"Mr. Michaelson," she said distinctly, "I am much too old to be playing necking games on the living room couch. I outgrew that sort of thing in high school. So, if you don't mind..." She moved her eyes meaningfully to the hand that still caressed her shoulder.

"Ms McVey," he returned patiently, his eyes very close. "We are both too old to be playing any kind of games." She caught her breath as his face leaned forward and she felt the brush of his lips across her nose. Then, unexpectedly, he sat up. "So why don't you return my courtesy and be as honest with me as I've been with you?"

She released a pent-up breath the moment his face was out of her range of vision. His hand still cupped her shoulder and his arm rested against the back of her neck, but now somehow it was more of a friendly gesture than a sexual one, and it was not quite so intimidating. His face was turned toward her and it took all of her concentrated courage to meet his gaze coolly, to refuse to retreat behind blushes and confusion. She had never wanted a cigarette so badly in her life, but she did not quite have the courage to reach for one, so she simply sat there eating candy and trying to ignore the warm sensation that was flooding from his cupped hand down her arm and all the way to the tips of her fingers. So he wanted honesty. She could give him honesty. She said in a moment, quite pleasantly, "This is quite a modus operandi you have for yourself. You have legal entrée to countless women's homes, you have ample opportunity to check them out, then you return later to press your advantage. Is there much profit in that sort of work?"

Far from being insulted, her barb only seemed to amuse him. He responded, "I hope you locked up your silver."

She scowled. "Why did you come back here tonight?"

"Why did you let me in?"

"I thought you wanted to be honest," she challenged. This was not going at all the way she had wanted.

"I will be," he answered blandly, "as soon as you are." And then, with a very slight lift of his shoulders, he apparently decided some sort of compromise was in order. "I am not a burglar," he told her easily, and never once did that slightly amused gaze flicker from hers, "a pervert, or a rapist. I meet lots of people, and I try to get to know as many as I can. Sometimes I meet someone I want to know more than any of the others, and you were one of them. That's why I came here tonight."

"Love at first sight?" she taunted dryly.

"No," he responded seriously, although his lips curved into just the faintest hint of a wry smile. "Lust at first sight, maybe, but love is much too serious a word to be tossed about like that."

"Well," she declared, "at least now we're getting somewhere! You admit then that the only reason you came here tonight was to see whether or not I would—to use a crude term—put out for you. You liked what you saw this afternoon, and you thought you'd try for more."

Keith's eyes were frankly laughing now. That both infuriated her and reassured her. Jessie did not believe she had ever met such a stimulating man. How was it that he could make her feel safe and intimidated at the same time? She knew she should have put an end to this absurd conversation and this uninvited visit long ago, but she really, deep down, did not want to. He was puzzling, fascinating, infuriating, yet—in a strange sort of way—fun.

He said, "You're a very suspicious person, aren't you?" His tone was conversational. "But to answer your question—at least I think it was a question—if you were to ask me to go to bed with you, I wouldn't say no. I'd like very much to make love to you, and I intend to—eventually. But as for this evening, all I really had planned was to ask you to have dinner with me."

"Oh." Deflated, embarrassed, completely at a loss for words, she could not maintain the eye contact. But when she heard his soft chuckle her eyes flew to him immediately, angry and defensive, stiffening for harsh words.

He headed her off with one upraised finger that approached her lips just as they parted for a stinging condemnation. "I'm not laughing at you, darlin'," he assured her. His eyes were very warm. "I'm laughing with you, and it's a compliment. You're so incredibly good at the kind of verbal handball we've been playing, I really couldn't resist teasing you a bit." And the dancing laughter in his eyes faded to a warm glow as he added, "But I prefer we cut through the frills and get back to basics. I like you a lot, Jessie," he said softly, and there was absolutely no doubt in her mind that he was sincere. How could anyone doubt the sincerity of a man with such clear, unaffected purpose in his eyes? Like a child, he had no fear of rejection, no concept of deception; he would lay his heart on the line in this and any other matter without hesitation and expect all others around him to do the same. Openness was instinctual to him, and the very prospect of reciprocation frightened Jessie. "I liked you the minute you opened the door and started screaming at me this afternoon, and I liked you more by the time I left you. I liked the way your eyes glowed when you talked about your art, and I liked the way you rushed to help your friends when they called, and I liked the way you rescued that little bag of bones from the storm. When we kissed it was like morning sunshine, and I guess from that moment on I haven't thought about too much other than making love to you."

It was not an invitation, simply a statement of fact. It made her breath catch and her stomach tighten, and for just one moment—one moment too intense and too ephemeral to capture—she thought about it too. For what seemed like forever she could do nothing but stare at him, letting his warm, comfortable gaze penetrate her and caress her and draw her close, and she thought, very vaguely, *I like you, too . . . a lot.* Then she said abruptly, "I think recreational sex is a highly overrated pastime." And she turned her attention to slipping another piece of candy into her mouth, tasting and chewing slowly with a casual enjoyment she was far from feeling.

He was watching her with an odd, patient scrutiny. She got the impression that he was reading more from each gesture, each word and inflection, than she would ever have wanted him to know, and it made her uneasy even as it fascinated her. It made her feel as though the few hours they had known each other had been years, and though she consciously tried to deny the easy companionship she was beginning to enjoy with him, the feeling was there nonetheless.

He agreed thoughtfully, "That's true. It is, however, a very effective way to express affection and to break down the walls that people like to build between each other."

She lifted eyes to him that were not quite frightened, but a little more than startled. She was not at all certain where that comment was leading. He seemed to be taking what she had meant as a lighthearted remark very seriously; the intensity in his eyes proved it. She tried to inject a note of brightness into her tone, but she stammered as she repeated, "W-walls?"

He took a strand of hair from her unruly ponytail and began to wind it about his finger, answering soberly, "You have a great many of them. Defenses that shelter your inner feelings, protect you from other people— and keep you away from what you want. Honesty and openness break down your wall, so you avoid them as much as possible. That's why you won't be honest about how you really feel about me—about my being here— and you won't admit to yourself what you really want."

Even as he spoke she felt herself retreating, stiffening. Her eyes widened in amazement and insult. What an incredible man! What arrogance, what conceit. . . . But as she looked at him she knew it was not conceit, and if there was arrogance in his nature it was not an intentional affectation, and that knowledge only plunged her further into confusion. Jessie retorted sharply, "I told you, I don't feel anything about you—except perhaps utter antipathy. As for what *I* want—why don't you take your own advice and be honest about what you *really* want?"

He smiled—softly, unexpectedly. His finger stopped its gentle twining motion but remained entangled in her hair. He said easily, "What I want right now is to kiss you. But I think we have more important issues to deal with first."

"Like what?" Her tone was stiff, and so were her shoulders where they met the curve of his arm. She continued eating candy, deliberately, one piece after the other, not tasting it. It became a challenge to continue to meet his eyes.

"Like what it is you're hiding behind your wall," he answered mildly. "Why you're making this so incredibly difficult, why you feel you have to be on guard against me."

"Well, pardon me for making it difficult for you! There's something peculiar about a woman who's on guard against a man who walks into her house with the announced intention of seducing her?"

His smile was so easy and relaxed. It was totally unfair that he should be so comfortable when every nerve in her body was threatening to fray. She had never felt so ill at ease in her life.

"So, we're back to that again," he said. "It really throws you off-balance when someone is up front with you, doesn't it? Well, be forewarned, I'm going to tell you right now where I stand. I'll be perfectly honest with you, and all I ask is that you do the same for me."

She watched him cautiously. The candy had lost its appeal completely and was in fact beginning to make her a little nauseated, but she continued to bring a piece occasionally to her mouth, just to give her hands something to do. And he went on smoothly, "There are too many situations in life, Jessie, where we're forced to put on false faces and build our little defenses against the outside world; personal relationships shouldn't be one of them."

When he said that—*personal relationships*—something quivered deep within her. Did he mean to imply he wanted some kind of relationship with her? It had been so long since any man had wanted a relationship with her, it had been so long since she had even considered it . . . and she must be crazy to consider it now. She barely knew him. He had just walked in off the street, an unknown repairman, and through some subtle sorcery had in a matter of a few hours made her feel as though she had known him all her life, made her start thinking she might *like* to know him the rest of her life. . . . It was crazy. He wasn't even her type; there was nothing about him that should interest her at all . . . and in some totally incomprehensible way he was making her forget all that.

"We can spend weeks or months playing the game," he explained reasonably, "each of us trying to impress the other and put our best foot forward, and all we'll end up doing is being something we're not—building little walls between what we really are and what we want the other person to think we are. Or we can cut through all the nonsense, relax, and be ourselves and admit right now that there's a physical attraction, and just let it happen."

She stared at him. His ability to capture in a few phrases the very essence of the complicated courtship ritual, to disarm and expose it so shamelessly and guilelessly, amazed her. "Good heavens," she said somewhat weakly. "Are you for real?"

"I assure you I am." He smiled faintly, and his eyes were clear and frank. If this was a line, it was a very original one—and very effective.

"But I told you," she returned somewhat indignantly, "I'm not attracted to you at all. In fact, I find this whole conversation somewhat ridiculous."

He shook his head slowly, his lips tracing a faint smile as his eyes dropped, half-closed in a gesture of exasperation. "Jessie," he said on a low, amused breath, "you are exhausting."

"So are you," she retorted, and popped another candy into her mouth.

"I'm beginning to think it's useless to try to talk to you."

"And I'm beginning to think you're crazy."

He had been watching with amused absorption the automatic path her hand made from the candy in her lap to her mouth, and now he commented, "You're a very oral person, aren't you?"

She opened her mouth to retort, and then she caught the double meaning. She gulped down the last swallow of the tasteless chocolate and felt heat creep from beneath the opening of her sweat shirt slowly up her neck. All of a sudden the moment between them wasn't so comfortable anymore. All of a sudden she didn't think she could survive another moment without a cigarette. She said abruptly, "How long have you worked for the telephone company?"

Once again his hand came out to cover hers as it reached for the pack of cigarettes. "Six months," he answered. The other hand patiently uncurled the fingers that were clenched about the candy in her lap. "These," he pointed out, dropping the candy back into the dish, "will ruin the taste of your wine."

Her eyes, as they met his, were half belligerent, half frightened. Beneath his expert orchestration, the atmosphere had changed from pleasantly conversational to subtly electric, and the transformation was smooth and effortless. "I don't want any more wine," she told him.

"Fine." His eyes reminded her of warm toffee, sheened like satin on the outside, soft and malleable within. The gentle pressure of his hand on her shoulder increased as he once again leaned toward her. The other arm slipped about her so that it brushed just beneath her breasts, and his fingers spread ever-so-lightly against the curve of her waist. His face moved very close, but he did not kiss her. He simply sat there, looking at her with a gentle smile, as though waiting to see what she would do.

She tried very hard not to press herself back into the sofa cushions because she did not want him to think she was afraid of him. She *was* afraid of him. She must be, for why else would her heart be jumping so crazily and her lungs contracting so painfully on each breath? Sincere or not, it was intensely obvious what he wanted from her, and equally as obvious that he had every confidence his perseverance would be rewarded. Oh, he was very smooth, and she was very out of practice for handling such situations. It was becoming harder and harder to remember why she had so diligently avoided them.

She said, "I thought you were going to ask me to dinner."

He smiled, "After all that candy, you're still hungry?" His finger stroked her cheek; it was useless to try to ignore him or his intentions. Desperate danger signals began to go off because it would be entirely too easy to enjoy this, to open herself up to him and in the process to bare herself to an endless cycle of pain and involvement....

She said very calmly, very forcefully, "Stop this. I told you I'm not interested."

And to her very great surprise he sat up, took her hand, and pulled her to her feet. "All right then," he said equitably. "Dinner."

Jessie was taken aback, uncertain whether she was relieved or disappointed at the sudden change of course the evening had taken. She stammered, "Oh, well, thank you, but I didn't mean—that is, it's rather late, and you have to go to work in the morning...."

"No, I don't," he replied mildly. "As of this afternoon, I'm afraid the Bell Telephone system and I have come to a parting of the ways. I am once again swelling the ranks of the unemployed."

Now she really didn't know what to say. "Oh, that's—too bad." She tried to regain her equilibrium. She was not the type of woman who went out with strange men—or allowed herself to be kissed in her own kitchen by them, for that matter. This unorthodox encounter had gone far enough, and she now had the perfect opportunity to break it off. Only she wasn't entirely sure she wanted to break it off.... "Keith..." she began hesitantly, unconscious of the fact that a troubled light had dimmed her eyes and that she had crossed her arms over her chest in a blatantly protective gesture.

"Oh-oh," he said softly, and there was a gentle light in his eyes that might have been meant to be teasing or reassuring. It was neither. "You're worrying again. Want to talk about it?"

"There's...nothing to talk about," she said tensely. "It's just..." She felt herself floundering with unfamiliar words and alien ideas. "It was nice of you to ask me to dinner and to bring the wine and all, but I think you should know..."

"That you're not going to pay at the end of the evening with your body," he supplied mildly. "No problem."

She was once again thrown completely off-balance. She stammered, "I—that's nice, but there's really no point to it. What I mean is," she clarified rather desperately, "I'm sure you're really very nice and I'm...flattered by your interest, but you're really not my type."

And just as she realized how awful that sounded, he burst into laughter. He laughed with his whole body; mouth, eyes, shoulders, even his hair, took on a sort of dancing gleam, and the air around him seemed lighter when he laughed. "That's okay," he said, and reached for her hand. "You're not my type either. Shall we go?"

Jessie gave him one brief, helpless look, and then turned in resignation to put on her shoes and coat. He was a very difficult man to argue with.

The rain had turned to a cold drizzle as they stepped outside, and the air was dank and unwelcoming. Keith led her to a rust-bitten Chevy van, circa 1967, whose dented off-white frame was only flattered by the phosphorescent filter of the overhead street light. He held her waist to help her inside, advising, "Careful now, there are probably tools on the floor." Tools, wadded newspapers, and old beer cans, Jessie discovered as she tried to push some of the litter under the seat with her heels and clear a place for her feet.

Keith hoisted himself into the bucket seat beside her and explained, "I'm not the only one who uses it. You'd be surprised how popular you become when you own a van."

Jessie smiled a little and settled back onto the worn upholstery, not knowing what to say. The motor throbbed into a comfortable hum. As he pulled out into the street she could not resist the temptation to glance at the back of the van. Among other objects she could not identify, there was an ice chest, a tool box—and a sleeping bag and a couple of hastily folded blankets. She could not help wondering who else used the van, and for what.

Then Keith said thoughtfully, "I think you should know I have no intention of making this into a platonic relationship."

She looked at him, startled. "I think it's a little bit early to assume this is any kind of relationship," she said.

In the flash of another car's headlights she caught the corner of a half smile. His voice was silky smooth, sensuous, vibrating with confidence. "Oh, no, it's not."

She moved uncomfortably in her seat, lacing her fingers together in her lap, staring straight ahead. "You're awfully sure of yourself, aren't you?" She tried to keep her tone on the same conversational level as his.

Keith glanced at her. "One of us has to be, Jessie. I know it's been bothering you since I kissed you this evening," he went on easily, "so before you work yourself into an ulcer over it, let's get it out in the open. I still want to make love to you, and I'm going to teach you to want it too."

The way he said that was maddening. Not *I'll try,* or *I hope,* but I'm *going* to teach you.... She said, only half joking, "Does that mean if I say no I get to walk home?"

The smile, she knew, was meant to be comforting, but the dusky interior of the van was suddenly charged with electricity, and she had rarely felt less comfortable in her life. He said mildly, "You call the shots. I'm not going to pressure you, and if I do unintentionally, you'll let me know. Is that fair?"

She could not answer because her eyes had fallen on the length of his slender wrist as it rested on the steering wheel, and the delicately boned hand that was attached to it, and she was suddenly wondering what it would feel like to have that hand brushing over the soft flesh of her thighs.... She jerked her eyes back to the shiny black asphalt before them.

"All I'm asking from you," he went on gently, "is honesty. Let's not build the wall any higher than we have to, huh?"

He looked at her for just the moment he allowed himself to take his eyes from the road, his glance so tender, so sincere, so utterly open that she knew instinctively it would be impossible ever to be anything less than honest with this man. It would be absurd to expect anything less from him. And so she said calmly, "Then why did you come back? What do you really want from me?"

She knew the following silence was not an artificial affectation. He was considering his answer, choosing his words with care, as he always did. "Just a chance," he responded at last, "to be good to you."

Something unsettling clenched at her stomach just below the area of her heart. This man could be dangerous, a dim voice warned from far back in her mind. This whole thing could get out of hand.... But he smiled at her, and the power of her early-warning system dimmed and gradually began to fade.

"So," he demanded abruptly. There was a teasing note in his voice to which she responded immediately. "What is your type of man, New York lady?"

She settled back, a mischievous little smile tugging at her lips as she glanced at him through slanted eyes. "Oh... tall, dark, and handsome, naturally."

"So far so good."

"Rich."

"Oh-oh."

"The white-tuxedo type with a continental flair."

"A Maserati in the garage and a gold ring on his pinky?"

Her eyes twinkled. "Right."

"I think I saw a man like that advertised in the Nieman-Marcus catalog," he mused, and she laughed. The lingering tension dissolved like motes of dust within the warm interior of the van.

Keith took her to a small home-style café where the booths were covered with blue-and-white checked vinyl cloths and the overhead lighting was bright and cheery. The atmosphere was casual and chatty; the small room was filled with the clutter of clinking utensils and the hubbub of voices and good smells from the grill. The waitresses greeted Keith by name; and Jessie knew he must come here regularly.

"This is nice," she said as she slid into the booth, and she meant it. She was unaccountably relieved that he had not taken her someplace dark and secluded, with wine and flickering candlelight.

"I like it," he agreed. "They don't fuss over you here. They bring you your meal and leave you alone. Now that," he pointed out, "is the trouble with your New York restaurants. Stuffed-shirt waiters bringing you water ten minutes before you get thirsty and peering over your shoulder to anticipate your every need—"

"That," she retaliated, "is called good service."

"That," he returned, "is a royal pain in the butt."

They ordered cheeseburgers, french fries, and Cokes, and she asked him if he had ever been to New York. "Often enough to know I'm not missing anything," he replied. "Once," he clarified with a grin. "As a teenager on a family vacation."

Jessie asked him about his family, and she learned that he had a brother living in Florida and a sister who was married to an insurance salesman in Arkansas. He had been born right here in Tennessee and neither of his parents was living. She told him she was an only child and her parents were divorced. Keith asked about her husband, and she told him briefly that he had been a junior vice-president in a company that specialized in the manufacturing of farm implements and that he had been transferred to Hawaii shortly after the divorce. He did not pursue it.

The cheeseburgers were delicious. She settled back against the booth, thoughtfully crunching the crushed ice that remained in the bottom of her glass, and she inquired, "What are you going to do about a job?"

"Something will turn up."

"Any leads?"

Keith was leaning back against the booth, one arm resting casually on the table. The sleeves of his dark sweater were pushed back to expose his fine-boned wrist, light hazel in color, shaded with smooth dark hairs. One hand was curved gracefully about the base of his nearly empty glass, and a slender forefinger traced a pattern on the molded amber surface. He said, "Actually, I have quite a few options. The gas station down the street needs help, but that's only part-time. There was a sign in the beauty parlor for a cosmetician, but I think I'm overqualified for that." His expression was perfectly bland, and she could not be certain he was teasing. "Of course, there's always waiting tables, but I think tomorrow I'll answer the ad I saw in the paper—male stripper."

"Sure you're not overqualified for that?"

He grinned. "I'm sure."

She tapped another cluster of ice into her mouth. "You don't seem very concerned about it."

He shrugged. "I try not to get too uptight about things that aren't important."

She stared at him. "You don't consider employment important? What are you, independently wealthy or something?"

He assumed a thoughtful attitude. "I don't know. Do total assets of thirty-four dollars and seventy-eight cents qualify me as independently wealthy?"

"Hardly," she returned dryly. "You see, it's like this, Michaelson. You don't work, you don't eat. It's the law of the jungle. And I should think imminent starvation is something you might find just the least bit important."

He smiled at her, and the light in his eyes was clear and untroubled. His confident lack of concern made her former statement seem pompous. He made her feel as though she had just tried to tell a child there was no Santa Claus—only to find out the child knew more than she did. "There are worse things," he assured her.

Jessie was not sure she wanted to find out what things he considered worse, so she lifted her glass again. There was a sudden glint in his eyes as he watched her. "You know what chewing ice is a sign of, don't you?"

She lifted an eyebrow, and he obligingly informed her. "Sexual frustration."

She set the glass on the table with a thump and almost choked on a piece of melting ice. The indignant embarrassment in her eyes was so automatic that he laughed, and his dancing eyes only grew merrier as she glared at him. "Do you know what your real problem is?" he demanded at last, sobering a little.

"No," she retorted sarcastically. "What's my problem?"

"You're too damn responsible. You work two jobs. You give your dinner away to a stray cat. You go in for a sick friend when you've just gotten out of bed yourself. Someone needs to teach you how to play."

"And you're just the person." She couldn't keep the biting edge off her voice.

He lifted his glass to her in a mild salute. "The expert."

"That I don't doubt." It was hard to stay irritated with him. She met his eyes in what she hoped was a challenge. "So why did you leave the telephone company?"

His eyes were still vastly amused. "We had a, ah, difference of opinion over company policy."

"They wanted you to get your hair cut," she stated flatly.

He grinned and reached for her hand. "Come along, darlin', it's time for your first lesson."

For a moment as his hand clasped warmly over hers she experienced a lurch of alarm, wondering which of his two lessons he was referring to: the promise to teach her how to make love, or how to play. Or perhaps they were the same thing to him.

Fifteen minutes later Rod Stewart pounded out suggestive lyrics to the deafening roar of a hundred wheels on a hardwood floor. Jessie cried in alarm, clutching at him, "But Keith I told you—I don't know how to skate!"

"That's all right, darlin'," he shouted back. "I do!" And he pushed her off.

Two hours later Jessie was reflecting wryly that this man knew more than one way to leave a woman bruised and battered—beginning with the ego and working outward. "That was not fun," she informed him darkly as she inserted her key into the lock.

There was a residue of mirth in his voice as he leaned against the door frame and responded, "Don't worry, honey, you'll get the hang of it. You're just a little stiff."

"You can say that again," Jessie mumbled, fighting the urge to rub her aching posterior. The lock turned and she withdrew the key; then she hesitated. Nervous trepidation fluttered in her stomach as she turned to him uncertainly. This was it, then. The rest of the evening had been so easy, but it had all been leading to this moment—the infamous good-night scene. The time when a girl either got kissed or politely brushed her date off, the time when she had to decide whether to extend the evening by another hour or so or to end it at the door. And he simply stood there, lounging against the door frame with his hands stuffed into his pockets, watching her, waiting... waiting for what? The golden aurora of porch light spilled over them, and his eyes seemed to hold an alert amusement. She swallowed dryly.

Keith broke the silence with a lazy drawl. "No, thanks," he said. "I can't stay."

Her lips tightened with a reluctant smile. "I suppose I could make some coffee," she conceded.

He did not wait for a second invitation, but politely reached around her to touch on the kitchen light and gestured her inside.

Jessie put on water for instant coffee and then wondered if he would construe that as a hint that she would prefer not to prolong his stay. There was something about the amused flicker in his eyes as he watched her take down the cups that assured her he did. He made himself useful by spooning coffee mixture into the cups while the water heated, and she found her eyes unwillingly drawn to his hands, so beautifully expressive even while performing such a mundane task. The kitchen light gleamed on his soft, black hair and showed her the movement of muscles beneath the light material of the clinging sweater. She could see the padded softness of chest hair outlined beneath the material, and she wondered what it would be like to press her hand against the springy texture. She wondered whether the roughness would tickle her palm through the fabric and whether she could feel the heat, and if his heart would be pounding out its own wild rhythm as it had the last time he had held her. . . .

And then she became aware that he had filled the cups and that he was watching her, his own gaze thoughtful and aware and examining her thoughts without judgment or criticism. Under such a gentle perusal it was ridiculous to be embarrassed, but when he handed her her coffee, she spilled a drop, and said quickly, "Would you like something to eat?"

"No." His hand upon her shoulder was a brief caress as he gestured her toward the living room, his tone filled with too much knowledge and just a trace of amusement. "But I'll bet you would."

"Are you suggesting that my appetite is unladylike?'' Her voice was so bright it was almost brittle.

"I am suggesting," he responded smoothly just as they reached the sofa and she was reaching for a cigarette, "that your constant need to have something in your mouth is a sign of—" he paused just long enough to indicate to her with a quirk of his brow that what he was about to say was not precisely what he meant. "—nervousness."

She remembered all too well his opinion of her oral habits, and she decided to forgo the cigarette for the moment. She perched on the edge of the sofa, cradling the coffee cup in her hands, and he folded his long limbs beside her, setting his coffee on the table to cool. His smile was companionable, though she thought she caught a hint of teasing in his eyes as he demanded, "Well, how's the evening been so far? As bad as you expected?"

"It was the roller skating that did it," she said glumly. "Promise me, Keith, no more. I'm getting too old for that sort of thing."

He chuckled softly. "I told you, hon, you're just a little stiff. And you're only as old as you feel."

"Which is ninety-two right now."

A tiny mewing sound startled her. She had forgotten all about the stray kitten. She giggled as she saw the little animal making its way from some unknown corner across the slippery hardwood floor toward them. Its stomach was so swollen from the feast that it practically dragged the ground, and it walked lopsided. Jessie could almost believe it had done nothing but eat the entire time they had been gone. Its gray and white fur was drying in absurd spikes and clumps, and the determined pace with which its tiny legs ate up the expanse of floor was comical. The kitten made its way unerringly toward Keith, fastened its claws on the hem of his jeans, and began to climb up his pants leg.

Keith patiently bent down to pluck him off, holding him with his back paws dangling in the air as he brought him to eye level. The kitten regarded the bearded man with alert, curious blue eyes, and Keith said pleasantly, "You're a dumb-looking little beast, you know that, Delbert? Just look at you. Don't you have any pride in your appearance?"

Jessie giggled helplessly. "Delbert?"

Keith turned the kitten toward her. "He looks like a Delbert, doesn't he? Revolting animal."

"I take it you don't like cats." It was amazing how comfortable she felt with him. From the moment he had walked in the door this afternoon it had been like that, and it was totally inexplicable—as though she had known him forever. She knew that could be dangerous.

"Can't stand the nasty little critters," he replied. "However..." He moved the kitten away from his face, where it was batting at his beard. "They seem to have an inexplicable attraction to me." He placed the kitten on his thigh, where it immediately curled up and went to sleep. Jessie watched the soothing motion of his slender forefinger as it absently stroked the tiny animal's back, and then he inquired, "What happened to your marriage?"

She didn't have to answer that. There was no reason to go into that with him. She said, "It didn't work out."

"Tell me about it," he invited.

Once again she hesitated. She had never been able to talk to anyone about it, not really. Even Celia, her best friend in New York, did not know the worst details. How could she confide in anyone the humiliation of failure, the trauma of rejection, the slow pain of watching love turn to disappointment, disappointment to hate, hate to emptiness.... And why should she suddenly be moved to confide in this stranger now?

"We had nothing in common," she began carefully. "I suppose it was one of those impulsive things that, if either of us had stopped to think about for even one minute, we never would have done. Then we were married, and it was too late. We...just weren't compatible, in bed or out." She stopped suddenly and ventured an embarrassed, slightly self-deprecating glance at him. "I don't know why I'm telling you this."

"It's the bartender in me," he assured her.

His smile and his tone were so relaxed that she began to relax again herself. "Bartender?" she inquired.

"One of my many jobs. It's true that people will tell their bartender things they won't tell their psychiatrist." And then a slight frown of concern troubled his eyes as he insisted gently, "Jessie, didn't you know this before you married the guy? Didn't you recognize the problem?"

She moved her eyes back to her coffee cup. She replied somewhat shortly, "Do you mean didn't I do any shopping around before I bought? No." Frank had been her first lover, and the experience had been disappointing at best. At worst it had taught her that sexual vulnerability meant emotional vulnerability, opening herself to rejection and humiliation and failure.... She heard her own voice, soft and rather quarrelous, confessing, "He was...cold. He didn't like me to touch him, you know? Everything I did was wrong."

Jessie looked at Keith quickly, but found only friendly interest in his eyes, a willingness to understand, sympathy in the truest sense of the word. That look warmed her to the very depths of her soul. Still, she tried to shrug it off negligently as she finished, "It lasted a year."

"Sounds as though he had a real problem," Keith commented soberly.

"I suppose," she agreed quietly. "But I don't blame him, any more than he blamed me. He couldn't help the way he was."

"But you blame yourself."

With the razor's accuracy of an experienced marksman, he had cut straight to the heart of the matter. Blame herself? In one swift blow it all came back: the desperation, the failure, the frantic trying again, the exposure and the vulnerability. The rejection of the most intimate offerings and the slow painful crushing of self-esteem on both his part and hers. The pain. How long had it taken her to stop blaming herself? Had she ever completely stopped? "I sacrificed everything to that marriage," she said quietly. If there was a note of bitterness to her voice, she had not meant it to be there. "My career, my life in New York...everything I wanted out of life. And when it was over—" she looked around her with one more derisive shrug "—I was here, with no place to go, nothing to show for it." And lacking the courage and the self-confidence to try again. Everything of value had gone into the package trade—her heart, her soul, her ambition, and her self-esteem—and she was left poorer but wiser for the experience.

His hands cupped her shoulders gently. "I'm sorry, Jess," he said simply. All-purpose words with an abundance of meaning when he said them. When he said them, she knew they were sincere; they had the power to comfort and reassure and, for the moment, to make her forget.

With a slight increase of the pressure upon her shoulders, he brought her back against the length of his chest, and she sank against him. For a time he simply held her. She could feel the soft, steady rise and fall of his chest. She felt warm and snug. She wondered what it would be like to sleep with him, just to lie beside him and have him hold her. And then he bent to place a slow kiss upon the curve of her jaw.

She stiffened automatically and drew away, reaching for a cigarette. True to his promise of no pressure, he let her go. He sat with one arm crooked casually along the back of the sofa, and he watched her with absolutely no expression on his face at all. Then he said mildly, "You should know that your daily consumption of cigarettes will increase in direct proportion to your level of frustration."

She lifted her chin, met his gaze coolly, and lit the cigarette. He smiled. "Say it."

"This is not going to work, Keith," she obliged him firmly.

"Why not?" He took up his coffee cup and sat back with it, watching her steadily, waiting for a reply.

She sighed. "It just won't," she said rather sharply. "We have two different backgrounds, two different sets of values; we have nothing in common. Why do you want to bother with me, anyway?"

His smile was complacent and undisturbed. "That's a loaded question. Are you sure you want an answer?"

She drew again sharply on the cigarette and crushed it out with a fluttering motion in the ashtray. At the same moment he replaced his coffee on the table, and when they straightened up, his hands floated to her face. As gentle as her half-drawn breath his fingers captured her and held her a helpless victim beneath the warmth of his liquid-cocoa eyes. Her heart fluttered in her rib cage like a frantic moth beating its wings against a windowpane. Softly he said, "Lady, I don't think you know what you want."

Keith's thumbs caressed her cheekbones just beneath her eyes, the third finger of each hand brushed across her lashes and ruffled them closed. Then his hands moved downward, cupping her chin, a forefinger on either side tracing the corners of her lips. He kissed her gently.

Jessie sat looking into his soft smile, her parted lips still warm from the brief contact with his, unable to react or to say a word. His voice filtered down to her through a misty haze of half contentment and half yearning, more tender than a caress. "What do you want, Jessie Dee McVey?"

What did she want? The question whirled nonsensically, darting numbly into little-used corners of her brain and blurring into indistinct, unfamiliar patterns. What did she want? Her cozy house, her few friends, her peaceful life.... No, not this. Not this quiet place and this gentle man....

He lifted lifeless fingers between his and brought them slowly to his shoulder, to his collar. Warm textured flesh fell against the coolness of her fingertips; his breath was slow and deep as he brought his face to rest against hers. His beard was like silk against her cheek. Her fingers moved against the skin of his neck experimentally, an almost imperceptible caress. She felt his lips curve into a distant smile, and he inquired huskily, "So bad?"

Her breath quavered in her throat as she moved her hand slowly around his neck, beneath the thick curl of silky hair, and cupped it there. What did she want? Maybe no more than this moment....

Keith's fingers glided down to her throat, lightly stroking the extended cord there. He kissed her very tenderly on the cheek, and upon the corner of her mouth. "I'll never leave you hurting, Jessie," he said.

Those were the best words she had ever heard.

He looked down at her, and his smile was sweeter than a kiss. Quiet, confident, steady, his eyes held her in a lingering caress, and he advised gently, "Think about it."

Her hand was still about his neck, and her fingers captured a strand of long dark hair. She looked up at him quietly, her eyes wide and solemn and ... vulnerable. Then, without her knowing who made the move, her cheek was resting against his shoulder, his arms holding her, protecting her. What did she want? It hardly seemed to matter anymore.

She sighed in contentment mixed with resignation. "When are you going to get a haircut?"

He pushed her away a little, though the twinkle in his eyes was severe. "When are you going to stop smoking?"

She laughed and snuggled back against his shoulder. No, it hardly mattered at all.

Chapter Three

The sky outside the boutique was a water-color blue broken by slow-moving popcorn clouds. Occasionally the crystal sunlight that spilled over the counter where Jessie worked would be diffused into a silky fluorescence by one of those clouds, making it difficult for her to be certain she had gotten the exact shadings and textures she wanted on paper. She was working by sunlight because five minutes ago Keith had obstinately turned out all the lights and hung the Closed sign on the door.

At last, reasonably satisfied, she held up the sketch of the newspaper layout she was designing for his approval. "Lovely," he acknowledged somewhat dryly. "Now, can we go?"

"Do I detect a trace of cynicism in your tone?" she responded archly, and made a few pencil-line adjustments to the sketch.

"Forgive me, darlin', it's just that I don't believe the state of mankind will be irreparably damaged if a few dozen women more or less are not persuaded to lay out their hard-earned cash for dresses they don't need and can't afford. Are you ready?"

She put down her pencil and looked at him gravely. The pale shadow that fell across her sketch pad was a reflection of the cloud that crossed her mind. It was always like that with him. When she was with him she was happy and warm; it was easy to ignore the luminescent clouds high in the atmosphere. When she was alone those shadows lengthened, stretching over the sun to remind her that this contentment couldn't last, it wasn't real, she did not belong within the sparkling glow of his carefree life-style, and he had no place in her world.

He stood there, reading her thoughts with a patient adeptness she had learned to know so well, and his smile was gently reproving. "Another brick in the wall, Jess?" he challenged softly.

She lowered her eyes and picked up her pencil, watching a small pattern of lead-point dots form on the blotter beneath her absent tapping motions. It was no use. How could Jessie expect Keith to understand about dedication, about ambition—him, the man who had had three jobs in the past two months and was once again unemployed? She felt good when she was working. She got an almost sensual thrill from putting her ideas on paper and knowing that those ideas—a personal part of her—would eventually move into other people's lives and influence their behavior. That she would make a difference, somehow, some way. How could he *not* understand that?

She lifted her eyes to him stubbornly, and he was waiting for it. His stance was casual, his expression relaxed, his eyes a reflection of mild, unhurried interest. "There's something wrong with enjoying one's work?" she returned evenly. "Is ambition a dirty word in your vocabulary?"

"You know as well as I do, love," he replied, "that in the overall scheme of things Madison Avenue will not change the world in any meaningful or lasting way. And I can't see the point in working yourself to a frazzle over something that won't make any difference ten years from now."

"It changes the world every day," she muttered, dropping her eyes again. It was impossible to pick a fight with him. He was so damn...reasonable. She looked up at him once again rather hopelessly. "Keith, I like my work. It is important, maybe not to you and maybe not right here and now, but it's a chance...to go for something higher, you know what I mean?" She struggled for the words that always managed to fall like honey from his tongue. On paper she could capture the most abstract ideas and complex thoughts with a few deft strokes of her pencil. But when it came to communicating to the person whom it suddenly seemed desperately important that she convey the one idea that was more important to her than anything else in the world, she was helpless. "All I've ever wanted," she tried to make him understand, "was to do something important, to go as high as I could go. It's not just convincing women to lay out their hard-earned cash for dresses they can't afford. It wouldn't matter if I were convincing kings and presidents to lay out their hard-earned cash for countries they couldn't afford. Don't you see, it's the concept. It's doing what I do well and knowing that there's no limit as long as I'm doing it. It's reaching for the stars. Can you understand that?"

"Darlin'," he said patiently, reaching for her hand, "what would you do with the stars if you had them?"

He pulled her around the counter, and she sighed helplessly as he dropped the strap of her purse over her shoulder. He ran one finger along the curve of her cheek with light affection and he teased, "See what working under all that starlight has gotten you? Pale cheeks and puffy eyes. You need a strong dose of fresh air and sunshine."

It was useless to protest, and Jessie tried not to think about how Anna would react when she found she had closed the shop early on a Saturday afternoon. There were so many things she tried not to think about when she was with Keith.

The April rains had left a long stretch of balmy weather in their wake, forecasting a bright warm May. Jessie reacted to the thrill of springtime come at last with the same exhilaration as the rest of the population, experiencing for perhaps the first time an actual touch of spring fever. She stood on the glittering white sidewalk and let the warm breeze run its hands over her cotton sundress and caress her bare legs, and she thought that Keith was right, this was no day for working.

"You could have at least let me pack the lunch," she said, making a pretense of complaining as he helped her into the van.

He grinned at her. "Don't trust my cooking?"

"Since I have no doubt your 'cooking' consists of a quick stop at the deli," she retorted, "I can't say that I do."

That, of course, was not strictly true. She had been privileged to sample his talents in the kitchen on one or two impromptu occasions at his apartment, and he wasn't half bad. But when she had attempted to return the invitation—whether she felt sorry for him because he was a bachelor or whether she felt guilty because she knew he was constantly spending money he could not afford on her—he accepted only on the condition that she would allow him to bring the food and prepare the meal. It was an unspoken rule between them that when she was with him she was not to concern herself with anything, she was not to be pressured by even so small a responsibility as shopping for and preparing a meal. How could any woman fail to react to such tender care as that? He had the art of courtship down pat, and he was keeping his promise of teaching her how to play.

Those few visits to his apartment had proved very educational. She found herself perfectly at ease alone with him in his home, perhaps because there was nothing calculated or contrived about it. He made no effort to create a seductive atmosphere or to impress her with his domestic talents, and even though quite often they began the evening alone, they very rarely ended it that way. Keith had more friends than it was surely legal for any one person to have. They were constantly wandering in and out of his apartment, seldom bothering to knock, often staying for a drink or a meal or an impromptu party. The phone never stopped ringing, and there was simply no opportunity for intimacy when Jessie was at Keith's apartment. She found his friends fascinating and was constantly amazed by his effortless ability to attract people from all walks of life—students, businessmen, professionals, laborers, all of them gravitating to Keith's small apartment as though it were a second home, hailing him on the street, sharing their table whenever they went out. He had a way of making people feel comfortable and at ease, he could communicate with anyone on any level, and his innate, uncomplicated honesty in a modern world was something that inspired trust and drew people to him like a magnet. It was all part of his natural charm, which Jessie was beginning to know too well.

They went to the state park, less than an hour's drive away. Once there they skirted other couples and picnicking families who had had the same idea, weaving through bands of teenagers with their Frisbees and disorganized softball games. The first few weekends of spring would not find anybody indoors, and Jessie despaired of ever finding an unoccupied table or spot of grass. But magical things always seemed to happen when he was around. He paused for about thirty seconds to join a group of giggling elementary-school girls and boys in a game of kickball; then he took the canvas picnic bag from her hands and led her unerringly down a small incline, along a random wooded trail, and into a small sun-and-shade dappled clearing just large enough for two. The sounds of other revelers were muted by the soft wooded enclosure, and the air was perfumed with the heavy scent of pine and earth. "Lucky find," she commented, looking around her appreciatively. "Or—" she tried not to glance at him too skeptically "—have you been here before?"

He grinned at her. "Jealous, sweetheart?"

She scowled and turned quickly to begin unpacking the picnic bag. "Of course not." But that was another thing that bothered her. She knew for a fact that he had not seen any other women in the past two months because every spare minute was spent with her. Was she supposed to make sense of a man who would deny himself the obvious pleasures of another woman's company to spend unfulfilling and unsatisfying time with her? Was he going for some sort of endurance record or something? Or was he simply trying to endear himself to her through sacrifice?

"One weekend," he told her, spreading a worn, khaki-green army blanket over the pine straw-littered ground, "we'll go to the mountains, when we have more time. Do you like to fish?"

"I've never been," she admitted, taking a bottle of still-chilled wine from the insulated bag and unwrapping the glasses.

He laughed in astonishment. "You are a city girl, aren't you? Well, it's long past time your horizons were broadened. It's a definite date."

"I'm not much for camping out either," she warned him.

"Not to worry, babe, this particular little resort comes complete with fishing cabin and all the amenities."

Once again she could not prevent her eyes from slanting toward him skeptically. "A romantic little hideaway in the mountains, hmm?"

His eyes danced. "If you consider long weekends spent with a group of smelly, beer-drinking, dirty-talking men romantic, I suppose so."

She carefully laid out bread, fruit, cheese, and thick-sliced ham, and she said casually, "I might be going to New York this summer."

He sat down on the edge of the blanket, one arm propped loosely on his upraised knee, and looked at her with the sun playing in his eyes. "Oh, yeah? What's up there?"

Such innocence. Such a simple, untroubled view of the future in his eyes. The throb of city life, the hum of purpose, the lights and the glitter all seemed to fade as she tried to answer his question, and in a moment she smiled a little and shrugged. "Nothing, I suppose." Only a way of life.

Keith looked for a moment as though he might say something more, but then that lazy smile crept into his face and softened his eyes, and he let it drop. Jessie was glad. She did not know why she had brought up the proposed trip at this moment, but she realized now that the last thing she wanted to talk about—or think about— was New York. It was too nice a day to argue.

Replete with food and sunshine and two glasses of wine, Jessie lay back upon the blanket and lit a cigarette as Keith put away the remainder of their feast. His eyes were faintly mocking as he dropped down beside her and watched the breeze scatter wisps of the gray smoke across low-hanging pine branches. "Ah," he murmured dryly, "there's nothing like the crisp scent of burning tobacco on a balmy spring day."

Jessie made a face at him and defiantly blew a thin stream of smoke in his direction. He rolled over on his back beside her and plucked up a blade of grass, chewing lazily on the juicy stem. "That's a nasty habit," she said.

"Not as nasty as yours."

"You'll get liver worms."

"You'll get—" the spark in his heavy half-glance implied an explicit second meaning "—relaxed."

The combination of full stomach, cool wine, and lazy sunshine was a potent drug. Jessie felt the pinkening fever of sun kisses on her arms and bare shoulders and across the bridge of her nose, and when she closed her eyes she saw the pattern of leaves whose shadow fell across her face against a blushing background. She watched a small yellow butterfly weave its own intricate pattern against the patchwork of blue and lacy green and puffy white above her head; the scent of baby grass and crushed pine straw was intoxicating.

"Sheep clouds," Keith murmured beside her, and she turned her face lazily to look at him.

"What?"

His eyes were half closed and barely focused on the

patch of sky within his range of vision. "That's what we used to call them when we were kids. Sheep clouds."

She ground out the cigarette carefully in a patch of damp earth an arm's reach away and turned her head again to follow the slow-moving path of shiny white fluff across the brilliant blue horizon. "You must have had a nice childhood."

"The best in the world."

Like now, Jessie thought somewhat dreamily. *These are the things childhood is made of....*

"We also used to separate the dirty clouds from the white ones, and when it rained, we pretended we were giving the sheep a bath."

She giggled. "What else did you do?"

"Oh...made haunted castles out of empty closets, watched ant wars...."

"Do ants have wars?"

"Hmm-hmm. They're the only species besides man capable of large-scale organized behavior."

"What else?"

He stifled a yawn. "We held off regiments of British soldiers from a snow fort and sailed a regatta across the sun porch on rainy days...dug for gold in an abandoned quarry and dove for sunken treasure in a muddy pond...fell asleep in the sun with clover up to our ears...."

His voice wandered off into the lulling drone of a honeybee circling overhead, the distant orchestrated buzz and hum of smaller insects, and the faraway background of occasional human laughter and voices. She watched with sleepy fascination the slow, ponderous course a woods spider was making along the edge of the blanket; she felt the honey-baked warmth of his body beside her, their shoulders brushing, the dark hairs of his long forearm mingling with the pale hairs of hers. She turned sun-dazed eyes upon him and observed him with silent solemnity. His dark hair fell from a graceful center part across a smooth forehead; his eyes were closed by a short fringe of dark lashes. Tiny lines radiated from the corners of those eyes like the rays of the sun in a child's drawing. Patches of shadow played in a lacy network over the silky texture of his skin, and drops of sunlight caught streaks of mahogany in his beard. There was one freckle on his right temple just beneath the tapering of a satin brow, and she was suddenly overcome by an almost irresistible urge to touch it.

He was wearing the pastel blue T-shirt with its rendering of Delbert on the front that she had given him as a joke. He had groaned and complained that he received enough grief from that monster as it was, he'd be damned if he would have him plastered on his chest. But he wore the silly shirt on every possible occasion purely to tease her, and only someone with his unmistakable masculinity could get away with it. The pale fabric caressed his shoulders and contrasted with his dark beard, flowing like a second skin over the rise of his chest and the flatness of his abdomen. He was wearing tight-fitting bleached out jeans that formed a smooth, unbroken line of sensuality from waist to ankle. Her eyes traced that line with lazy, unobserved pleasure, finding art in the beautiful symmetry of the male form, the flat hips and taut, slender thighs, the curve of the knee and the firmness of calf. The jeans were pure white in worn places, at the knees, the front of the thighs, on the pockets, and down the front of the fly, and she quickly jerked her eyes away to study the tips of his battered boots, with their run-down heels. What an enigma this man was. What a sweet, gentle, utterly mind-twisting character. A man of quick, scathing intelligence and innumerable aptitudes, smooth, natural charm and prosaic philosophy... how easy it would be to let herself want this. How easy to imagine it was possible between them.

She turned on one elbow, looking down at him studiously. She captured a piece of pine straw that had become entangled in his hair and drew it with an absent, thoughtful motion across the flutter of his lashes, over the curve of his cheek. "What do you want, Keith Michaelson?" she said softly, and mostly to herself.

The slow smile in his eyes and the gentle curve of his lips told her he had not been asleep after all. But his voice was drowsily husky as he replied, "Besides you, you mean?" His long fingers closed over hers and removed the piece of straw. His hand held the warmth of the sun and the roughness of experience. His eyes were daylight clear. "Mostly," he answered easily, "whatever I happen to have at any given moment."

Simple, uncomplicated. Nice.

His eyes examined her face in the same leisurely enjoyment with which she had studied him only moments ago. He brought their interlaced fingers upward and traced a lazy pattern on her chin with his knuckles. The sun, cozy and enervating, felt like a hot blanket on her shoulders and the back of her hair.

He shifted position slightly, and she felt his hand upon the small of her back, his long fingers spreading above and below, her waist snuggled into the crook of his arm. Watching her with interest and affection, he extracted two of his fingers from the lock with hers and applied warm pressure upon the side of her face to guide her mouth downward. She did not resist.

Sun-dappled kisses met her lips, soft and slow and feather light. Far away a strident mockingbird called to its mate, and branches rustled in joyous reply. A warm breeze crawled over Jessie's bare legs, and the insect chorus hummed a discordant melody. His lips sought and tasted the honeyed warmth that clung to hers, and time was only a figment of her imagination.

His hand released hers and stretched over the plane of her face, his calloused tips roughening her downy skin, rubbing a slow erotic circle on the corner of her mouth, parting her lips as his kiss deepened. Her own hand fluttered awkwardly over his upper arm, brushing his bare flesh and sinewy muscle, then moved quickly away to curl against a handful of scratchy wool blanket. His lips curved against her cheek. "I won't slap it, you know," he said softly, and he recaptured her hand. "It's all right, Jess, whatever you want." He brought her hand to his chest and left it there, giving her the freedom to touch and explore and express tentative desires without fear of rejection or scorn, and she floated into the experience with the mingling of their breaths and the sure warm mating of their mouths as his hand slipped about her neck and guided her to him.

She was melting inside, soft and glowing like liquid caramel. It was so easy with him. Rising awareness was more intense than the blush of the sun, yet just as natural, and the sensation that grew within her was sharp and delightful, like the taste of a rich confection on a painful sweet tooth. The rippling of his breast muscle beneath her open palm was an erotic sensation in itself, the wine-drowsy heat radiated through the thin material and the soft padding of hair, and she felt the expansion of lungs and the tightening of power as he moved his arm up her back and spread his fingers along her shoulderblade. She wanted to feel his skin against her hand and tangle her fingers in the silky hair; she wanted to feel his heart rush, as hers was doing. She let it happen, this hazy wanting, this goodness that glowed in the center of her and radiated outward, not resisting, not thinking; just being for the moment right with him. She let him control the rhythm of her breathing with the warm wet explorations of his tongue across her lips and her cheek and her chin—and then inside her mouth, where her breath caught in a sharpening tempo and the honey in her veins turned to liquid fire. And she gave herself to it, for it was impossible to do otherwise. The scents of crushed pine straw and damp earth receded into the taste of wine and masculinity; the tweetering and rustling of the birds dimmed into a soundless rushing inside her head as she met the sweet certain probing of his tongue and felt the hardening of his mouth against hers, the intensity of his fingers sculpted around her skull as though it were a thing of exquisite beauty and priceless fragility. She let him control the rising flush that tingled over her limbs and her face and dampened her neck and burned in her stomach; she let him tell her heart when to beat and when to stop, and she let him, with one smooth graceful movement slip one arm about her and pull her on top of him.

Keith's breath cooled Jessie's scorched cheek, and his beard was a stimulating abrasive as he rubbed it against her face, slowly and tenderly, his skin a silky smooth contrast. His fingers traced the twining pattern of the braid that fell straight to the nape of her neck and moved to circle her ear, opening up a whole new vista of delicate sensory response. His eyes were warm and rich, lit with lazy affection and deep tenderness, and he murmured, "You have gold in your hair." One finger, as light as a butterfly wing, brushed across her eyelid. "And stars in your eyes."

She could feel his long length beneath her, the shape of his thighs, his chest flattening her breasts, his hardness pressing into her stomach. She touched a trembling finger to the freckle on his temple, and his eyes met hers steadily, adoringly, filled with lazy delight. Her fingers spread along the side of his face, caressing his smooth skin and silky beard, threading through the satiny texture of his hair. She touched his earlobe and traced the semicircle behind his ear, wondering if he experienced the same tingling sensation she did when he did it to her. She saw the deepening light of pleasure in his eyes as her finger traced a kiss upon his lips, and it was a heady sensation. His hands floated to her shoulders, freeing her head for movement, waiting for her. She touched her thumb to the side of his mouth, caressing; she let her head drop slowly forward.

It was no routine thing for her, this sharing and giving, the intricate lover's dance of aggression and passivity into which he led her with such natural ease. Demanding nothing but allowing everything, his unspoken signals were sure and gentle. He was pleased with her. It was an intoxicating thought. Her simple gestures and inexperienced responses excited him; he somehow found cause for celebration in her very ordinary body and unassuming character. He made it easy to give.

His hands roamed down her back and his kiss deepened, slowly and by stages pushing her toward the place where pleasure faded and desire flamed. With purpose and decision, long fingers explored the dip of her waist and without hesitation the rise of her buttocks, deep massaging motions pressing her into the prodding awareness of his body beneath her as his head lifted a little and his tongue invaded her mouth. Deep, plundering kisses, his and hers, punctuated the sharp rapping of her breath and hazy delight fell away into quick, hot awareness as his hands moved lower.

Her skirt remained bunched up above her knees from the deft movement that had arranged her on top of him, and her breath melted away into a tiny, high moan of delight and discovery as she felt his sensitive fingers brush against the back of her thighs. There was a moment of intense, frozen awareness at the sensation of calloused male hands against unsuspecting flesh, and then those hands began to move upward, the material of her skirt falling over them like a veil shrouding their secrets from a magnanimously amused sun.

She had to break the contact of their mouths in a vague instinct to capture breath. Her chest was tight and swollen, and her heart hammered out a choking rhythm. His tongue flamed quick hot awareness from her ear downward and outward, and his hands slipped over the silky material of her bikini underwear, delicately massaging the soft fabric into her sensitized flesh; then with a movement so deft and natural it was almost unnoticeable, they slipped beneath the elastic and against her bare skin. Long fingers circled and cupped, experienced fingertips pressing and kneading, abrasive palms burning little-touched flesh. The need to press herself into him, to take all he offered and to give in return, was so powerful it hurt, and a wave of dizziness swept over her, blotting out the day and chilling the sun with its burning flush. Jessie dropped her head to his shoulder, helpless.

Keith's hands moved slowly away, and upward to rest against the small of her back, his long fingers floating down the curve of her bare waist. At some point she became aware of his breath, warm and somewhat uneven, on her cheek; now she could feel the pulsing of his heart against the trip-hammer racing of her own. His hands held her, gentle, secure, waiting. He pressed a tender kiss on the side of her throat.

She would have remained like that forever, buried beneath his hands, hovering just this side of safety, but dread began to mingle with anticipation, and she knew it couldn't last. Reality seeped back in muted colors and deafening sounds; the raucous voices of a nearby family, the irritable chattering of a squirrel, the breeze chilling the dampness of her legs and her face. The uncomfortable awareness of his body beneath hers, her irritated nipples stinging with his heat, the almost obscene pressure of male power against her abdomen, the readiness in each of their bodies for something that would not be fulfilled. She became aware that her fingernails were digging into his shoulders with what was surely enough force to draw blood, and she uncurled them slowly. She raised her head to look at him, the woman with kiss-rouged lips and desire-flushed skin and stars in her eyes, and she did not know what to do, what to say. It was useless to lie to him. Foolish to try to hide her response from him. Cruel to keep teasing him....

And as usual, he saved her the trouble. He made no attempt to disguise his emotions from her—frustration, irritation, unquelled desire, and even a small amount of hurt—but he somehow tempered it with a curving smile and a gentle teasing. "Shall we go back to the parking lot? Let me show you what else the van is used for."

She rolled off of him slowly, sitting up, drawing her

knees up to her chin and covering her ankles with her skirt. She sat with her back to him, her face buried in her folded arms, and there was a long silence.

Pine straw crackled, and shadows moved as he sat up. There was no accusation in his voice, only tender curiosity. "Are you embarrassed? Hurt? Darlin'..." His hand brushed across her shoulder, fingers touching the back of her neck. "I can't tell what you're thinking if I can't see your face."

Handprints still tingled on her back and legs and buttocks, her lips still throbbed from his kisses. She could not look at him. She wanted to answer him, but sound was choked in her throat like a lump of tears. God, how could he be so forgiving? How much longer could his gentleness endure? It wasn't fair that he should be so good, so perfect in so many ways.... It wasn't fair to either of them.

Firmness tempered the care in his voice as his hand fell away. "Jessie, we need to talk about this."

"There's nothing to talk about," she choked out to her knees. Hadn't she said everything to be said on the subject? Hadn't he been forewarned?

She heard a sharp breath and knew he planned to say something, but it was followed only by a ringingly poignant silence. The sun went behind a cloud.

After a long time he said, almost casually, "Are you too tired to go out tonight?"

Somehow she managed to lift her face, to straighten her knees. She still could not look at him. "That... would be nice." Her voice sounded almost normal. Why did he keep setting himself up for this torture? Why did she?

They folded the blanket and gathered up the picnic bag in silence, and then, as he lifted a branch for her to pass in front of him onto the trail, he smiled at her, quietly, unexpectedly, comfortingly. "We are going to talk," he assured her.

She stepped onto the trail with sudden urgency and did not look back.

Chapter Four

Three times Jessie almost called Keith to cancel the date, and since he had only allowed her an hour to shower and change, that was quite a bit of emotional vacillation within a compact space. A hot, stinging shower could not erase the flush of his kisses from her mind nor the touch of his hands from her body, and when she thought of seeing him again she went hot with anticipation and cold with dread. Why was it he could make her believe in fairy tales; how could he draw her so easily into the web of his dreams.... Why did she continue to do this to herself?

She hesitated before her closet, her damp feet leaving an imprint in the colorful shag throw rug before the door. And in a moment of defiance she jerked out a deep purple crepe dress printed with tiny pink rosebuds—one of those boutique garments Keith would have said she didn't need and couldn't afford. It was true that since she had been seeing him she had had no opportunity to wear it or anything like it. But she was tired of blue jeans and sweaters, and tonight she wanted to dress up.

The dress was a wraparound with a single shoulder button and a tie belt. The cut of the shoulders was too deep to allow either a bra or a slip under it, and she boldly discarded both garments. Her legs were still flushed attractively from the afternoon sun, and she did not wear stockings, either. And, as she slipped white sandals over her bare feet she wondered what she was trying to prove. Independence? A graphic display of the diversity of their life-styles? Or was it just barely possible that she had put on the clingy, revealing garment with its criss-cross V-neckline and its bare shoulders for the same reason any other woman would have....

Keith's slow appreciative grin when she opened the door told her exactly why she had worn the dress. It made her heart start pumping again and drew a watercolor pink from the tips of her tingling cheekbones down to her fingers. She felt silly, and she felt pleased. But he only teased her. "You're overdressed."

"It would be hard not to be, with you," she retorted. But in fact he looked marvelous to her. The inevitable blue jeans were topped tonight with a western-cut shirt of indeterminate color in the deceptive porch light and an open denim vest. The cuffs of his shirt were turned back to reveal smooth brown forearms; the day in the sun had brought a golden tint to the tan he had acquired earlier in the season working on a construction crew. There were copper highlights in his hair. His eyes were onyx-colored and glowing. His smile was heart-meltingly beautiful. And as Jessie stepped outside, pulling the door closed behind her, his hands suddenly captured her, shocking a gasp from her, weakening her legs with the swift caress of a hundred fingertips from shoulders to waist to hips, sheer fabric a fluttering barrier against her skin. Then he wrapped his arms about her and held her to him, a painfully tender gesture, affectionate and secure. But it was only for a moment, and her breathing was quick and uncertain as he stepped back and smiled down at her. "Sometimes the element of surprise works wonders," he said. He kissed her on the nose. "You feel marvelous."

The glow that had only died to coals since leaving him this afternoon recaught like kindling, and it lasted the rest of the night.

He took her to a club in one of the less-publicized districts of Nashville, and when she saw the exterior of the sunshine-yellow concrete block building—it seemed to lean to one side—she was certain she was overdressed. The small parking lot was crowded with battered pickup trucks and dusty cars that would have been late-model ten years ago, and a couple of lanky cowboys lounged under the purple glow of a neon sign that said simply, The Place. Jessie would not have felt safe there with anyone but Keith.

Inside, however, she was pleasantly surprised. It was the type of place he liked to frequent, crowded, smoky, and with the pulse of a live band expanding the thick walls before they even reached the door—the type of place where no one fussed over you. The crowd, though filling the small room to capacity, was not unruly. The dance floor was standing room only, and couples made miniscule undulating motions against one another in a constantly shifting knot of humanity that was somehow erotic. The occupants of the maze of six-inch wide tables and ice-cream parlor chairs were unusually courteous and self-controlled, talking quietly with one another or listening to the band, which was quite good. Keith smiled and lifted his hand to several people he knew, and when he guided her to a table a waitress was there almost immediately with two glasses of Liebfraumilch and a very personal smile for Keith. Jessie started to ask him how well he knew this woman—just out of conversational curiosity, of course—but he had turned his attention to the small stage where a four-piece band was performing with electric guitars and amplified keyboards, and she restrained herself.

Jessie was impressed. The band was a cross between country-western and soft rock; their sound was a brilliant display of high technology that was almost too good for the type of music they were playing. They had a natural empathy with the audience and such well-honed skill that Jessie wondered whether they might really be some very successful group straight off a hot record label that was playing this dive incognito. She understood why Keith had brought her here.

When the band wound down into a soft instrumental number before ending their set, she turned to Keith, thrilled with the performance. "They are fantastic," she said. "What are they doing here?"

His eyes were still fixed on the stage with an intense concentration, but now he slowly brought his attention back to her and smiled absently. "They are good, aren't they? It's electronic sound."

"Do you know them?"

"Um-hmm." He seemed to have lost interest in the performance that had so captivated his attention a moment ago as he looked at her. "I'll introduce you to them later, if you like," he added absently, and his eyes twinkled as he watched her light another cigarette. "That makes over half a pack since we left the park this afternoon. Something bothering you, Jess?"

She stared down his insinuating gaze defiantly. "Yes. I'm hungry."

"You," he murmured as he lifted his hand lazily for

the waitress, "are a woman of insatiable—and intriguing—appetites."

And she was becoming more aware of them every day...as he well knew. "Are you going to sit here and talk dirty to me all night?" she demanded archly.

Keith's eyes danced in the shadowy candlelight as he leaned toward her, blocking the movement that brought the cigarette to her lips with the placement of two fingers lightly upon the full curve of her mouth. "Do you want me to?" he teased. "Or what if I just show you something better to do with your mouth?" And without warning he pressed his own lips over hers, firmly, gently, and briefly—and she felt a delightful rush of response that left her wanting more as he pulled away.

She loved it when he kissed her. The whole world seemed to dance when he was around, and he turned her values and her common sense and even her ability for conscious reasoning into flickering fireflies against the powerful beacon of his personality. Maybe all the wine she had had today was having a cumulative effect, maybe she was simply losing her mind, but she felt high and happy and dangerously content. She tried to hide those emotions with a feigned insult, and she said coolly, "Public displays of affection are very low-class, Michaelson."

He leaned back easily, watching her with obscurely amused eyes, and he informed her, "That was not a display of affection. That was a display of pure animal lust. You're driving me crazy, lady."

For a moment she was startled. He had never said that before. She was not certain whether the announcement was exciting or intimidating; she wasn't sure how to react. She recovered her composure in the few seconds it took her to snuff out the cigarette in the ashtray and responded pleasantly, "Is that right? And here I was thinking you were made of steel."

His eyes glinted as he suggested softly, "Would you like to go home?"

She could not be certain he was teasing, and fortunately—or perhaps it was unfortunately, she could not be certain of that either—before she could answer, the waitress arrived with a platter of sandwiches and a full bottle of wine. He had not placed the order; this was only another example of the type of efficient, no-bother service he liked. Jessie wondered rather uneasily whether he and this waitress shared some sort of unspoken method of communication, or whether he simply came here so often that all the waitresses had his preferences memorized.

She looked at the veritable mountain of sandwiches in dismay. "Would you by any chance be making fun of me?" she demanded suspiciously in a moment. "I can't possibly eat all this by myself!"

His eyes had traveled to some point over her shoulder. "You won't have to," he answered, and when she turned to follow his gaze it was to see the members of the band leaving the stage and making directly for their table.

They greeted him like a long-lost brother, with exclamations of "It's about time you showed up!" "We thought you'd deserted us, man!" and, with a friendly leer in Jessie's direction, "So this is what's been keeping you busy!"

Grabbing hands diminished the platter of sandwiches, there was much noisy laughter and joking as chairs were borrowed and robbed from other tables, and Keith made the introductions. The group called

Flame consisted of four nice-looking young men in their early twenties, Joey, Eric, Paul, and Carl, all indifferently dressed in jeans and T-shirts, all rather difficult to tell apart with their bland good looks and their floppy hairstyles. But they were fabulous musicians, and Jessie told them so.

Joey, the leader, grinned at her in a friendly manner. "Yeah, we know. The only thing standing between us and a number one hit is your fellow over there. See, one word from him to the right people and we'd shoot straight to the top, no doubt about it, but he's too damn—"

Jessie frowned in puzzlement. "I don't understand. What has Keith—"

"It's contacts, baby," explained Carl, divesting the plate of the remaining half of a sandwich she had managed to rescue for herself. "It ain't what you can do in this business, but who you know. And he knows them all."

Why should that surprise her? It would have surprised her had there been one person in Nashville Keith did not know. That his vast circle of friends and acquaintances should include show business greats should have been no cause for amazement.

Joey continued. "Didn't he tell you about Billy Marshall?"

It took her less than a second to recognize the name of the brightest star on the horizon of country music today. She could not help registering her surprise this time as she looked at Keith. "You know him?"

"Know him? He used to tour with him!"

Keith had tipped his chair back on two legs, lounging gracefully as he sipped his wine, following the conversation with only halfhearted interest. He shrugged. "I worked for him for a while," he admitted, "when he was first getting started. Managed the road crew, kept up the equipment...." But it was obviously not a subject that held much interest for him. He turned to Eric, lowering his chair and starting to rise. "Let's have a look at that sound board, I thought I heard a little fuzz on the lead guitar."

"Come on, man," complained Eric, wolfing down the last of his sandwich, "we've only got five minutes before the next set!"

"Won't take that long." Keith tapped him on the arm and insisted he follow.

Jessie turned back to Joey, an anxious curiosity urging her to make further discoveries about the man she thought she knew. "How did you meet Keith?"

"He designed our sound system." And then his grin was a little abashed. "Hell, he practically gave it to us—we're not exactly rolling in dough, I guess you can tell, and I guess he kind of gets off on working the electrical scene, so we ended up getting it for next to nothing." He shook his head a little. "I can't figure that guy out. Musicians are screaming for talent like his in L.A. and New York—hell, he could walk into any studio in Nashville and pick up a job paying a fat annual salary, but he'd rather give his work away to guys like us with nothing but a thank you to pay the rent." His shrug reflected the utter bafflement Jessie had come to know too well when she made the mistake of trying to understand Keith. Then he brightened and took her hand. "Say, do you want to see the system?"

Jessie couldn't tell one end of "the system" from the other, but it was fascinating to be caught in the stream of high-tech lingo that flowed back and forth between Keith and Eric with a rapidity that left her head spinning trying to decipher it. She was entranced by the sight of those delicate, competent fingers working beneath the beam of a high-power flashlight on the darkened stage, moving with intricate ease over miniscule multicolored wires and sockets. But more absorbing was the look of sheer concentration on Keith's face, an expression approaching almost rapture when he had finally achieved the sound from Eric's guitar that he wanted. He really loves this, she thought in amusement that was partly sheer bewilderment. Then why...

When Keith had commanded the band to get back to work so they could dance, she allowed him to lead her on to the tiny floor and take her in his arms. Keith placed her arms around his neck and drew her to him with his hands on her hips, and they were wrapped in the heated cocoon of humanity that swayed about them, every part of their bodies touching. She had never danced with Keith before. She had no idea how it would feel to have her naked breasts brushing against his chest and his thighs moving with hers in the slow, erotic movements of the dance. She was unprepared for the sensations caused by the trickle of warm breath against her ear and the softness of his beard on her cheek, and his fingers pressing into the curve of her hip brought back stinging, breathtaking memories of the afternoon. Her heart started to pump laboriously, and her breathing altered. She had never had any idea it was possible to become so aroused in a public place with a hundred other couples looking on.

It was useless to try to move away and futile to suggest he not hold her quite so tightly. If they were going to dance, it would of necessity be in close quarters. There was a heady gratification in knowing that their proximity was having the same effect upon his physiology as it was on hers, and she really did not want to stop dancing. But she tried to disguise her pleasure—and to perhaps distract her thoughts from the languorous, fantasizing direction they were taking—with conversation.

She looked up at him with a teasing smile. "I've discovered your passion."

The pressure of his fingers on her hips tightened, and he murmured, "I've never tried to hide it from you."

She fought back a rush of delighted color and kept her neck arched upward to look at him in defense against that sensuous voice in her ear. "Your work," she specified sternly. "That thingamajig you designed. I've never seen you get so excited about anything."

He grinned at her. "Haven't you?" He was in a very playful mood tonight. But at her mock scowl he assumed a very pompous tone that was delightfully incongruent with the erotic sensation of his lips moving against her ear, and he said, "Electricity, the great metaphysical link between man and his universe. A glimpse of immortality in the palm of your hand. All creation channeled between two thin wires...."

She placed her hands firmly on his shoulders and stepped back the few inches that were possible, looking up at him with a severity that did not disguise the bright awareness in her eyes nor the excited flush to her cheeks. "And this, from the man who only this afternoon told me Madison Avenue couldn't change the world? There is, perhaps, some intrinsic difference between what you find fulfilling in your work and what I do? I mean, is designing a sound system for a musical group going to bring salvation to the world?"

He grinned, his eyes catching flecks of the rotating blue and green lights from the stage. "Touché, darlin'.'' He held her close again and added, "The difference of course is that I do it for fun, you do it for profit. It's important to know where personal satisfaction leaves off and ambition begins."

She frowned a little, now genuinely perplexed. "Is that why you don't do it for a living? Do you have some sort of moral code against making a multidigit annual salary?"

The slight lift of his shoulders brought her only into closer, warmer contact with his body. "Who needs the rat race? One of the differences between you and me," he added mildly, "is that I get more satisfaction out of helping people out than exploiting them."

"That's not a nice thing to say, Michaelson," she murmured, but it was without real venom because his fingers had begun to trail absently down the curve of her buttocks and to the backs of her thighs and it was all she could do to keep her legs from giving way. Her arms tightened with an almost imperceptible convulsive motion about his neck, and she didn't breathe at all until his hands moved slowly and with exquisite exploratory deliberation back to her waist again.

"I know," he murmured, answering the statement she had almost forgot making. "And to apologize, I'm going to show you how to sell those wretched dresses of yours so you'll stop worrying about it."

She laughed, low and throatily, against his shoulder. The band had moved into another number, but they did not stop dancing. "You?" she mocked. "Show me?"

"If there is one thing I do know, dear child," he assured her, very close to her ear, "it's how to sell anyone on anything."

That, she acknowledged somewhat dizzily, she did

not doubt. He had started out selling her two telephones she did not want and was now on the verge of selling her something else she had had no intention of ever wanting. . . .

His matter-of-fact tone summoned her back from disturbed, somewhat incoherent reflections. "You need to go for the soft sell," he told her. "Low-key, honest, unpretentious. You know your prices are ridiculous. Make your customers want the product *because* of that, not in spite of it. Good old-fashioned honesty. Works every time."

She felt a small thrill of something very near to adoration—not because it was such an original idea or because he had thought of it first—but because it had come from him so easily, so generously. Because he cared. Because for the first time their two worlds touched and the subtle blue-arc sparks that grazed across the horizon were explosive with promise.

And then he kissed her on the nose, smiling. "And that's the last venture I make into the corrupt world of commercial gain, so don't get your hopes up."

Jessie laughed, purely and simply because she was happy.

They stayed until four A.M., long after the club had closed, drinking wine and talking with the band, and the night passed so quickly that Jessie did not have time to get tired. The energy that sparked between Keith and his friends was invigorating, and she was renewed by the contact. Or perhaps it was just being with Keith himself that made her wish the evening did not have to end.

His arm was around her waist, and she leaned lazily against his shoulder as he escorted her up the walkway to her door. Her head was spinning with soft lights and subtle colors, her senses alive with the star-dusted night, and her mind was full of a cacaphony of discoveries and impressions—all of them centering about Keith Michaelson. Curiously she asked, "Do you really know anyone who could help them get started?"

"Probably," he answered negligently as she straightened up to retrieve her key from her purse. His hand caressed her shoulder. "I suppose there are one or two producers in this town who would kill for a chance to get at talent like theirs. It's only a matter of time before they're discovered."

She hesitated before inserting the key into the lock, looking up at him with a puzzled frown. "Then why don't you help them out? If you really can, I mean," she added on a slightly derogatory note.

He grinned and touched his finger to her chin, a teasing, indulgent gesture. "Because," he answered, "they're shark-bait, just like you. They've got the talent, the ambition, the thirst for power and success— but they don't know how to handle it. Let them loose on the world, and they'll be gobbled up in less than a year."

She stared at him, uncertain whether or not she completely understood his reasons for lumping her into the same category as his ambitious friends. Shark-bait. What was that supposed to mean? She wasn't entirely sure she wanted to find out, so, mustering her best superior tone, she said simply, "Oh, the great judge of human character. You really enjoy controlling people's destinies, don't you?"

He took the key from her and opened the door. "Darlin', I'm too tired tonight to control anybody's destiny, and so are you. Let's solve the problems of the world another time, shall we?"

He touched a switch, and the pole lamp in the corner glowed to amber light. Delbert, who was curled up asleep on the sofa, stretched and blinked and uncurled his pink tongue in a mighty yawn, then sprang directly for Keith's knee. Keith plucked him off, looked at him for a moment seriously, and then told him, "You're starting to wear out your welcome, cat. Why don't you go find some other house to plague?"

Jessie patiently rescued Delbert from Keith's threatening clutch and locked him in the bedroom. When she returned, Keith greeted her with a glass of wine—the last, Jessie promised herself sternly, of the evening. She was beginning to feel a little woozy, and she wasn't sure how much of it was from the wine and fatigue and how much was due to Keith.

She slipped off her sandals and curved her feet beneath her as she sank to the sofa, lighting a cigarette even though her throat was sore and dry from having smoked too much today already. She did not seem to be able to be around Keith without smoking, and of course he was right. What she wanted when she was near him had nothing at all to do with tobacco. She smiled at him as he filled his own glass and came over to her. "I had a nice time tonight, Keith," she said. "In fact, all day."

"It's called playing as hard as you work," he replied, "and you're not doing too bad—for an amateur."

He sat on the floor beside her, his elbow resting on the sofa cushion near the curve of her knee. She playfully took a long strand of his hair and spread it over his shoulder and across her knee, loving the tickling sensation against her bare flesh. "When are you going to learn to work as hard as you play?" she teased him.

He leaned his head back, more silky hair brushing

against her leg, and he sipped his wine indulgently as he replied, "You could get to be a real nag, woman."

Silence fell, warm and easy. It was four thirty in the morning and only right that he should be here, that they should be together sharing the peace and the still-ness of the predawn. She felt drowsy and good and a little light-headed; it was a wonderful feeling.

She crushed out her cigarette in the ashtray and snuggled down against the cushions, studying the half inch of wine that remained in her glass with an ab-sorbed air. "Liebfraumilch," she said thoughtfully. "What does that mean, I wonder?"

"Ummm...." The sound of her voice had appar-ently brought Keith away from peaceful thoughts of his own. He considered her question. "Well, I know *Lieb-estraum* means 'dream of love'...*frau* means 'woman' or 'mother'.... 'Dream woman's milk'?" She giggled, and he projected seriously, "'Love of mother's milk'? My German's not too good."

"I always thought 'lieb' meant little," she suggested with as much control as possible, considering the fact that bubbles of laughter were dancing in her head like Champagne.

"Little mother's milk? Little cow's milk?"

She let the fit of silly giggles overtake her. "I think you're a little tipsy," she accused, and her giggles turned to shrieks as he turned dancing eyes upon her, fastening his hands about her waist and dragging her to the floor with him.

"I think we both are," he returned, and she made only a token resistance as he pulled her to him between the circle of his legs, both of them laughing as she tried to keep her wine from spilling and her dress from hik-ing up about her waist, and he showed absolutely no regard for either concern. The wine did spill, but she managed to keep her skirt in a somewhat decent position, and her face was flushed and her breath was short when she at last found herself cradled half on his lap and half on the floor, her head supported by the arch of his bended knee.

His eyes were glowing with boyish pleasure, but his tone was serious as he reproved, "You really should stop smoking. You have no stamina." He laid his hand very lightly against her chest, just beneath the curve of her breast. "See how your heart is pounding just with the effort of getting from the sofa to the floor?"

Her peripheral vision caught sight of her wineglass swaying tipsily on its rim, and she said woefully, "I'm going to have a stain on my rug."

"I'll buy you a new one."

She looked up into the familiar, gentle face, the pleasant curve of his lips, the dark affectionate eyes, and a movement of her hand brought his face to hers. Slow kiss, soft and wonderful. And when she looked into his eyes again the tenderness of his smile was closer than any embrace. She could have looked into those eyes forever, seeing nothing but gentleness and affection, sharing and understanding. How was it possible that one man could make her feel so good, so right about everything? So... natural.

He said her name very softly, and when he said it something in her face seemed to give him enormous pleasure. There was a widening of his eyes and a deepening as he looked into hers, a leap of something very close to adoration. A slim finger traced a path from her brow to the curve of her cheekbone; then the fingers spread to thread through her hair. With each movement his eyes were drinking in her expression as his fingers reverently explored new sensations of temperature and texture, and she was mesmerized by the delicacy of her response as his hand trailed downward over her face, around her ear, to her throat, caressing her shoulder. She thought nothing. She hardly breathed. She gave herself over to the moment, letting it happen, experiencing it, loving it.

His hand floated down to her waist; an adept, graceful movement untied the belt that bound her dress. His fingers fell between the two layers of material, separating them, exposing the prickling flesh of her abdomen to the cooling night air. And all the time he was watching her, his eyes steady and unrushed, alert for any signal of objection or protest. Her lips parted with a breath as she felt warm, work-roughened fingers playing with fascinating delicacy across the silken expanse of her bare flesh. Sensitized muscles contracted and curled, warmth spread from his touch downward in a lazy, welcoming pleasure even as her chest tightened and her heart began to race. She tried not to breathe because she was sure he would notice the trembling of her lips if they moved for the passage of air. His head bent downward; one by one he closed her eyelids with a kiss. She started breathing again when his hand moved upward, exposing by lingering inches her skin to the touch of his fingers and the brush of the air. Her breasts filled with awareness and pulsed with longing before she even felt the pressure of his hand.

Slow sinking dizziness flowed through her with the warmth of his fingers caressing and curving about her breasts, their delicate circular patterns teasing stiff nipples and with slowly tightening pressure cupping, molding. The racing of her heart shook her entire body; each brush of his fingers or movement of his palm tightened the thin wire of anticipation, and it was wonderful, what was happening to her. It was a free-floating feeling of drowning pleasure to move with this experience, to let it carry her....

"Jessie," he said softly, "open your eyes."

In a moment she did. It was an uncertain fluttering motion that stung new heat to her cheeks as it gradually brought his face into focus. Her cheeks were stained with pleasure, her eyes deep and luminous, her lips parted with shallow breaths, and for a moment he simply looked at her. He was smiling. "You are lovely," he whispered, and he kissed her.

Her hand fell against the side of his neck, crept beneath his collar, fingers straining and tightening to draw him closer, reveling in the sensation of his flesh beneath her hand and yearning to drink him in and to open herself to him.... I'm falling in love with him, she thought as though from very far away, and it was a beautiful, strangely welcome realization that floated just the other side of conscious acceptance, not threatening, not frightening. She hadn't sought it, she hadn't invited it, yet it was there, as certain as the coming sun and as formless as the wind—yet, like the wind, just as indefinable. For of course it couldn't be, this incredible thing that she imagined was happening inside her...it only felt so right to pretend it could be, for the moment.

The depth of his kiss left her lips throbbing and her flesh tingling as he drew slowly away. He slipped his arm beneath her shoulders and shifted the position of his leg, arching her toward him, exposing the full length of her throat to the deep pressure of his mouth and the wet, tantalizing brush of his tongue. She shivered and then gasped as the warmth of his mouth

met her breast. Immediate electric shock signals re-
layed pulsing awareness to her lower regions; the secret
flesh so long dormant swelled with life and need. For a
moment everything brightened, colors were sharper,
the sound of her own sharp breathing incredibly clear,
every cell of her body heightened to swift awareness.
Then it all melted together into a slow, swirling, golden
sweet glow, like caramel candy left too long in the sun,
oozing goodness and delight. His tongue traced a tingling course over her nipples, his hands cupped, his
mouth drew long kisses from her firmness. His hair
tickled her chin, and his beard rubbed against the sensitized nerve endings of her breasts, a gentle abrasive
she found unbearably stimulating. When he lifted his
face, her lips were aching for him; she wound her arms
about his neck, she felt the hot unsteady fan of his
breath across her face as she dragged his mouth to hers.
She thought she could taste a very faint hint of her
perfume on his tongue.

Her palms curving about his neck pressed against a
throbbing pulse, smooth-textured skin protecting a
fragile vein that was engorged with power. Its rapid
rhythm beat a counterpoint to the hammering of her
own heart, the erratic puffs of breath that flared her
nostrils. Unconsciously she turned to press herself into
him, her hips making subtle yearning motions as he
stretched out beside her. His jeaned leg slipped between hers, and her abdomen met the warm metal of
his belt buckle, her breasts flattened against the textured, fabric-covered strength of his chest. His hand,
pushing away the remaining fabric, curved around her
bare waist, pressing, and holding. The thin cotton of
her panties met the stiff material of his jeans, and his
lips were on her hot face, silky beard caressing, warm

breath and moist tongue pouring over her ear. His hand moved downward, over the shape of her hip and along her thigh, and she felt control slipping; she felt herself plunging headlong into the blinding white light of discovery where there was no time for thinking, no room for questions, no will for conscious decision, only the overpowering need to give in to yearnings.

It was desperation, sudden fear in an echo from the past, which gave her strength. "Keith," she whispered. Her voice was husky; she was hardly even aware of what she said. Jessie only knew from far away that she needed time—time to think—time to regain control or she would be lost. Her breath was little more than a gasp, sentences punctuated by the pounding of her heart. "You should know...I'm not...that is...I don't...use any contraception."

He moved his face slowly to rest against her shoulder. Horror and relief swept her when she realized what she had said, what she had done...and then dread grew as she felt his chest expand with a long deep breath; the dread was mixed with a sharp stab of loss. For a long time he was very still against her; she could feel stiffness creep into his muscles. Alarm gripped her as he moved, and then she realized incredulously that his shoulders were shaking with laughter. He brought both hands up to cup her face, his dark eyes were filled with mirth, disbelief, and something very faintly like bitter self-derision. "If you are trying to scare me," he said, "it's not working. I happen to love children. And if you're trying to break the mood..." He sat up, the firm grasp of his hand on hers pulling her with him. "It's working. Okay, Jessie, talk to me."

She couldn't. She could only fumble to arrange the folds of her dress about her naked body and the shreds of her dignity about her vulnerable heart and try to hide behind her misery as she felt his probing eyes upon her.

At last he removed that condemning gaze, and she felt safe enough to glance at him. He was sitting in profile to her, his arm resting across one upraised knee, the beard hiding the expression of his face and long shadows from the lamplight concealing his eyes. But she could feel the tension. She could see the soft rise and fall of his shoulders with each breath. She wanted to crawl away and hide.

He said, "It's times like these I wish I smoked."

Perhaps the comment was meant to lighten the mood, but there was nothing light about his tone. Her cheeks were raw with draining color, and her lips felt swollen and abused; she ached all over. She said stiffly, "I think you'd better go."

Keith looked at her slowly. He made no attempt to spare her feelings by disguising his emotions. His eyes were hard and his lips were tight and there was controlled fury in every inch of him, yet he spoke quietly, distinctly, and very evenly. "If you don't want me, that's fine. If you don't feel comfortable telling me why, that's okay, too; I can accept that. But you will *not* lie about it. That I won't tolerate. Talk to me, lady," he commanded quietly.

Jessie felt herself sinking deeper and deeper into despair. Talk to him? How could she? He knew that she wanted him; he knew that she could not commit herself to him. He did not know the terrible risks involved in such a commitment, the exposure of the heart, the threat of rejection, the danger of failure... and he would not understand if he did know.

Still in that same even tone, his temper carefully controlled, he said, "All right, I'll go first." His eyes were like flecks of coal, the hard surface shielding a soft inner crust that flaked away bit by bit as he spoke. "I feel lousy. I'm angry and I'm disappointed and I hurt like hell. You did this to me, and I have a right to know why."

She caught a breath low in her throat, and her eyes narrowed. It would have taken less than that challenge to snap away the thin thread of control she had been grasping so desperately; primal emotions surged and seethed within her and demanded an end to the tension, an end of the fight. She said softly, "It's all just a game to you." Her eyes were glittering. "Divide and conquer, and the prize is my body. Well, you've been a gallant soldier; you've proved yourself through sacrifice and determination, and God forbid that I should withhold your prize now!" Her hand fluttered to the single button at her shoulder with a jerky motion, tearing at it. All vestiges of control slipped away and she screamed at him, "Here, you want me, take me! I'm tired of fighting you!"

Hard gripping fingers closed over hers in a swift, ruthless motion and he breathed, "No theatrics, Jessie. This is too damn serious, and you know it."

For a moment she struggled with him, stupidly, all capacity for reason and logic sucked away into the black tunnel of pain, leaving only the instinct to strike out, to hurt—herself, him, anyone. And in that breathless moment she saw his eyes soften, pity and understanding seeping through the thin shield of anger, and she could fight anything but that. He pried her fingers away from the button; she dropped her head in humiliation and defeat as scalding tears filled her throat. "Go away," she whispered brokenly.

"No." There was gentleness in his tone, softness in his touch, as he brushed away a strand of hair from her damp cheek. And then a long sigh and he shook his head slowly. "Lady, you have more defenses than a Green Beret on night patrol, and I wonder if even you know what you're defending yourself against. You had one clumsy lover, and you let the bastard destroy your marriage, your self-esteem, and damn near your life. Jessie, you're no idiot. You know what happens between us will have no resemblance whatsoever to the way it was with your husband. You're just using that to fortify the wall you're trying to build between us. But why? What are you so afraid of?"

She got very slowly to her feet. Her legs were still shaky. He was not telling her anything she did not already know. How long had she been using her bad experience with Frank as an excuse to avoid a sexual relationship with any man? Because a sexual relationship meant a personal relationship; it meant exposure, vulnerability, risks to the heart and soul she could not afford to take. She had built her fortress carefully, painstakingly, and until now no one had ever threatened it. It was exhausting work, defending the heart, especially as she began to suspect her most dangerous enemy was herself.

She said tiredly, "It has nothing to do with Frank." Or at least not much. "It's you and me. Us. Together." She made a small helpless motion with her hand, not looking at him. "It wouldn't work."

He was standing very close behind her. She almost imagined she could feel his breath upon her neck. "It's good between us, Jessie," he said softly, "you know that. It has been from the first minute. Aren't you getting tired of lying to yourself?"

Yes, she thought wearily. So tired....

"Are you afraid of an uncommitted love affair," he added quizzically, "or are you afraid of making a commitment? Which is it, Jess? Can't you tell me that?"

No, she couldn't tell him that. She stood rigidly with her hands clasped before her, wanting nothing more than to sink back into the gentle protective embrace of his arms and let him make the hurt go away.

And he said in a very odd tone, "I never would have taken you for a coward. I knew you had been hurt, I knew you had a need to protect yourself... but basically you're not a coward, Jess. Why won't you look at me?"

Coward? she thought. Yes. If I weren't, I would be lighting a fire on Madison Avenue instead of hiding away in this safe little place, or... Her eyes went with bleak yearning toward the display of political cartoons on the wall. Had she ever had the courage to go for what she wanted? It had nothing to do with one bad lover or one failed marriage. It was the pattern of her whole life.

She felt his hands, very lightly, upon her shoulders. He inquired softly, "What can I do, Jess? What is it you want?"

It took all her willpower to keep herself from turning into his embrace. What did she want? That was easy. She wanted success, fulfillment, security... she wanted her life to take a straight, uncomplicated upward path, and she had no room for the distractions of a futile love affair. She wanted him....

She said, hardly above a breath, "Time." The word was almost choked out. "Time—alone."

She felt his gentle smile as evidenced in the barely perceptible pressure of his lips against her shoulder. "No," he said huskily. "That's not what you really want. But I'll give it to you anyway." He dropped his hands. She felt a lurch that tore at the pit of her stomach as she knew he was leaving.

She watched his familiar figure cross the room, and a sudden swift fear stabbed her that he might never come back. Urgency parted her lips, but fear choked off the words, and he opened the door. He stood for a moment silhouetted in the murky gray of a reluctant dawn, and when he looked at her his smile was bleak.

"Congratulations," he said. "You've just spent the night with me."

There was perhaps another moment's hesitation in which her eyes met his in confused despair, and then he was gone—before she could call him back.

Chapter Five

It was one o'clock on a Friday afternoon. Anna was away on a buying trip, and the store had been filled with customers all morning. Jessie was spending her lunch break trying to catch up on the paperwork, and Sammy had already called twice, soliciting her help with the latest design she had delivered for him. When the phone rang again she snatched it up and practically barked her greeting.

It was Celia, calling from New York. "You won't believe what I have for you," she breathed excitedly.

"If it's a two-week all-expenses-paid vacation to Hawaii," Jessie said, cradling the phone with her ear as she used her hands to punch prices into the tickets with the printing machine, "give it to me straight. I can take it."

"Better," avowed Celia. "I have arranged an interview for you on August third with Mr. James Massey of the famous Madison Avenue address...."

Jessie hesitated for just long enough to catch her breath. "But I haven't decided for sure I'm even coming to New York this summer!" she exclaimed impatiently. "What do you mean, you arranged—"

"It's a chance of a lifetime, Jess. He's seen your work and wanted to meet you; you can't possibly—"

The edge of the ticket maker caught her finger and drew blood. Jessie swore softly and stuffed her finger into her mouth, then interrupted her friend snappishly, "For goodness sake, Celia, don't you think I'm old enough to make my own decisions and arrange my own interviews? I'm not even sure I want to make the trip this year—or that I can afford it! Will you for heaven's sake give me a break?"

There was a very brief pause; then Celia said reasonably, "Don't you think you're old enough to take control of your own life? You've got to go after what you want, Jessie. Mr. James Massey—nor anyone like him—is not going to come knocking at your door in Nowheresville, Tennessee. You've got to go to him."

Suddenly Jessie felt overwhelmed by the enormous burden of pressure. Decisions were piling up on her, and she was not prepared to make them. The tinkling of the bell on the boutique door announced the arrival of another customer, and she could not cope with this right now. "Look, Cele, I'm working and I can't talk right now." She swept the blank tickets and ticket maker into a drawer before turning to see her customer. "Someone just came in, and I have to get off the phone."

"I'm not going to cancel the interview," she warned.

"Do whatever you like, I—" Jessie turned and looked straight into the deep brown eyes of Keith Michaelson. "I have to go," she said weakly, and hung up the phone.

In the five seconds she looked at him fifteen days of isolation, despair, and heartbreak flooded past her eyes like the last visions of a drowning man. Fifteen days of telling herself morning and night that she had gotten what she wanted, that it was for the best, of trying to ignore the very certain truth that all she had succeeded in doing was punishing herself—again. Fifteen days. She had never thought he would leave her alone this long. He had promised her time, and time he had given her. And for fifteen days, morning and night, hour after hour, staring at the telephone, straining for the sound of the chugging engine of the battered van pulling into her driveway, she had been hauntingly aware that he had not promised he would come back. But he had come back.

He had come back, and the sight of him was the last-minute lifeline thrown to that drowning man. The sight of him made her heart start pumping again and told her lungs to reach for new air. Jessie looked at Keith, and it was like stepping out of the shadows into a bright summer day. Absurd happiness began to tingle in her toes and spread all the way up to the roots of her hair, and suddenly everything was just right, just the way it should be. Colors shifted and brightened and fell naturally into place; the temperature-controlled air about her was warm and balmy, and she found her own equilibrium just by looking at him.

He was settled lazily against the counter, his weight partially on his forearm, and he was smiling. "Hi," he said. "How's business?"

The loose wavy hair, the satiny dark beard, the curving lips, the warm, coffee eyes. All of him, the jeans and the long-sleeved plaid shirt over a navy T-shirt, the beautiful hands arranged with such negligent ease upon her counter—all of him was like a long, refreshing drink to a parched throat. She could not control her absurd smile of pure joy, and she knew her eyes were glowing. She began to babble. "Oh, just fine—terrific, actually. I used your idea about the soft sell; did you see it in the paper Sunday? 'You can afford more, because you're worth more.' We're already beginning to get some response, although I'm not sure how much of it is due to advertising techniques and how much is just the usual summer rush. This place has been a madhouse all week."

She had to pause for breath, and his lips curved slowly into a deeper smile. His eyes were moving over her, touching her eyes, her nose, her mouth, her chin, neck, shoulders, breasts, hands—and everywhere his glance rested, it was like a caress. Her whole body began to tingle, and she felt herself blush. It was good, so good to see him. He said, "Looks like I got here just in time, then. Sounds like you could use some R&R. What are you doing this weekend?"

At that moment she would have cancelled an audience with the Pope to be with him. But she pointed out uncertainly, "Well, I have to work tomorrow of course, but—"

"The point of R&R," he informed her, "is to avoid work as much as possible. You've got those dark circles under your eyes again, darlin', and your tan is starting to fade. Time for more fresh air and sunshine before you fade right away into a mere shadow of your former self."

Even as she smiled she knew that the dark circles had little to do with overwork, nor did her pallor. Many sleepless nights and restless days had taken their toll, and she was still amazed that he could do that to her, that any man could do that to her.... Love could be a physical thing, as well as an emotional one. If that was what it was.

And he added casually, with absolutely no change in his expression or tone, "I'm going to the mountains this weekend. Do you want to come?"

For just a second she caught her breath. For just a second she had an absurd impulse to specify, "Do you mean the *whole* weekend?" But she knew very well what he meant. She looked into those soft, patient, totally nonjudgmental eyes, and she knew several things. First, the casual manner with which the invitation was issued in no way implied that he did not understand its significance. Second, he did mean the whole weekend, day and night. And third, he would not ask her again. If she said no it did not necessarily mean he would walk out of her life never to appear again; he might continue to see her, but their relationship would be vastly altered. He was calling for a decision from her, right now, this minute, no more games, no more walls. Wasn't this the man, she thought in a sort of low-key panic, who had once promised her no pressure?

She floundered, trying to buy time, "Well, there's the store.... Anna's out of town, and it's my responsibility.... I can't just lock up and go away for the weekend...."

The slight, momentary shadow that crossed his eyes told her that while he might have expected this answer from her, it was not the one he wanted. Still, he smiled as he straightened up. There was so much to read in that smile, but she was too rushed, too flustered, to catch any of it. "Right," he said. "Take care of your responsibilities, Jess."

He started to turn, and she rushed on, "Besides, there's Delbert. I can't just lock him up and leave him for a whole weekend—"

There was amusement mixed into the quizzical expression on his face as he pointed out, "One small cat can't run your life. Leave him a pan of dry cat food and a bowl of water and lock up all your valuables."

She looked at him for a long moment of creeping helplessness and sinking despair. He was backing her against a wall. He had never done that before. She had wondered so long where his patience would end, and now she knew. He had never promised her he would wait forever. She had never asked him to. All this time she had held the rule book, and he had guided her along, letting her grow used to feeling safe with him. Now he had volleyed the ball directly into her court and she was in control, completely. It was not a safe feeling.

Her eyes were pleading as she looked at him. Jessie already knew he would understand, that was not what she sought from him. Forgiveness was not what she wanted. She knew there would be no second chance. She didn't know what she wanted. "I—I can't," she said in a very small voice.

His lips tightened slightly in acknowledgement and acceptance. "Okay," he said easily, and started for the door. "I'll give you a call sometime next week."

What do you want, Jessie McVey?

He had reached the door before she said urgently, "Keith."

He turned, and for just a moment as she looked at him she thought he did know, he did understand, what a great deal it required of her to listen for once to her heart and not her reason. To reach out for what she wanted. She smiled at him rather uncertainly. "Could you—could you give me time to change first?"

His eyes welcomed her, his smile fortified her. "I'll stop by your place in an hour," he said.

Precisely an hour later Jessie handed her overnight

bag to him with a nervous little smile and stacked her paint box and canvases on the front floorboard of the van. "I thought I'd better not waste the chance to capture the scenery," she explained. "Who knows when I'll get another chance to see the Smoky Mountains."

"Chances are where you make them," he told her. "We can go back anytime you like."

From the first moment he had arrived, Jess had been trying to ignore the pleasurable light in his eyes everytime his glance swept over her. In that very first moment she had wished desperately that she had worn something other than the low-cut, navel-emphasizing shorts and the knit bandeau top that had a tendency to curl down every time she bent over. The day was hot and sticky, and it had seemed appropriate attire at the time, but was she being too obvious? Was this really the first time he had seen her in shorts? She wished at least she had a better tan, and that she had paid more attention to her exercises these past weeks. Once again, to avoid his gaze, she turned her eyes to the leaden sky and commented, "It doesn't look like the weather is going to be very cooperative."

His eyes snapped with amusement as he saw through her feeble attempt to distract him—and herself—from the real purpose of this weekend. He placed his hands firmly on her waist and assured her, "The weather is not affecting my view of the scenery in the least." He kissed her on the nose, and his tone was kind. "Relax, Jessie. I'm supposed to be taking your mind off your problems, not creating more. And—" he slapped her playfully on the bottom as he turned her toward the van "—if you don't stop chewing your fingernails so loudly, you're going to scare the fish away."

She managed a nervous little giggle as she climbed

inside. "I hope," she added severely, "that you've planned an alternative menu besides fish. I told you, I've never done this before."

His quiet look told her that he understood this was a first for her in many ways—that he understood, and accepted. That he was with her, not against her. That one look told her many things, and in that brief solemn moment wiped away all residual fears and uncertainties, leaving her only glad to be with him, happy and comfortable for perhaps the first time in her life.

And he said as he started the engine, "Do I look like a complete idiot, Jessie McVey? I wouldn't think of going more than ten minutes away from the heart of civilization with you unless I'd packed enough food to fortify an army. And to begin with…" He reached into the back before putting the van into gear and tossed a large bag of peanuts into her lap. His eyes twinkled. "Keep your mouth busy until I'm free to offer you a substitute."

She made a face at him and tore open the bag.

Jessie was disappointed in her first view of the mountains. The day was so dreary that visibility was limited, and the smoky blue-gray colors were swallowed blandly by an even deeper gray sky. The tops of the mountains were flat, like rounded topiary bushes with the top halves sawed off. It was just as well there was not much to see, for the treacherous twisting roads—little more than paths in some places—that Keith negotiated with such competent ease required all her concentration to keep her heart out of her throat. At one point they turned sharply, and from her window she saw nothing but a sheer drop into foggy nothingness. She said weakly, "Oh, God. This is not relaxing me, Michaelson."

He grinned at her and turned abruptly onto a wooded dirt trail.

She felt safer there, possibly because even though the edge of the mountain might well have been just inches from the back tires, she could not see it. The van bounced and jerked on worn shocks, and low branches squealed against the roof and slapped the window, causing her to flinch. They moved from deep shadow into patches of subdued light, frightening little animals and screeching birds. The air was rich with the dampness of pine resin, cloying honeysuckle, and the fresh, woodsy scent of kudzu. The pervasive heat that had clung to the lowlands was lighter here, but humidity wrapped itself around them like a tropical veil. Patches of velvet-frond ferns brushed against the van's tires, and little islets of wood violets peeked out from beneath tangles of blackberry vines that were ripe with dark fruit. "Can we eat them?" inquired Jess excitedly, twisting about to pinpoint the exact location of the sagging vines. "I mean, are they real blackberries?"

"Darlin', if you want to fight the wasps and the snakes for them," he replied indulgently, "you're welcome to them. As for their being 'real'—" he shot her an amused look "—plastic blackberries only grow in suburban supermarkets."

She gave him a look of totally feigned insult and turned her attention back to the window.

The slow progress of the van ate up the hard-packed rutted path and patches of dry grass and weeds, sprinkling the still-life scenery with a fine powder of red dust. Jessie's senses were busily trying to absorb it all, searching for a way to capture the lazy hot stillness and the heavy hush of colors on canvas. There was a quality of unreality provided by the thick heat and the diffuse light, as though they had come unexpectedly upon a secret part of the world and caught it during siesta time.

The road ended abruptly before a large clearing, and Keith stopped the engine. A glassy slate lake stretched to the west, and tall evergreens tangled with leafy branches of less ambitious timber before the whole of it blended into the dusty green swell of a mountainous incline. Various lengths and textures of grass shaded the ground from deep emerald to pale gray, and the occasional rippling motion was the movement of some small animal seeking a deeper shelter from which to observe the intruders. A single surprised black-eyed Susan brushed against Jessie's door as the vehicle rolled to a stop, and bordering the lake were snatches of color in clumps and waves of plant life—red, orange, bright yellow, dark blue. She had never known there were so many species and varieties of wildflowers.

Directly before them was a narrow footbridge about four feet long constructed of raggedly-hewn lumber placed on either bank and protected on one side by a rail of twisted, bark-covered pine. And directly before that was the cabin, surrounded on all three visible sides by the buttercup-yellow glow of wild daisies.

"Oh, Keith," she said softly. "Look at the daisies!"

She opened her door and sprang lightly to the ground, disturbing a swarm of lazily droning green bottle flies. The cabin itself was a scene depicting crumbling Americana. Its overall dimensions were perhaps ten-by-twelve. It was set on concrete blocks, and the small space between foundation and ground was a tangle of creeping ivy and dry grass. The brown paper shingles on the sides were peeling, the tin roof curled up at one corner, the metal chimney pipe was lopsided. The window frames were of gray, weather-worn wood and so was the door. And everything was so silent. The absence of the customary background noises of civilization—distant traffic, airplanes, the constant low-key hum of industry and life—was so striking it resounded. The resulting silence was heavy and indolent.

The scraping and sliding of the van door was an abrasive intrusion into the scene, and it startled two curious crows overhead into a noisy flight. Jessie watched their departure and their indignant reproofs in amusement as Keith handed her her suitcase and invited, "Go ahead and explore if you like." He removed an ice chest from the back. "I'm going to put some of this food in the spring."

She glanced at him. "Spring?"

He grinned at her naiveté. "Nature's great refrigerant. Back in a minute."

She crossed the sagging footbridge carefully and was relieved to notice it protected not more than six inches of clear gurgling water. She pushed at the weathered door uncertainly, and it swung open slowly on creaking hinges.

The inside was not much different from what she had expected. The windows were covered with billows of burlap tied back with fraying cord, the walls adorned with peeling gray-white paint. There was an old-fashioned potbellied stove dominating one corner that fascinated her. The interior smelled very faintly of fish, and it was stifling hot, but the room was clean. A long counter took up one wall, its bare wood sagging in the middle. In one corner of the counter there was a tangle of fishing lures, a pair of pliers, and a reel of fishing line. Beneath it were curtained shelves that proved to be bare except for a few forgotten paper cups and one plastic fork. The room contained a small wooden table, several ladder-backed chairs, and one double bed whose metal frame supported a gray-ticked mattress and two matching pillows.

Jessie looked at that bed for a long time, and she suddenly had a flash of the elegant Bahamian hotel suite in which she had spent her honeymoon. And for some strange reason that brought a silly grin to her face. She tossed her overnight bag onto the bare mattress, smoothed a strand of hair away from her sticky face, and went back outside with a step that was almost bouncy.

She made her way to the edge of the lake, where she knelt down in the scratchy grass and watched with clear-eyed fascination the silvery darting of minnows close to the shore. She felt Keith's step behind her just as he slipped his arms around her waist from behind and drew her slowly to her feet. He tickled her chin with a daisy and she giggled, taking it from him as she sank back against his strong length, holding his arms in place around her bare midriff, sighing as she leaned her head against his shoulder. "Oh, Keith, it's so peaceful here."

His beard tickled her neck where it was bared by her ponytail. "Have you been inside?"

"Hm-hmm."

"What did you think?"

"Not exactly the Waldorf-Astoria. There's no running water," she pointed out.

"Sure there is. About fifteen yards away; it runs right down a gulley and into the feeder stream."

"Where's the little girl's room?"

She could feel his grin, as warm as sunshine, against her neck. "You follow this little path around the cabin, down a small incline, and straight to a big fluffy bush marked 'Hers'. You can't miss it."

"I assume there's an attendant on duty."

"Yes, but you tip her in hickory nuts."

She giggled. "Nice system."

In a moment he added, "I assume you noticed the bed."

For a second something ridiculously like nervousness tightened in her stomach. She nodded.

His soft beard nuzzled her ear. That did not do anything to alleviate the sudden fluttering sensation that had begun in her chest. "You are not, I hope," he said matter-of-factly, "laboring under the delusion that I intend to sleep on the floor."

She shook her head, unable to speak.

"*You're* not planning to sleep on the floor?"

Jessie turned in Keith's arms, smiling, and dragged the daisy playfully across his forehead and down his smooth cheekbone. "Why don't you show me how to put a fishing line in the water before all the big ones get away?"

He kissed her on the nose, and then on the lips, and her automatic swelling response almost irradicated the brevity with which the gesture had been planned. She felt his fingers tighten slightly on her bare back, heard his soft intake of breath, saw a momentary brightening and question in the depths of his eyes. But it was gone so quickly she might not have noticed it at all, and when he turned away to scoop up the fishing poles he had left on the grassy bank, her heart was racing and her skin felt damp.

"It's really very simple," he explained to her, handing her a pole. "You bait the hook, throw out the line, then lie back on the bank and close your eyes and hope to hell the fish don't bite and wake you up."

She looked at the complicated rigging of pole, hooks, and sinkers in her hand, and then to him suspiciously.

"I hope you're not expecting me to put anything gooey and squiggly on this hook."

He grinned. "After due consideration of your lack of experience in such matters, I decided to use for bait something that is neither gooey or squiggly. Cheese."

She looked at him dubiously. "Do fish like cheese?"

"It's a gourmet delicacy," he assured her, releasing her hook from the cork handle of the pole. "Besides, if I used worms, I have no doubt you'd call the ASPCA on me."

She laughed, and the answering spark in his eyes made her warm all over.

He spent the next half hour trying to teach her how to cast and finally decided such an enterprise was entirely too dangerous. He cast both lines into the water and propped the poles up on forked sticks planted into the side of the bank. After instructing her carefully to keep an eye on the red and white floats that were bobbing from the lines, he started for the cabin to open the windows and unpack the remainder of their supplies. "What if I get a bite?" she called after him in some alarm.

"With cheese as bait?" he scoffed. "Not a chance!"

As it happened, he was right. By the time he returned to supervise the fishing poles she had gotten bored and retrieved her art supplies from the van. She settled herself on a stump some distance away from him, the feathery grass brushing her knees, and set to work capturing on canvas the scenery that she knew instinctively she would remember the rest of her life.

The hazy sun faded gently into a purple twilight as Keith dozed stretched out on the bank and Jessie waved honeybees away and scratched insect bites absently, completely absorbed in her airy pencil sketches of the rolling mountains, the impertinent daisies, the stately cattails and the lacy watershrubs that lined the lake. She wished she had the skill to sketch Keith. She wanted to remember him forever as he was now, his long length stretched out in the fragrant grass, scuffed boots crossed at the ankles, arms folded under his head, face shielded by a tattered straw hat.... She wanted to explore with her pencil the lean masculine body her hands had not yet discovered.

At last Keith sat up lazily, reeled in the lines, and called to Jessie that it was time to start thinking about dinner. It was getting too dark to sketch anyway, so she reluctantly put away her things, rubbing at a few more new insect bites, which were really becoming annoying. Part of the great outdoors, she supposed.

He lit a kerosene lantern and built a campfire in a circle of rocks a few yards away from the cabin in the best Boy Scout tradition. She complimented his outdoor skill, and he complimented her sketches as he examined them in the fading daylight. She put her sketches on the counter inside the cabin and came back outside, irritably scratching her arms and a new welt that had appeared just above the snap of her shorts. "I don't suppose you included a first-aid kit in your list of survival equipment, did you?" she inquired.

He looked up from stoking the fire with immediate concern. "What's wrong?"

"The woodland creatures are eating me alive. Do you have any insect repellent, by any chance?"

He took her hand and led her to the lantern, where he examined the small red rows of bumps on her arms and legs and stomach with steadily darkening features. She did not like that look. "Mosquito bites?" she asked hopefully.

"No." His tone was grim. "Chiggers."

She almost laughed at the funny sound of the word, but his expression kept her from it. "What is that?"

"A bug." His eyes were full of regret and self-blame. "Lord, honey, I'm sorry. I should never have let you come out in these woods dressed like that...." And his lips twisted into a rueful half-smile. "I guess I was too busy enjoying the view to think about the consequences."

She shrugged, trying not to scratch. "A few bites. No big deal."

"They're not bites, exactly," he started to explain, but there was a flicker of bitter amusement in his eye as he finished simply, "Never mind. I don't think you really want to know. And you are not going to like what I'm going to have to do to you now."

That was a very alarming statement, to say the least, but before she could question him he had disappeared into the cabin. He returned in a moment with a mason jar half full of a thick brown liquid.

"Oh, God!" she gasped when he opened the lid. The odor that assaulted her was like the first unsuspecting taste of Chinese mustard; it made her eyes water and stung the back of her throat. She took an automatic step backward, waving at the air. "You're not going to put that on me! What is it, skunk oil?"

She thought she caught the edge of a grin as he dipped his fingers into the jar. "You don't want to know. Hold still, now. Believe me, the alternative is much more unpleasant."

Jessie screwed up her face as he began to smear the thick paste over the welts on her legs. "What's the alternative?" she choked.

"I don't think I'll tell you that, either."

He pasted the noxious stuff on her arms and legs, the few bites that were visible on her chest and stomach, and then he commanded impersonally, "Lower your shorts."

She stared at him, wide-eyed, for just the second it takes to blink, and he explained patiently, "These things can crawl under your clothes, you know." Then he grinned. "Don't worry, darlin', there's something about the smell of this stuff that has an automatic neutralizing effect on the libido. Hurry up, now, so I can wash my hands."

She unsnapped her shorts and lowered them to the bikini line. He found several more welts on her stomach and back and attended to them efficiently, then went to wash his hands in the stream, advising her good-naturedly to please sit downwind of him for the rest of the evening.

Jessie tried not to be depressed as she watched Keith prepare a savory camper's stew that she could neither smell nor find an appetite for. It was just a silly thing that could have happened to anyone. Romance and adventure in the great outdoors. Sure. At least the itching had stopped.

She felt better when Keith began to tease her and talk to her, and she laughed as tears ran down his face while he was peeling onions. He threatened her with the fact that chigger-bites did not necessarily exempt her from KP duty and that she was just as capable of peeling onions as he was. He wiped his eyes with the back of his hand and immediately had to go splash water on his face to stop the tears. Jessie finished peeling the onions. Her eyes were already stinging so badly with the odor of the insecticide that she did not even notice the new pungency.

When he handed her a plate of steaming stew she looked at it dolefully in the yellow firelight. "How do you expect me to eat anything with this awful smell all over my body?" she complained. "How long do I have to keep this stuff on?"

He looked at her frankly in the flickering shadows. "Until the bugs die," he said.

Whatever appetite Jessie had managed to preserve completely vanished. She set her plate aside.

She started to light a cigarette, but Keith advised against it, telling her he wasn't sure exactly how combustible the ingredients of the insecticide were. She tried to eat a few bites to appease her rumbling stomach, but mostly she looked longingly at the gently lapping water while Keith consumed his meal with relish, complimenting his own cooking lavishly and telling her she did not know what she was missing.

"Do you suppose," she suggested at last, "it would be safe to bathe in the lake?" He surely could not expect her to spend the rest of the night swathed in this smelly mixture; if not for her sake then for his, a bath was of first priority.

"Perfectly safe," he assured her, rinsing the dishes at the edge of the lake. "As long as you don't get your feet tangled in the undergrowth, you shouldn't drown, and I understand water moccasins can't bite under water."

"Water moccasins?" She looked at him for one moment of bleak despair and then she turned away, staring angrily into the spitting flames. "I think you brought me up here just to make fun of me, Keith Michaelson. Just to torture me and scare me and show me what a helpless, incompetent pioneer woman I would make."

He laughed softly behind her. "Poor little city girl. Is this the most disgusting thing that has ever happened to you? Are you embarrassed, humiliated, miserable? A nice warm shower would make you feel better, wouldn't it?"

She turned hopefully at the mention of the word shower, and was greeted by a bucketful of cool lake water emptied in a flood over her head. She leapt to her feet, gasping and sputtering, but he had ducked into the cabin before she could verbally register her indignation.

When he returned only moments later, she was ready for him. She laughed out loud at the startled expression on his face as she tossed a bucket of water over him, and he stood there for a moment, rivulets of water running from his beard and the ends of his hair, gasping and wiping his eyes, soaked to the waist. Then he looked at her, and the malicious gleam in his eye made her take an automatic defensive step backward. "See if I ever do anything nice for you again," he said, and between his fingers he held a tantalizing bar of soap.

She gave a gasp of delight and wrestled him for it. He gave her a good fight, but victory was soon hers. She eagerly began to soap her arms, her legs, every inch of bare flesh that was tainted by the smelly mixture, while he went to the edge of the lake to refill the bucket.

He set the bucket at her feet and moved to stand before her. He had taken off his wet shirt and T-shirt, and for a moment she was captivated by the sight of his naked chest. As she had suspected, it was covered all over in a thick net of dark hair, sheened now with his recent dousing and glistening in the firelight. She followed in fascination the lean curve of his broad shoulders, the knotted muscles of his forearm, the well-defined bone structure of his collarbone. Her eyes traveled downward across the tight musculature of his breasts and the dip below his sternum, the smooth flatness of his abdomen and lower, to the point where the narrowing triangle of hair disappeared below his belt buckle. She wondered what he would do if she reached her hand out and touched the soft dark tangle of hair, if she spread her fingers through it and sought the warmth of his chest. She wanted to do that very badly.

He smiled in acknowledgement of her wandering eyes, and that brought Jessie's already-tingling senses into new awareness of his closeness, his masculinity. Her heart began to race as his hand fell lightly upon the soapy silkiness of her bare shoulder, trailed down the course of her inner arm, and he said huskily, "Do you always shower with your clothes on?"

She shivered as his fingers slipped beneath the stretchy material of her top just below the curve of her breast and began to tug gently upward. At his soft command she lifted her arms and let him slip the top over her head.

The skin of her breasts puckered with sudden exposure to the night air, her nipples rapidly hardening. She shivered again as his fingers touched a light pattern on her collarbone. His eyes held hers tenderly. "Easy, love," he said softly. His fingers threaded through the hair at her temple, releasing it from the loose braid. "Are you okay? Are you cold?"

She started to nod, then changed her mind. She was neither cold nor okay. She was shivering and melting inside as his hand slipped down with easy skill to the snap of her shorts and the brief zipper. Her chest hurt with the reverberating pounding of her heart, and it was enormously difficult to catch her breath. Long fingers gathered the material of both shorts and panties and in a single graceful movement tugged them down over her hips.

The warm night air crawled over seldom-exposed flesh as she stepped out of the constricting material around her ankles, forcing her to shiver violently. She stood there before him, naked and vulnerable and trying hard not to shiver, and felt his eyes touching each part of her body with the delicacy of a caress. Quietly he said, "Jessie, darlin', you are beautiful to me."

She was beautiful to him. The words filled her with warm, glowing delight, and she wanted nothing more at that moment than to step into his arms, to feel his body surrounding every part of hers. To be loved by him.

Keith's smile caught her eyes as he took the bar of soap from her lifeless fingers. It was a smile of slow affection, tender encouragement, and it drew ripples of pleasure from the center of her stomach outward. He worked up a lather in his hands and spread it over the silky smoothness of her shoulders, drawing a low gasp from her as the slippery sensation moved to her breasts, with rounded repetitive massaging motions that gathered and released, concentrating attention stroking and drawing throbbing nipples that strained to meet him. Fine quivers strained within her, and she struggled to control her breathing as butterfly fingers moved over her rib cage and her abdomen, light, slippery up and down motions, slow and sure and tender. And all the time his eyes were on her face, holding her, watching her, delighting in her pleasure.

Soapy hands curved over her buttocks, stroking, rounding, gripping lightly, then down her legs, around her calves, upward to brush very lightly between her thighs, and her head roared. Her knees weakened, and she stiffened to keep her balance. Then gently, very gently, his bare forearm circled her waist from side to back, and his lips brushed like a whisper across her mouth. "Don't, love," he said softly, and it was a command to relax, to open herself to him and the freedom of the balmy night's caresses, to let herself be.

He left her for a second, and she tensed in anticipation and uncertainty; then she felt the trickle of water over her shoulders, guided downward and around by the cupping motions of his hand. She leaned her head back and a soft sigh of contentment escaped her parted lips as tension was washed away like the foamy residue of soap and was replaced by a honeyed languor that spread with a seeping sweetness through her weightless limbs. The sensation of cool water flowing over her body was erotic yet soothing, the caress of his hands in its wake welcome. When he stepped in front of her she linked her arms instinctively about his neck, and his hands slipped just as naturally beneath her armpits, thumbs spreading with a light pressure to her breasts. His face was hot against hers, his kiss long and adoring and tasting marvelously sweet. He brought her slowly against him, his hands sliding over her wet body to circle her waist, her breasts brought with an ever-increasing pressure against the warm abrasive texture of his chest. She could feel his heart beat. She could feel the heat of his face warming hers, and his warm, moist tongue sliding against hers and the strong pressure of his fingers against her bare skin drawing her ever closer.

His hands moved slowly to cup her face, feathering over each curve and indentation they encountered on their upward course, then molded themselves around her cheeks, thumbs touching beneath her chin. He tilted her head backward slightly so that she had to look at him, and all she had ever wanted was in the warm melting depths of his eyes, the tenderness of his smile. "Darlin'," he said very softly, "I don't want to compete with the bugs for your attention. Let's go inside."

She walked in the circle of his arm the few steps into the cabin, and he laid her down gently on the bed, which he had made up with fresh linen this afternoon. Her damp body left an imprint on the crisp muslin sheets, and the bed was marvelously soft, smelling of sunshine and evergreen. She lay there listening to the sound of her heart and the movements of his undressing, the whisper of a zipper and the rustle of denim, the muffled clink of a belt buckle against the wood floor. She heard the creak of two steps, the stirring of bedsprings as he rested his weight on one knee beside her, and then felt the hard muscles of a furry thigh brushing against her hip. His hands floated around her face, smoothing back her damp hair, and each moment was a slow, thudding heartbeat tight with concentrated attention and waiting as he simply looked at her. He looked at her forever.

"Jessie," he whispered. One slender finger carefully traced the arch of her brow. His eyes were beacons in the misty night, searching for and rescuing a floundering soul. "Tell me you want this as much as I do. Tell me."

Jessie looked at him, reaching for him, finding in him all she had ever wanted...finding the courage to reach for it. Her breath was a thin stream through barely parted lips; her hands fluttered to his neck and clasped there, holding him. "I do," she whispered.

His breath caught softly, his head bent slowly, and

their mouths met at once, eager this time, giving freely now. She felt his full length beside her, his long muscular legs, strong embracing arms, radiant heat spreading outward like an exploding sun. Slim competent fingers slipped beneath her shoulders, lifting her a little so that her neck arched backward, and his mouth, warm and wet from their kiss, traveled an excruciating course downward. His hand slipped forward to cup her breast, shaping it to his mouth, exploring it with his tongue in lazy circles and specific probings until her breath was no more than an erratic memory and every nerve in her body was stretched to its finest extension outward from the center of his attention. And as she waited, suspended in anguish and taut with yearning, his lips moved to the aching hollow of her throat and his hand brushed downward. Strong beautiful fingers moved between her legs, seeking with utmost delicacy her most sensitive parts, exploring with musical grace the profundity of her need.

Jessie felt herself melting, drawn to him with the sharp sweet clarity of need, spreading like honey into the misty night, where nothing existed except him and her and even the raucous chirping of the crickets faded into a faraway dream. The scent of him, sunshine and perspiration, the sound of his breathing intermingled with her own, the hot dampness that bathed her body and the salt she tasted on his lips. The endless loving promise of delight that was in the silky explorations of his fingertips, and the emptiness and urgent yearning that built deep within her, which only he could fill. She moaned out loud and whispered his name as her arms circled beneath his to grasp his shoulders. She felt the dampness of the warm patches of hair beneath his arms and unconsciously she arched her hips toward him.

"Keith," she said, loving the sound of his name. And again, through a burning haze of rising need, "Keith."

He lifted himself over her as at the same time those fingers slipped beneath her, circling her hips. Very far away she was aware of the muffled thud of her heart and the roaring fog in her head as she waited, rapt and suspended, for him. She felt the soft, heated blanket of his chest over her, the brush of silky hair against her breasts, and the strength of hard muscles, and his mouth covered hers. And at last, at last, she felt the slow deep filling of her aching need, the flooding warmth, the gasping welcome, an end to wanting, an end to emptiness.

Jessie squeezed her eyes shut and curled her fingernails into his shoulders, swept with a sensation so sweet, so rapturous, it was almost blinding in its power, so all-consuming and all-encompassing it was frightening. She clung to him and let him lead her into regions she had never dared imagine before, his natural rhythms a magical match for her own. It was as though from the beginning of time she had been fashioned only for him—she had been born with a natural void inside her only he could fill—and all this time, all these wasted years, she had been waiting for him, wandering the earth in search of him, never knowing that he was all the time as close as her outstretched hand. She opened her eyes and in rapturous amazement saw the same look of dark wonder reflected in his eyes, so close to hers. She had never seen that look in a man's eyes before. Tenderness and adoration, slow sweeping delight that transported them both as they made shared discoveries on the dim borders of reality, things they would not have believed until now, things only guessed at before now. His whispered breaths and his drawing kisses spurred her further outward into the far boundaries of herself and then sharply in again, tantalizing her with secrets she could not see and promises she ached for. Thrusting outward and drawing inward, reaching for the stars, circling ever closer to the golden promise, and then suddenly, like a rocket bursting through the clouds or an eagle soaring into the sun, it was hers, this place she had never been before, the place where she lost herself to the outer regions of reality—the place where she lost herself and became part of him. And the secret was that that was the way it was always meant to be.

Twisting and spinning, floating in fragmented scraps of consciousness and half-imagined glimpses of daylight, she was for a long time suspended in that wonderful never-never land between waking and dreaming, where muted sensation is supreme ruler and the fibers of rational thought tremble beneath its golden glow. And then gradually she became aware of his heavy breathing near her ear, his warmth engulfing her, furry legs entwined with hers, and that was a new sensation of delight in itself. She could feel the slow steady jerking of his heart when she moved her hand with awesome languor to the heavy thicket of his chest, the slickness of their perspiration-oiled skin against each other, the dampness of the sheets beneath them. And wonder like she had never known filled her, heavy contentment, soaring delight. She wanted only to get closer to him, to hold him and never again be separate from him, to make this mystical feeling last forever.

His lips brushed across her eyelid as she snuggled closer. She could feel his smile, which was a reflection of her own. "Do you want a cigarette?" he inquired, and she shook her head as she burrowed her face into his shoulder, filling her nostrils with his scent, tasting him on her lips.

His voice was teasing. "Are you hungry?"

"No," she murmured. Those long, beautiful fingers were stroking her from waist to hip as she lay on her side against him, soothing her and worshiping her even as they unintentionally aroused her again. Some unwanted part of her mind assured her that this was the way it was supposed to be when the loving was good, that the magical swelling feeling inside her was only natural and expected, but that did not make it any less special to her. That did not make it any less magical or wonderful or enduring.... She lifted her face to him, and she knew her eyes were glowing and her face alive with rapture, but she wanted him to see, she wanted him to know the deepest secrets of her overflowing heart. "Oh, Keith," she whispered, "is it like this for everyone?"

His eyes were lowered as he bent to place a kiss of exquisite tenderness atop her tousled hair. "No, sweetheart," he answered softly. "Not for everyone."

She pressed herself close to him and lifted her face to receive the fullness of his kiss. She could never have enough of him, of what they were together. Not ever.

Her fingers tangled lazily in his hair, moving over the silkiness of his shoulder, her **lips ta**sting the clinging salt on his skin as they moved over his throat and the sharpness of his collarbone; she gave herself over to this timeless pleasure, the endless wonder of knowing him. He propped himself up on one elbow beside her, his own fingers beginning a contented, unhurried, renewed exploration of her body, and she could see his smile in the darkness; she could see the deep light of contentment. And her own eyes reflected it. "Hey,

Jessie," he said softly, and his eyes deepened with something like amused certainty as he drew his finger in a tickling path across her chin. "It's all right to say it, you know."

She turned her face to nuzzle his chest, hiding her deepening smile of delight. "Everyone says it in bed."

His fingers teased a rippling path down her spine; his voice was indulgent and amused. "That doesn't make it illegal."

She shook her head and shyly let her own fingers roam, telling him in actions rather than words what he wanted to hear. The urgency of their first coming together was gone, but their new explorations were all the sweeter for their timelessness. When he moved over her he looked at her for a long time, every part of his body brushing lightly against hers, his hands cupping her face, the deep light of his eyes drawing her very soul outward to meet him. And he said, very quietly, "I love you, Jess."

Her fluttering sigh of happiness was the scattering wings of the last vestiges of doubt, and she drew him down to her.

The next morning Jessie was awakened by what sounded like pieces of gravel bouncing in a pie plate. Slowly she recognized the scent of rain washing away red dust and the earthy fragrance of pine and damp grass. The lake soothed a repetitive rhythm as it lapped against the shore; wet wings fluttered just outside her window as a bird sought shelter in the rafters. And then, very gradually, she became aware of something else: a warm male form in the bed next to her, lean and muscular and hairy, the mingled delight of perspiration and masculinity blending into the other earth-rich aromas of a rainy summer morning. Keith said, his voice a husky drawl in her ear, "You sleep like a rock, lady."

She stretched slowly, uncurling her smooth legs from the tangle with his, and stretched her arm across the flat breadth of his waist, pressing her breasts luxuriously into his chest before withdrawing, turning on her back, and opening her eyes. Gray morning light washed over the tacky little room, and the face of the man she loved filled her eyes. "Good morning," she murmured.

"Good morning yourself," he retorted, his eyes sweeping over her with the lazy light of his smile. "I'll have you know I've already been out and about scavenging for your breakfast. You didn't even notice when I got back into bed and put my cold feet on your bottom."

She started to giggle, then turned her eyes to the murky uncurtained window overhead. "It's raining," she pointed out.

"It wasn't two hours ago." He turned with a squeaking of the bedsprings and reached for something on the floor. She sat up with a bounce of delight as he presented her with a bowl of fresh blackberries.

She did not notice that in her enthusiasm the sheet had fallen down around her waist. He made her aware of the fact with a warm cupping motion and a deep kiss planted squarely in the center of her left breast. "You taste even better," he murmured.

"Better than blackberries?" she teased, demurely rescuing the sheet as her eyes danced and her face glowed with new life.

"Better than ever." He sat up and slipped his arm about her waist, drawing her toward him.

She protested laughingly, shielding the bowl, "You

can just get that amorous look out of your eyes until I've had my breakfast—I'm starving. Besides, blackberry stains won't come out of white muslin."

But even as she spoke she offered him her mouth, and the kiss sent new streams of syrupy warm wonder through her. It had not faded. What she had feared might be a dream was just as clear, just as rich and abiding in the light of a new day, and in some ways even more wonderful. It sent bubbles of sunshine-bright happiness bursting through her and the reluctance with which she left him was tempered by the knowledge that at any time he was just within the reach of her fingertips, and the adventure had just begun.

As though reading her thoughts, he settled next to her with his arm about her bare shoulders, smiling as he pressed a dewy moist blackberry between her lips. Nothing had ever tasted sweeter to her... except perhaps his kisses. They sat in wonderful warm silence for a time, eating blackberries and listening to the mesmerizing pinging of rain against the metal roof. He took a strand of her hair and drew it absently across his face, tangling the light brown with the dark brown of his beard, and he said casually, "I've been meaning to ask you—did you ever do anything about that little problem you mentioned the last time we met?"

For a moment she was confused, but the mischievous light in his eyes reminded her just as he specified, "Shall I expect a joyous announcement in a month or two?"

She couldn't help blushing, and she concentrated her attention on nibbling away the last blackberry before she replied with what she hoped was a passable imitation of sophisticated nonchalance, "As a matter of fact, I did do something about it. No surprises waiting in the wings for you this time, Michaelson." She ventured a glance at him. "Relieved?"

His face was thoughtful. "Not really. I told you, I love kids. However—" his smile was slow and loving, and it confused her even as it enraptured her "—there's consolation in knowing that you didn't let me talk you into something on the spur of the moment. That you wanted this and planned for it and—" now there was just a hint of question in his smile "—that you're not sorry?"

"No," she whispered, watching him, loving him. "I'm not sorry."

The bowl on her lap slipped to the floor as he moved over her, gathering her to him as she arched to give him her kisses, and he met them with dewy soft adoration and languorous motions of love. She smiled against his bare shoulder, her eyes shining with a secret light and her body glowing as his fingers began their musical explorations of delight over her limbs and her torso. "Is this the way we're going to spend our first full day in the wilds of the Smoky Mountains?"

He nibbled at her throat. "There's not much else to do in the pouring rain. I'm sorry the weather couldn't have been more cooperative."

Jessie thought the weather had been most cooperative, and as his lips moved lower she tangled her fingers in his hair and murmured, "Oh, is it raining? I hadn't noticed."

"Darlin'." He moved his face upward to place a sweet, infinitely tender kiss upon the corner of her mouth. "I want to fill all your days with sunshine."

Jessie tightened her arms around him and determinedly ignored the fretful clouds that were gathering on the horizon of their future. She refused to listen to the voices that warned her this couldn't last, that neither a physical act nor an emotional commitment could solve the problems nor change the circumstances that must inevitably keep them apart. Very far away she knew that it couldn't last, but for now, at this moment, she had her arms around the only thing she had ever really wanted, and it was enough....

Chapter Six

Bright morning sunlight fell in yellow shafts over the rumpled covers of Jessie's bed on a Monday morning three weeks later. Keith groaned and flung his forearm over his eyes, turning over on his back to dislodge the kitten who had been stalking a stealthy course along the side of his hip. Delbert dug his claws determinedly into the side of the bed and scampered back up again, pouncing determinedly on Keith's chest. In a movement Keith captured him and deposited him none too gently upon the floor. "Darlin'," he drawled without opening his eyes, "if you don't do something about this cat you are going to be witness to an extremely unpleasant old-style gangland-type execution."

Jessie, who had been watching him sleep long before Delbert's playful awakening, smothered a giggle in her blue-and-white cornflower print pillow. "He's just hungry," she replied, her eyes dancing. "Like me."

Keith turned his head, opened his lazy eyes, and smiled at her drowsily. "What are you hungry for, love?"

Jessie loved the sight of his dark hair tangled on her feminine pillowcase, the shadow of his lean form beneath her frilly sheets. She loved the morning languor in his eyes and the sleep-warmed muscles of his arm as it slipped slowly around her waist. But she pulled her lips away from his reluctantly and said with a regretful shake of her head, "No time. I have to go to work."

He slipped his hand between her legs, and a playful spark lit his eyes at her automatic shiver. "What did you say? I didn't quite catch it."

The flush that spread over her whole body was both uncomfortable and delightful. She tried to wiggle away. "No kidding, Keith. I have to open the shop today. I can't be late."

He fastened his hands firmly upon her hips and drew her on top of him. His body was warm and firm and naked beneath her; she loved the feeling. He held her with his long fingers spread over her back and her hips, and he looked at her gravely. "I don't like watching you go to work in the mornings. Almost as much as I don't like going to work myself."

Her lips dimpled mockingly. "When you do," she pointed out. "Do you have an alternative that would keep both of us sheltered and clothed and reasonably well fed?"

Keith nodded. "You should stay at home and create poignant, brilliantly memorable political cartoons, and I should invent new and magnificent ways to harness electricity, and between such earth-shattering endeavors we should make long, slow, beautiful love." His fingers trailed over her buttocks; his lips nipped her chin.

She shivered in warm delight. Her eyes were sparkling. "We'd starve."

"There are worse things."

"Keith..."

He lifted his face to look at her again, his hands still.

"Do you know what else I don't like?" he added seriously.

"What's that?"

"Going home at night. Going home in the morning. Taking you home at night or taking you home in the morning. There has got to be a more efficient way of managing our lives."

Everything within her stilled. She did not move; for a moment she did not breathe. She tried very hard to keep her expression neutral. She did not know how long she had been expecting this, nor how long she had dreaded it. She did not know why she should dread it, nor why every time she allowed herself to approach this relationship in concrete terms she was filled with such helpless confusion. She only knew that she spent every waking moment away from Keith, trying to keep worrisome, oppressive thoughts at bay, trying to shelter the fragile dream from the cold grip of reality. She said cautiously, "You mean . . . live together?"

A flicker in his eyes told her she had not been successful in keeping her thoughts from him. He was so sensitive to her every mood, every infinitesimal change of expression or momentary pause, that it was impossible to keep anything from him. He was entirely too sensitive. Yet he kept his voice casual as he inquired, "Do you have something against marriage?"

Marriage. Her heart began to thud again. She forced herself to relax. She knew he couldn't be serious. She formed a dry little smile and retorted, "Do I look like the kind of girl who would marry a long-haired, generally unemployed dropout who doesn't even own a suit?" Surely he couldn't be serious.

But as she watched his eyes going slowly over her face she was no longer quite so certain. As usual, he hid nothing in those eyes, but mounting trepidation prevented her from reading the message there. He said thoughtfully, "And what if I cut my hair, got a regular job, and bought a suit?"

She caught her breath. For just one brief moment she imagined he was serious, she let herself think it could be. "Keith," she said softly, "would you do that for me?"

He looked at her soberly for another moment. She imagined she saw all sorts of things in his eyes. And then he grinned, suddenly and wickedly. "Hell, no," he said, and slapped her none too gently on her bare bottom. "Get up, woman, I've got to go to work."

She rolled off of him, gasping in a mixture of laughter and indignation, but as she watched him step into his jeans and move toward the bathroom the laughter tasted suddenly of the sting of bittersweet tears. Impatiently Jessie brushed the irrational emotion aside with a toss of her head and a deep breath. She looked lovingly at the imprint his body had made on the pretty sheets for a long moment; she ran a hand lightly over the lingering warmth. She tried not to think. And then she got up and made coffee.

But it was becoming less and less easy not to think these days. The best she could do was to try not to get depressed about it. She had known very well what she was doing when she had let Keith patiently wear down the barriers that protected her heart. She had known exactly what she was getting into when she had let herself love him. Nothing had changed. Still, two more disparate people could not be found if you searched the world over. Still, their values and their needs were poles apart. They were forever doomed to live parallel life-styles because of who they were and what they wanted. They had nothing in common but loving each other. Day by day she tried to keep those cold truths at bay. Day by day she concentrated on living for the moment, on taking all the happiness that life offered with a timelessness that would last as long as she let it.

And why shouldn't she be happy? For the first time, Jessie had taken a positive step in controlling her own life. She had not let love slip away; she had reached for what she wanted. She was learning to see life through Keith's innocent, uncomplicated vision, and it was beautiful. When she was with him there were no worries, and everything was easy. She had her pleasant little home, work that she enjoyed, good friends, and a man who loved her. Everything was perfect. She had everything she wanted... and not quite.

It was almost predestined that in the midst of these reflections the telephone would ring and that it should be Celia. "Sorry to call so early, love," came the ever-cheery voice, "but I'm still on California time. Didn't wake you, I hope."

"You're talking to a working girl, remember?" Jessie heard the shower stop, and she poured two cups of coffee to cool. "We get up at the crack of dawn."

"So when has the working girl scheduled her vacation this year? I'm arranging my August schedule, and I've got to know."

"Oh, Celia, don't rearrange your schedule for me—"

"You know I will." Her voice was firm. "I'm not taking the chance of being out of town when you finally decide to grace us with your presence. Besides, someone has got to be here to show you around; it's been so long, you've probably forgotten how to hail a cab."

Jessie heard the blow dryer going, and she smiled a

little. It was true enough: He might as well move in. They spent almost all their time together anyway, and their possessions were equally divided between his apartment and her house.... It would definitely be more convenient. But living together implied more of a commitment than simply convenience and....

"Come on, Jess, I've got to have a date."

Celia's voice dragged her back to the present. "At this hour of the morning?" Jessie hedged. She opened a can of cat food and emptied it into the dish. Delbert came scampering when she placed it on the floor.

A short breath revealed her friend's frustration. "Jessie, for goodness sake, what's the big deal? You've been putting this off for months—for years. You know you want to come, and if it's money—"

"No, it's not that." Of course she wanted to come. For the first time she was absolutely sure that was what she wanted. A chance to go home again, to face the memories, to experience again the high-powered, fast-paced life she loved...even if it was only for a little while.

"Good." Celia was decisive. "I've got it all worked out. You'll stay with me, of course...."

Celia's voice faded out as Jessie thought about it—really thought about it—and her heart began to pump with excitement. Yes, it was what she wanted, and now she was strong enough to go for it. There was a subtle sense of elation that came with that realization, a discovery of her own strength and her determination. Of course she had known all along New York was what she wanted; it had just been a matter of time while she regained her confidence and recovered her losses.... And of course she had known all along that she wanted it for more than a two-week visit, but that was something she still could keep on a subconscious level. She did not have to make that decision yet.

And then Celia said, "Of course, you've got to keep in mind the interview the first week of August and schedule your time accordingly...."

The *interview*. Jessie had forgotten. But the reminder set her heart to speeding again, even as a small wisp of dread formed in her stomach. It was a chance. A chance to prove herself, to try it again.... Rising excitement pushed away rational concerns, and she was already flipping through the pages of the colorful kitten calendar that was pinned next to the refrigerator. It didn't necessarily mean anything, she told herself. Probably nothing at all would come of it, but it was a chance.... She told Celia, "What if I make reservations to leave the last Sunday in July and return the second Sunday in August?"

"Perfect!" exclaimed Celia. "All right, now, I'm writing it in ink, so don't you dare back out on me. I can't believe this—I've finally gotten a decision from you!"

And when Jessie hung up the phone, she was beaming with triumph and excited anticipation. It felt good to finally make a decision, to know she had set her feet on the road that led to what she really wanted. And then she turned to see Keith standing there, and some of the excitement faded.

Even dressed in the jeans and T-shirt he had worn last night, he looked fresh and clean and rested. He looked beautiful to her, and when she looked at him, there was a small stab of longing in the pit of her stomach, which was irrational but nonetheless refused to be pushed away. He said casually, "Who was on the phone?"

She opened her mouth to reply, but somehow the words just wouldn't come out. Why couldn't she tell him? He knew she had been planning a trip, it was no big secret, she would have to tell him her plans were definite sometime... but not this morning. For some reason she just couldn't tell him this morning. She found herself replying, "Oh, just an old friend." And as he moved past her to take up his coffee, she slipped her arms about his waist, stopping him.

He bent to kiss her hair automatically, his hands curving over her hips, but she lifted her head to meet his lips. He tasted like peppermint and sunshine, and she loved him. "Umm." He smiled, tasting her lips one more time. "Nice." He started to move away. "But I thought you were running late."

A low desperation started to form deep within her; she was aware of it, but she did not understand it. She wound her arms more tightly about his waist and tasted the clean soapy fragrance of his neck. Her hips unconsciously swayed, pressing into him as her hands moved downward over his jeaned hips and forward to his abdomen and chest. She felt his breath go uneven beneath her caresses, and when he slipped his hands automatically into the front opening of her robe, she melted into him. That was what she wanted, that was all....

"Darlin'," he murmured against her ear. His hot breath sent tingles down her spine. "I don't have to be at work till ten, but you've got to open the shop...."

"I'll be late," she whispered, and lifted her mouth in a kiss so passionate that there was no longer any room for doubt about how she wanted to spend the morning.

As the days and weeks passed, Jessie tried to rationalize why she continued to delay telling Keith. Perhaps it was because their time together was so precious she did not want to spoil it with intrusions from the outside world. When she was with Keith it was difficult to think of anything else—the trip to New York seemed like a hazy and somewhat absurd dream. When she was with Keith she forgot all the reasons she really wanted to go. They simply lost their significance against the warm spell of contentment he generated. And perhaps she was thinking very far in the back of her mind that she might change her mind at the last minute, for it would be very difficult to leave Keith, even for a few weeks....

But she knew she would not change her mind. She simply tried not to think about it, that was all. She knew her place was in New York, serving her ambition and doing what she knew best, and she had always known that eventually she would end up back there. She also knew that the day was approaching when she would have to make a permanent decision and she looked forward to that decision with mounting excitement and dread. She was ready for it. She was ready to tackle the world, to pick up her life where it had been interrupted by a disastrous marriage and her own failing courage; she was ready to grasp her destiny and mold it to her wishes. It was a good, firm feeling. Of course there would be problems, but those were the things she tried not to think about. Something could be worked out. Perhaps Keith would come with her. Something surely could be worked out, but she did not have to deal with it now. She needed the time in New York to think, to work out the details, and then...well, then she would make a decision. Then she would talk to Keith.

But then the day came when she could no longer put off talking to Keith, or avoid making a decision.

She and Keith were experimenting in her kitchen

one Saturday evening with a recipe Jessie had clipped from the Sunday paper. Keith neglected to tell her that the eggs were supposed to be separated before they were added to the bubbling sauce mixture. and, giving him a withering look, Jessie volunteered to go out for another dozen. The trip to the corner market did not take more than five minutes, and when she returned he was as she had left him, slowly stirring a fragrant wine sauce that was waiting for egg yolks. He greeted her without looking up, "The airlines called. Something about changing your flight time. You'd better call them back."

Slowly she put the package on the counter, and her heart began to thump a dry rhythm in the pit of her stomach. It was impossible to see the expression on his face in the shadowed light of the vent hood.

She opened the carton of eggs and responded with a passable imitation of casualness, "Thanks. I will, right after dinner."

He looked up with a wry lift of his brow. He did not seem angry. "Thinking of running away from home, Jess?"

"Oh, Keith of course not!" Her voice was overbright and desperation was knotting in her chest. "I was going to tell you, only . . ." She swore softly as a bright speck of yellow appeared in the egg white she had just separated.

"Only what?" His voice was mild. Too mild.

She busily poured out the mess she had made in the bowl and tried again. She did not look at him. "There didn't seem to be any rush. I hadn't made up my mind—"

"You made reservations. That sounds like a lady

with her mind made up to me. What were you afraid of, Jess?''

The challenge in his tone was very bland, but it was there nonetheless. She looked up at him, and he was leaning against the stove, strong and confident and utterly at ease, his expression composed and his eyes alertly interested. There was a sheen of perspiration on his skin from the overheated kitchen, and the lingering summer day and his hair gleamed in the overhead light. Her throat jerked with sudden longing, and it was a moment before she could reply. In that moment she saw him observe and catalog the changing expressions on her face and something about his own demeanor seemed to change very subtly—as though he became at once more cautious and more gentle, definitely more alert.

She said, keeping her voice even and almost detached, "Maybe I was afraid you would be angry."

He smiled, and it was a smile that mocked her inaccuracy even as it teased her for trying to get away with it. "More likely, you were afraid I would give you another one of my scathing lectures on the vice and corruption of the big city, and that this time it might sink in."

"Maybe," she said stiffly, and deliberately turned to crack an egg on the side of the bowl. Her stomach was churning and defenses were building. She was not certain whether the emotion that was thudding in her heart was suppressed anger, dread, or simple fear. She would have done anything to avoid this conversation. "Maybe I just got tired of hearing it."

"Does that mean I have your permission to say it one more time?''

She had known it was coming. She and Keith never really argued—it was impossible to argue with a man who did not lose his temper—but the closest they ever came to it was when she talked of New York. Then, with a few pointed words, he could plunge her into confusion and uneasiness, and that was the only time she ever felt uncomfortable with him.

"You don't belong there, Jessie," he said flatly. "It all looks pretty and inviting from a distance, but you'll be swallowed whole. And by the time you find out that what winked and glittered so temptingly is really nothing but gilt-edged tinsel, it will be too late. Don't make a fool out of yourself over greener pastures. Take a look at what you've got first."

She stared at him. He had never spoken to her so harshly before, and even though his tone was reasonable and his expression bland, there was a knife edge to each word he spoke. He had never attempted to disguise from her his opinion of her values and ambitions, but neither had he attempted to force his own standards upon her. Now there was no room for doubt about how he felt, and when he put those feelings into words, it sounded very much like an order.

A defensive anger smouldered in her, and she returned shortly, "Don't forget that's where I came from. I know perfectly well what it's like, and you have no right—"

"I think I'm going to say a lot of things tonight I have no right to," he interrupted, and she became aware for the first time of the atmosphere of subtly-charged tension between them. His voice remained calm, but there was a hardness in his eyes. She had never seen him look like that before, and it frightened her. "And the first one is that you know as well as I do, if you really belonged to the kind of life you left behind, you never would have left it in the first place. You've been living in a fantasy world, Jess, and it's gone on too long."

"Don't tell me where I belong and what I can do!" she blazed at him. "You know I didn't leave by choice, and you know that I always intended to go back!" It was with a stifled gasp that she realized what she had said, and the impact of her words registered in a flicker across his eyes. Horror and remorse flooded her, but she tried to stifle it as she turned away and took a wire whip to the egg yolks in the bowl. "Anyway," she said quickly, trying to keep her voice casual even though the dread and alarm were tightening in her throat and threatening to choke off her breath, "there's no need to get into that now. It's just a vacation—it's not as though I were thinking about a permanent move or anything!"

"Oh?" His voice was rather cool. "Did you cancel that interview your friend arranged for you?"

Color blazed to her cheeks as she looked at him, and helplessness cut off her response. She had mentioned that to Keith weeks ago, almost in passing, testing the waters before she'd lost her courage and been unable to tell him about the trip. She had thought he must have forgotten it. Now she realized that he had known all along what was going on and what she had been thinking, and the knowledge hit her like a slowly boiling panic.She suddenly wanted more than anything to forget this dreadful conversation had ever begun, to somehow turn the evening back to its innocuous beginnings....

She moved to pour the egg yolks into the sauce, but Keith turned off the burner and took the bowl from her. "The sauce will curdle!" she exclaimed, and he took her arm.

"Come along, lady," he invited mildly. "We're going to have a long overdue talk."

He led her to the sofa and removed a sleepily protesting Delbert, and all the while her mind was working frantically. She did not want to go into this with him tonight. She did not want to go into it with him ever, because she knew it meant they must fight. She did not want to fight with Keith.

"There's nothing to talk about," she began reasonably as he sat beside her. She folded one leg beneath her in a pretense of relaxation, but she could not help but notice that he sat several feet away from her, and the arm that he draped along the back of the sofa came nowhere near touching her. "I'm just going home for a couple of weeks—you knew I was thinking about doing it all summer. There's nothing wrong with that. If I had known it was going to upset you so, I would never have made the reservations without consulting you."

Though the words were said sincerely, a slight impatience in his eyes made her wish they were meant more sincerely. She had made the reservations without consulting him precisely because she knew it would upset him, because she knew it would lead to this....

He said, "I'm not upset about the trip, Jess. I know why you didn't tell me before. And if you don't think there's anything to talk about, fine. You just listen for a while, and I'll talk. Because what I have to say has been waiting too long."

There was gentleness in his voice, and there was no reason for the awful choking dread to start coiling in her stomach again. She looked into those kind deep eyes, and she did not know why she should have the sudden, overwhelming feeling that something terrible was about to happen. She clenched her hands in her lap unconsciously as he began to speak.

"I've been living in limbo since the day I met you," he said. His voice was smooth, and beneath his tender, open gaze she felt everything inside her begin to melt. She stiffened instinctively. "Wanting you, watching you drift back and forth between what you could have and what you thought you wanted, waiting for you to make up your mind. Hoping one day you'd open your eyes and see what's been there all along.... Well, honey, this has gone on too long. You're a big girl now, and it's time for you to face some realities. It seems to me you have two options. You can go back to New York and chase down your pot of gold—" there was the slightest pause, the very faintest softening of his eyes "—or you can share an entirely different kind of dream, and marry me."

It took her breath away. For a moment Jessie couldn't believe what she had heard. For a moment everything seemed frozen, even the blood in her veins, and then it all rushed back, swiftly, irrefutably, starkly clear.

He had seen the emotions racing across her face in those fleeting seconds, and he was not pleased. She felt him retreating from her even as he registered her reactions with a tolerant smile that nonetheless seemed to hold a trace of bitter irony. "Take your time," he invited.

She couldn't believe he had done this. He had given her an ultimatum. With no warning, no time to prepare, he was demanding a decision from her—now.

Marriage. As hard as she tried not to, she could not

help thinking about it. Marriage to him. Having him beside her day and night to love her, care for her, make her laugh and fill her days with sunshine.... Having his children, building a life together.... Marriage.

It meant forever. It meant Mr. and Mrs. on the credit cards. It meant two people sharing the space that was meant for one. It meant *one* life-style, not two. It meant overdrawn checking accounts and past-due bills and fighting over vacations. It meant forever, in this place, living this way.... He couldn't be serious. He couldn't mean it. Panic stirred its dusty wings within her, and she stared at him, trying to find some way to make herself believe he hadn't said it, to erase the past few moments from memory and to start all over. He couldn't be serious. He just couldn't.

"Keith," she said urgently, "why don't you come with me?" She placed both hands on his forearms, stroking, beseeching, tempting, even as her eyes begged him to put those strong arms around her, to give foundation to a sudden, far-fetched hope. "Just the two of us—a holiday, an adventure. You'd love it, I know you would, and that way—"

"No," he said. There was no trace of emotion whatsoever in his voice. Just *no.*

She withdrew her hands; she used them to clasp her own upper arms as though to capture a shiver. Her face was stunned, but inside she was feeling no surprise. She had known all along it must end like this.... "Why not?" Her voice was a croak.

Very simply, without elaboration, he went straight to the point. "Not now, not ever. That's your fantasy, Jess, not mine." How cold his eyes looked. It was as though he had looked into the future and seen what she was afraid to face. But his voice had a soothing, almost hypnotic aura to it as he suggested, "Shall we return to my question?"

Marriage. She could not believe this. She couldn't believe he was doing this to her. She struggled for a grip on the situation, and all she could do was try to make light of it, to try to convince herself he wasn't really serious and this wasn't really the moment that would change the course of her entire life. She cajoled him with a teasing, very false smile, "Now, Keith, don't be ridiculous. You don't want to get married."

An expression so blank crossed over his face that it frightened her. Her heart started to jump dully. She knew something terrible was going to happen, and as she desperately gathered her resources to forestall it, she could feel every nerve in her body stretching and drying and threatening to crack. "Try again, Jess," he said smoothly.

Oh, yes, he was serious. He meant it. Hadn't she known all along that this was a forever man, that he saw a future filled with simple days and quiet times; one woman, children, public schools, and a two-car garage and— Hadn't she always known? There was fear in her eyes and desperate tenderness as she said softly, "Keith, please let's not fight about this. You know it's impossible."

"Why?" he demanded in the same easy, carefully controlled tone. But his eyes were as hard as glass. "Why is it impossible?"

There was nothing else to do. She was going to have to hurt him, there was no way to save it. . . . Still, she floundered desperately, "You know how I feel about marriage—after Frank—I'm not ready to . . ."

He stood abruptly, uttering an oath so low and violent that she started, and he snapped at her, "Don't lie to me, Jessie!" His eyes blazed cold anger. "I thought we were past that stage. You know I can take anything but that. Now, try it again, and this time let's see if you can tell the truth."

She shrank back against the sofa, clutching her arms, her wide eyes suddenly stung by a wash of tears. She had never seen him like that, demanding, autocratic, his temper viciously controlled and directed at her. She said, "Keith, *don't*—this isn't like you—"

He whirled on her. "No, I guess it's not." His jaw was tight, his lips compressed into a pale line above his beard. His eyes were coal black, and his voice was a hiss of barely controlled rage laced heavily with contempt. "I'm supposed to be so rational, so easy going, so controlled and dependable. Well, I'll tell you something, Jessie, I've been giving too much and getting too little in return, and I don't feel very controlled right now. I feel cheated and impatient and hurt, and you'd better get used to the fact that I'm going to say a lot of things you don't want to hear and maybe a few I don't even want to say." And as he looked at her, some of the hard anger faded from his face. He released a short breath, dragged his fingers through his hair, and lowered his eyes briefly. When next he spoke his voice was somewhat gentler. "I love you, Jessie," he said. "When I said that, I meant it forever. And I meant all of you. But you've only been giving me half of you in return. The other half has been swept up in some hedonistic fantasy of life at the top, reaching for the stars and playing to the crowd.... I've tried to understand. I've given you space, I've tried to help you when I could, I've been here for you, waiting for you to make up your mind.... But honey, I've waited as long as I can. This can't go on."

And there it was. No more running from the shadows, no more ducking the inevitable. He had no right to do it, yet he had put it before her in black and white, and she must choose. She could have Keith, the one and only love she had ever known...or she could have her career, her ambition, her life lived to the fullest in her own way. He had no right to make her choose.

She stood, cupping her elbows in a futile, self-protective gesture that did not even stop the shaking. She circled the sofa until the length of it lay between them; then she turned. Very dimly she registered the caressing motion the cat made against her leg before he sensed his mistress's mood and leapt with a display of indifference back to the sofa. She did not know how she would make her voice work, but she had to try, one last desperate attempt....

"Keith," she pleaded. Her voice was hoarse, punctuated with airy breaths that left her aching lungs starved. "You know how important this is to me. You say you've been living in limbo—*I've* been in limbo since I left New York, wasting my talent and marking time, afraid to go forward and unable to go back...but you've changed all that, don't you see?" A note of tentative urgency came into her voice as she willed him to understand, to empathize, to give her once again the thing she had most loved him for—time. "You taught me how to go for what I wanted, you gave me courage—you did that! Don't you see I have to go on with it—I have to at least try! You can't ask me to turn my back on everything I've always wanted, everything I'm good at, and everything I belong to—not now!" And her words, so desperately sincere, so full of need and suffering and pleading, fell against the stone of his eyes and evaporated there. She looked at him, so remote and in control, so unmovable in the face of her most moving emotions, and very far away a painful rhythm began to pulse in her head: You are losing him... you are going to lose him.... She could not bear to lose him. She couldn't live with the void his absence would create; how could she make it without him?

She said quickly, "Not now, Keith. We can't talk about this now. You can't expect me to make a rational decision on the spur of the moment like this.... I won't lie to you about it, this trip—it will be a sort of testing period for me. I need to go, to get things in perspective, to get all my options in order and see if there's still a place for me on Madison Avenue, and if it's still what I want. But that's all it is—just a chance to see. I don't know how I'll feel when I get up there. I don't know what I'll find. I can't tell you anything until I get back. I know I have to make a decision...." She took a short, almost choked breath. "And I know that decision will affect your life, but I have no intention of making it now! You'll have to give me this time... to think, to see—"

He said quietly, "No, Jess. I won't be used that way."

She stared at him, stammering, "U-Used?"

A painful softening came over his face. It tore at her heart. "Yes, used. You'll use me as an excuse to refuse to make a decision about that job, and you'll use the job as an excuse to refuse to make a decision about me. You'll always have an out, and when you come back, you'll try very hard not to blame me for your having turned down the opportunity of a lifetime, but you will. You'll blame me for the rest of your life and succeed in destroying whatever chance we might have had together. I won't let you do that, Jess."

It was very difficult to catch her breath. Something awful and heavy was growing in the pit of her stomach, choking her. She looked at him, so tall and perfect in the yellow lamplight. The silky wave of his hair, the infinite depths of soft cocoa eyes. The tender mouth. The delicate hands. He had never been more beautiful to her. And even as he stood there so strong and solid before her, some trick of the imagination seemed to show him receding in waves, becoming smaller and smaller, and she whispered brokenly, "Hold me, Keith."

He stepped forward and took her lightly in his arms. His embrace was warm, but there was a reserve to it, as though he were keeping his emotions on a tight rein, afraid of crushing the fragile dream. And as tightly as she clung to him, she could not draw him closer. He whispered, "Don't do this, Jessie. I've got my arms around the only real and solid thing in my whole life. Don't make me let you go."

Hot moisture flooded her chest, burned her throat, stifled her breathing passages, and rubbed like sandpaper against the backs of her eyes. But she wouldn't give in to it. She had to be strong; she had to hold on to the dream this one time—perhaps the most important one in her life. "After I get back," she managed to say. "Don't ask me now. I need the time...."

And even as she spoke she felt him slipping. Very slowly, finger by finger, he released her. And just as slowly, just as deliberately, he withdrew from her—body, heart, soul, all of him, all that she loved, leaving in his wake a memory as elusive as the scent of daisies on a summer day. She couldn't believe this was happening. She couldn't believe that in the space of one half hour all that she had loved and shared and reached for and *wanted* for the past five months of her life was evaporating into dust before her very eyes. But she knew it when he spoke. She saw it in his eyes; she felt it in the renewed icy chill that spread slowly upward from the tips of her toes and prickled in her scalp. She knew it in the horrible sick feeling that clenched in her stomach. And he said quietly, "No, Jess. No time. If you have to think about it, it's no good. You already know what you want; I'm just waiting for you to tell me."

It sounded so final. It was final. Her fingers were icy, her cheeks numb. Her skin felt like dried cellophane, cracking and peeling to expose raw nerve endings and throbbing tissue all over. She couldn't bear to look at him, so close, within an arm's reach but a million light-years away. She started to turn away, and it was then that she realized her back was against the wall.

She looked back to him, and there was no avoiding the bleak truth that stared her in the face. It was time to choose. Choose between your love and your life.... How could she choose? Quiet days and love-filled nights; an endless succession of small successes and unfulfilled promises haunted always by the lure of what might have been.... Smothered ambition and wasted talent, undiscovered adventure. She did not belong here in this quiet place with this beautiful gentle person. He knew that as well as she did. There was too much calling to her out there, and there always would be, and she had known all along that she must inevitably turn her back on the whispers of her heart for the lure of greater things. "I can't," she whispered. She could not believe it was her voice, so ragged and hoarse, so beaten and defeated. She could not look at him. "I can't marry you."

She heard his breath. It was like the last wisp of life

from her own lungs. And when he turned, a sudden galvanizing fear forced her into one last desperate attempt. She raised urgent eyes to him and insisted, "It doesn't mean... it's over between us." Her hands were twisted together as though clinging to the last straw of hope. She did not realize that what her fingers were clasping was nothing. "We can still see each other, still be together, and in time..."

The sorrow in his eyes broke her heart. "No, Jess," he said quietly. "I couldn't stand to watch what you're going to become."

She heard his footsteps cross the room, and she knew it was true. It was over. He was leaving her. And there was nothing, absolutely nothing, she could do to stop him.

Somehow she found the courage to turn and to watch in slow churning helplessness as the only man she had ever loved walked out of her life. Jessie watched the sun fade and the dark curtain descend on the window of her heart, and there was nothing she could do about it. She had never had a choice.

Keith paused at the door. He looked at her, and for just a moment hope stirred, a second chance, the moment when she could have said something, done something, run into his arms and told him whatever he wanted to hear—something, anything, that would let her hold on to him for just one more minute. But that hope died before it had even taken its first fluttering breath. Jessie could not move, she could not speak. And the moment slipped past, empty and impotent, never to come again.

He said quietly, "No one will ever love you better."

When the door closed and she was left staring into the bleak gray corridor of the future, she let the tears come, bathing her face and splashing on her clasped hands, but their cleansing power could not purge the loss that would haunt her the rest of her life. "I know," she whispered brokenly to herself, all alone in the empty room. She squeezed her eyes shut, and the next breath that escaped her was only a fluttering prelude to an uncertain future. "I know."

SPRING 1984

Chapter Seven

"Don't worry, sweetheart, I know what you need."
Ray Jindrich's hand stole about her bare shoulder and
settled on her neck, kneading and caressing it, a hot,
firm pressure that knotted muscles rather than relaxed
them. "You're just tired, that's all, wound up over this
Greenway account. All work and no play, that's your
problem. You need to take it easy for a while, let your
hair down. Trust me, baby, I know just what you
need."

Jessie hated it when he said that. She hated it when
he put his hands on her, and she irritably shrugged the
insinuating massaging fingers away. And most of all
she hated the sleek elegance of the hotel lobby they
were crossing, the discreet, uniformed attendants and
the aura of proud ostentation that pervaded every
corner. The sight of it, the smell of it in rich leathers
and expensive carpets, the feel of the temperature-
controlled air clinging like a web to her exposed skin—
all of it settled heavily just beneath her rib cage, like a
rich meal she wished she had not eaten. She *was* tired,
but it was not the kind of tired Ray would understand.
It was the kind of tired that came upon her unexpectedly and with increasing frequency these days, and it

made her want nothing more than to crawl in a corner somewhere with her arms over her head and never have to face another day. It was the kind of tired that made brushing her teeth in the morning seem like a gargantuan effort, that made her face feel as though it would crack if she had to issue one more bright or sympathetic smile, that made the hands of the clock stick interminably between the hours of two and three in the afternoon. It was a tired that caused her to sit staring blankly at an empty wall of her apartment in the evenings, an untouched drink in her hand, not answering the telephone or the door, for hours at a time. It was the kind of tired that made her think she would surely scream if she had to face one more party like the one Ray was escorting her to.

The woman who was reflected in the gold-vein mirrors of the hotel lobby bore scant resemblance to the girl who had arrived from Tennessee with scars on her heart and fire in her eyes a mere five years ago. That girl had been driven by a secret pain to wrest her destiny from the world; this one had barely survived the battle. She was sleek and sophisticated, a perfect ornament upon the arm of one of the most successful advertising executives in the business. Her strapless black sheath with its diagonal spray of silver and lilac branches bore the label of one of the most exclusive houses in New York. The deep dip of the back was obscured by the silver shawl that draped from her elbows to the calf-length hem, and the silver-filigree chain she wore about her neck was a gift from Ray upon the signing of the Greenway account. It felt like an obedience collar, cold and heavy. Her hairstyle was an original—courtesy of "Clarence darling," as Jessie and Celia called him with a smothered giggle behind his back—

and maintained at an exorbitant price. It was shag-cut and waved in multiple hues of platinum and gold just above the collarbone and wisping away from her face and forehead; its sheen and brilliance were a secret only Clarence knew. Her "on-the-town" makeup was lavish and striking: glossy cherry-red lips, dramatically accented eyes, expertly highlighted cheekbones. She was a beautiful woman, and everything about her posture indicated she knew it; it was almost part of the job. Ray knew it too, and there was a proprietorial pride in the way his hand rested against her bare back beneath the shawl that suggested he would not be seen with her were she anything less. To Ray she was an asset, as socially necessary and professionally advisable as the late model custom Continental he drove or the discreet Dior tieclip he wore. He did not notice the grim lines about her rouged mouth or that the sparkle in her eyes was more like cut glass than sunshine, or if he did he did not care. But Jessie noticed, and she cared.

The elevator doors closed silently, and with a whispering purr they began their ascent. The folds of Jessie's perfume were wafted about on the delicately cooled air like a chiffon scarf, and she said abruptly, "I don't want to go."

Ray looked startled. It was not what she'd said—she had been saying the same thing all evening—but the way she said it. Her face suddenly looked pinched, her eyes dark and smudged, and her voice was as cold as ice. There was a harsh authority to her tone he had heard her use only once or twice with secretaries and underlings, and she was not behaving like herself at all this evening. Come to think of it, she had not been behaving like herself with increasing frequency the last few months, and for just a moment—a very brief moment—he was concerned. It occurred to him, for he was a man of simple solutions and direct lines of thought, that she had perhaps had too much Champagne at dinner—or perhaps not enough—and he soothed her with a caressing motion of his palm on her back, his fingers slipping inside the low sweep of her gown to caress her waist. "Don't be absurd, darling," he crooned. "You're going to love this. It's just what you need. Besides, I have a surprise for you, and you don't want to spoil it."

She said tightly, "Take your damned hands off me, Jindrich, or I swear I'll slap your face."

Jessie had no fear that he would take offense—nor hope of it. Ray Jindrich would not have been where he was today had he been the type of man to accept a rebuff. He simply rested his hand flat against her back again as he said smoothly, "The surprise, my dear love, is that this party is purely for fun—no business, no clients. Nothing to do but get high and enjoy the company of some of the most glittering names in show business today, and if you even once suspect that anything remotely resembling a business deal is coming together, you can leave that instant, no questions asked. Fair?"

She was surprised, with as much emotion as she was capable of feeling these days. For Ray Jindrich to do anything simply for the fun of it—outside the bedroom of course—must surely be a first. Already she was searching for ulterior motives and she registered the fact with one wearily lifted brow. "Show business, huh?" she said skeptically, thinking about the Broadway promotion the agency had handled only two months ago.

"Music business, to be more precise." The elevator

bounced to a foam-cushioned stop and the pressure of his hand on her back increased slightly for alighting. "Have you ever heard of Jackie Damien?"

Vaguely. Jessie rarely had time to keep up with anything outside her own carefully circumscribed field, and rock music was not her specialty. "I thought he was dead."

"Damn near. Talk is he's planning a comeback and I thought it would be a kick for you to get in on one of his notorious private parties. Now, tell me I'm not a hell of a nice guy; this kind of crap bores me to death."

She looked at him long and hard as the elevator doors swung slowly open. "This kind of crap is just another folder for your file of 'important contacts,'" she said coolly. "This kind of crap bores *me* to death; you eat it up. You just brought me along for window dressing, and unless you're planning to pay me overtime, I think you'd better take me home."

"Something tells me we've had this conversation before," he murmured, and he guided her before him into a brightly lit, deafeningly noisy foyer.

The conversation, the event, the entire scene. The loud music, the shrieking laughter, the scented smoke, the bright costumes—it was like a low-budget television serial that was played over and over again, and nothing ever changed but the faces. She could have closed her eyes and described the entire scene in detail. The mode of dress would range from the chic tuxedo look to leather and feathers, with a liberal sprinkling of faded designer jeans and oftwashed expensive running shoes to set the proper contrast against the room's elegant silkscreen wallpaper and crystal chandelier. Imported wines and twelve-year-old Scotch would be spilled liberally on the Aubusson carpet, and there would be a hospitality bar set up in a corner somewhere for those who preferred to take their comfort without a glass. Couples would wander regularly into the bedroom and would not necessarily return with the partner with whom they had entered. Somewhere there would be a sixteen-year-old girl trying to pass herself off as twenty-five and getting away with it easily. Elegant women and handsome men would be talking in bored tones and laughing at appropriate intervals, telling endless lies and trying desperately to have a good time. And suddenly Jessie did not think she could go through with it. For just a second something within her froze in violent protest, and she thought that if she took another step into that room, she would surely crack into a million plastic pieces.

But then Ray's hand on her back was urging her forward, his voice calling greetings to people he probably did not know, and all she could do was grit her teeth and say lowly, "Please, Ray, don't leave me alone in this zoo."

He laughed, although she had not meant it as a joke, and he bent to kiss her on the neck. "Dear heart, I would be a fool to leave you alone anywhere I didn't have to."

Ray and Jessie were not lovers, but they were the only two people in New York who knew it. Ray's bedding habits were notorious. He went about the business of seducing women with the same single-minded determination and smooth confidence with which he seduced clients, and his nickname, "Shark," was well earned for more than one reason. He had made a valiant effort to add Jessie to his list of conquests—more, she thought, than she deserved—but had finally ac-

cepted her rejection as firm, surprising himself as much
as he did her. His method of dealing with this assault
upon his ego was convenient and quite simple: he
merely pretended that public assumption was a fact,
treating Jessie with every consideration due a long
standing mistress and bolstering the deception so well
that Jessie sometimes suspected he believed it himself.
The charade suited them both perfectly. Being known
as Ray Jindrich's property gave Jessie the freedom to
choose and reject other offers of companionship, and it
allowed Ray freedom from what surely must be an exhausting attempt to end every evening in a connubial
manner. His private attitude was paternal, and sometimes they were almost friends.

But that friendship did not extend to baby-sitting
when Ray had more important things to do; nor did
Jessie expect it to. He supplied her with a martini and
took her on a token tour from one unfamiliar face to
the other; she put on her party mask and was very im-
pressive despite the fact that her nerves felt like
splinters and she had to forcefully restrain herself from
slapping the face of the next man who called her baby.
She met their infamous host, a man of thirty who
looked sixty, burnt-out, spaced-out, and desperate. She
found the encounter overwhelmingly depressing, and
when Ray left her alone she went to the bathroom to
try to recover.

There was a pair of bikini panties on the floor, and a
man in the Jacuzzi. Jessie braced herself with her palms
on the vanity and took exactly five deep breaths, making up her mind to get through one more evening. I am
not having a good time, she told herself grimly as she
went back outside, but somehow she found the detachment to face the rest of the evening calmly.

She arranged herself in a corner, sipping her martini, and tried not to think about the decline and fall of the Roman Empire. She tried not to think about whose husband would be leaving with whose wife and what famous personalities would end the evening in a ménage-à-trois and who would not be able to find his way home at all tonight. Careful, my girl, she told herself vaguely, sipping her drink. Your Peter Pan principles are showing again, and as she looked about the room she decided it really wasn't so bad. Certainly no worse than a hundred other parties like it she had attended over the years. In fact, it actually showed a little more restraint than some she was used to. No drunken strip-teases, no indecent exposure—but the night was young. There was a young man in a corner strumming his guitar and singing tonelessly to himself beneath the deafening roar of stereo music; there was nothing unusual about that except the fact that his head was shaved and his guitar had no strings. Two women had their heads together in the opposite corner, and Jessie wondered dryly whether they were exchanging recipes. A man in red velvet trousers and bare feet was sprawled out on the sofa, and the woman who straddled him and bent her face to his was in imminent danger of losing the thin scrap of T-shirt that protected nature's endowments from public inspection. In the crowded space between the sofa and the buffet perhaps a dozen couples danced in intimate, slow, undulations despite the fact that the beat of the music required more room for movement. Suddenly Jessie was reminded of another crowded dance floor and other couples moving like one in secluded intimacy, but that was a lifetime ago, and she did not want to think about that, either. She moved away when she realized that the two men who had been engaged in soft conversation next to her were holding hands.

Jessie had been aware for several minutes now that a blond young man had been staring at her. As she moved about the room and tried to ignore him he followed her, sometimes simply with his eyes, sometimes arranging himself to get a better look at her. There was nothing particularly unusual about that, and Jessie was not unprepared to fend off advances, but the odd thing was that he looked familiar to her. And if he knew her, why didn't he come over and speak up? She met so many people it was impossible to remember them all, but the more she looked at him, the more certain she became that they had met. She ventured a smile at him once, but he simply looked at her in troubled concentration, as though he, too, were trying to place a name with the face. She shrugged to herself and dismissed it, for she was certainly in no mood to spend the evening renewing business acquaintances.

It was perhaps half an hour later that she singled Ray out from the hundred-odd occupants of the room. He was standing near the sofa—the former occupants of which had apparently decided to seek more privacy—and he was engaged in a laughing conversation with a man who was wearing a Ralph Lauren shirt and a fringed buckskin jacket. Jessie felt no compunction about interrupting him.

The look on Ray's face told her immediately that if she intended to ask for an escort home, she had better arrange alternate transportation. He looked somewhat relieved when she said instead, "Do you see that man over there?" Both conversants turned to follow her gaze to the blond who was staring at her unabashedly.

"Do we know him? He's been watching me all evening, and he looks familiar."

Ray started to shake his head, but his companion supplied, "That's Joey Calvin." He lifted his arm to call him over. "Hey, Joey!" And he looked back to Jessie. "You know, the lead singer of Flame...." And it came together for Jessie with a jolt.

Of course she knew what had happened to the small-time band with the big sound who had once shared a six-inch table in a crowded room with her and eaten all her sandwiches as though they had been the final meal served to dying men. Three years ago—or was it four? All the years blurred together in retrospect—the inevitable success had hit them and they had shot to the top of the popular charts and stayed there without fluctuation all this time. One could not turn on the radio without hearing their name; their old hits were classics and their new releases sell-outs. Their biannual U.S. tours were riot-squad events. Oh yes, everyone knew Flame.

After all these years, Jessie found it easy to resist the urge to let her mind slip back in time to an evening in a crowded club, laughing and talking until four A.M. with this boy—now grown into a man—and his friends. It was all a lifetime ago, and mordant memories had lost their poignancy. There was hardly a spark of familiarity or a quiver of pain as he exclaimed triumphantly, "Jessie McVey! I knew it, I never forget a face!"

Jessie was surprised that he remembered her, and the flattery showed in her smile as she felt some of the isolation and sense of unreality that had pervaded her all evening begin to thaw. "Joey," she said. She realized that before tonight she had never known his last name. "It's good to see you again."

And just as Ray was saying alertly, "You two know each other?" Joey took her arm and propelled her away from the knot of people that had joined their conversation, his face smug and his eyes alight with curiosity and satisfaction.

"It's been driving me crazy all night," he went on. "I knew it was back in Tennessee, and I knew it was while we were still playing clubs, and it was right on the tip of my tongue...." He laughed, sharply and boyishly. "And they say all this high living has turned my brain to mush! Wait till I show you to the rest of the guys—bet they won't remember!"

She joined his laughter, feeling strangely relaxed and at ease, as though a breath of summer air had just cleansed the smoke-filled room. It was good to see him again, and if this unexpected collision with the past must hold inevitably painful associations, she was strong enough to keep them at bay for the duration. "You are amazing!" she agreed. "I don't see how you remembered me at all; we only met that one time."

"Mind like a steel trap," he admitted modestly. "Anyway, how could I forget the girl who..." He stopped and looked at her with curiosity mingled with amusement and amazement. "What the hell are you doing here, anyway?"

She lifted her shoulders negligently and sipped her drink. "Oh, I just wandered in with the rest of the crowd. I should have guessed," she added with a teasing smile, "that among all these high-power music business names yours would be the highest."

But he was looking at her oddly. "Then you don't...?" A sudden look of excitement crossed his face as he turned and shouted to someone on the other side of the room, and the secret anticipation in his eyes should have warned her as he grabbed her arm and began dragging her through the crowd. "You won't believe this. I mean, this is too damn unreal for words." He was practically chortling with self-congratulation. "I can't wait to see the look on..."

He paused before a couple locked in an almost obscenely intimate unmoving dance and slapped the man on the shoulder. The man mumbled something incoherent into his blond partner's shoulder, and Joey had to grab his arm to turn him around. Even then it took a very long time for the impression to sink in.

Jessie stood there for a very long time, looking. She had read about scenes like this, but she had never thought she would be a participant in one. She had never thought that the deafening rhythms of loud rock music actually could fade away into a dim ringing in her ears and the jostling, laughing, gaily colored crowd of humanity really could blur into a soft wash of watercolor with one figure painted sharply in the foreground. She did not know that frozen moments were a reality and not just a literary allusion—and that shock was a physical thing.

The beard was gone, and the face underneath was somehow not as she had imagined it would be at all, square and firm in definitive lines and unyielding angles with a sort of ruthlessness to it that was too hard to be handsome. The dark hair was precision cut and fell in loose attractive layers from a natural part to the point just above his collar. He was wearing a brown suede vest and no shirt, no shoes, and high-fashion tucked and pleated red velvet trousers. Her eyes went dully from the bare feet to the ridiculous velvet pants to the bare chest with its dark covering of silky hair, and something very far away jerked and tightened in her rib cage, a vise trying to squeeze the last drop of life out of a heart that was already dead. There was just one more moment when she could look upward through the blessed anesthetic of shock and see an unfamiliar face that registered only mild annoyance, the irritated curl of his lips as he looked from Joey to her... and his eyes. Eyes that had once been as soft and melting as a puppy's, eyes that hid no secrets and knew no lies... eyes that were now like two pieces of flawed onyx, glassy bright yet vaguely murky and revealing nothing beyond the slight exasperation and curiosity directed at his friend.

And her own voice, sounding small and faraway but amazingly steady, pronounced the single syllable, "Keith."

He looked at her, a puzzled frown slowly drawing his dark brows together, and it seemed to take forever before recognition registered. And during that time life was returning to Jessie in slow painful waves. Her feet tingled as though they had just been immersed in a tub of dry ice, her fingers hurt from gripping the narrow-stemmed glass, and her cheeks felt raw and cold. Her heart was thumping in a nauseating rhythm, and the pulse in her head was in counterpoint to the bass of the stereo. It was real, but there was a sickening feeling of unreality to it, an almost nightmarish quality, because if she had ever dared to let herself imagine they would meet again, it would have never been like this.

It hit him with a visible recognition on his face. His pupils, if possible, dilated even further, and there almost seemed to be some loss of color around his lips. He said quietly, dully, "My God. Jessie."

Something about the situation seemed to communicate to Joey that the two of them had best be left alone.

This was not, apparently, the way he had planned the reunion to go, and he registered mild disappointment and curiosity in a quick glance at Keith before he took Keith's abandoned dancing partner in his own arms and led her, unprotesting, a few steps away in a sensual shuffle that somehow struck a note of almost hysterical hilarity in Jessie. It was that jolt that prompted her to get a grip on herself and hold on fast, for she had not realized before then how close she was to giving into hysterical giggles or drowning shock, how devastating this, the final pull on frayed nerves, could be. It was happening; there was no denying that. The unthinkable had become a reality before her very eyes, and she must deal with it, as she always had. . . .

A small smile cracked her lips, and she tightened her grip on the glass until the delicate stem was in danger of snapping between her fingers, yet her voice was cool, pleasant, incredibly detached as she murmured, "Well, well. Look who I met on my way to the top."

He said nothing, and the witty enjoinder suddenly seemed vastly inappropriate, like black comedy. This whole thing was beginning to feel like a tasteless practical joke, the loud music, the suffocating decadence, the bright lights, and the harsh truth of this man—this stranger—who looked down upon her in what might have been mere shock or perhaps increasing horror, she did not know. She only knew that a low panic was beginning to grow in her, the need to run away warring with the sadistic compulsion to stay, to see it through, to try to convince herself that it was really happening. . . .

It was real, all right. She knew it was real because the pain was starting. She was intensely aware of the sharp division between the laughter and artificial gaiety that bounced and jostled all around them and the stark incongruity of this poignant moment, and all she could think of to say was, "What are you doing here?" Her voice shook a little as she said it.

He did not take his eyes off her. He did not exactly focus on her, but he kept looking at her, as though his vision was having some difficulty relaying the signals to his brain. As though he, too, were having difficulty believing it. And he said vaguely, "Umm...Jackie...." But he did not finish his thought. He simply stared at her.

Jessie had lived the past five years wrapped in an artificial world of false truths and bright packaging, where the only realities that mattered were those on Wall Street. She sometimes wondered whether the gilt edges of her professional life had not also contaminated her personal one, but she was not until this moment aware of how sheltered the tinsel world in which she lived was from matters of the heart. It had been so long since she'd felt any emotion that the faint stirring inside her now was shocking and intensely painful, like the slow agony that follows frostbite. But she had to hang on. She was not equipped to deal with this, not tonight...not ever.

She kept the artificial smile glued to her face, and she tried to distance herself from the pain, holding back the flood of memories with both hands, and she said lamely, "You cut your hair."

"So did you."

A half beat of silence. Desperation was rising. "You look good."

"So do you."

Inanities. Surface amenities that were pitifully inadequate for the occasion. Five years. A lifetime. Five years in which to carefully bury memories of white wine and daisies, the taste of sunshine and the sound of rain on a metal roof, five years of emptiness and veneer, and all of a sudden the memories she'd thought so carefully walled away came seeping through in a thousand places, like water through a rotting dam. There was no way to stop it, and she could only try to ignore it, but her strength was fragile and these emotions were too alien. She looked at him and she tried to make herself believe that once a girl very like herself had found the only joy of her life in this man's arms. This man with the hard face and the blurred eyes, the bare feet and... "Red velvet pants." She could not prevent the words from slipping out on a shaky note of incredulity, any more than she could prevent herself from staring at them. It was too much. This she would never have believed. Of all the things in the world, she could never have imagined this, and confusion and shock started to blur with the whirlpool of questions and unfamiliar emotions, and she did not think she could hang on much longer.

That statement seemed to snap him out of the trance for just a second and he made an abrupt gesture toward his outfit. "This? It's a joke...." Yet still he stared at her, his eyes moving over her with the same sort of dull disbelief she was feeling herself. The tension strained within her and threatened to crack. She suddenly wanted desperately to get away, to sort this out....

He released a short breath and gave his head a little shake as he dragged his long fingers through the beautiful scissor-cut hairstyle. That was when it all started to break inside her, and she knew she couldn't hold on one more minute. The sight of those delicate, slender-fingered hands took her back with the speed of a time vacuum to balmy nights and sweet-scented days, to a face she had loved more than life itself and eyes that held all the goodness of the world, to strong arms and a gentle voice, and suddenly she knew she was going to cry.

Keith said rather hoarsely, "Look...I'm sorry. You caught me off-guard, and I guess you can tell I'm a little stoned...." He was still staring at her, uncertainly, disbelievingly, as though waiting for her to evaporate into a shimmering mirage before his eyes. "I mean, I never expected...Jessie, is it really you? Are you really here?"

Somehow she managed to smile. Somehow she managed to make her voice work one more time. "It was really great seeing you again, Keith," she said. How normal her voice sounded. Just like that of any other woman who suddenly meets an old lover after five years.... "You're looking good." Another smile in his general direction, and she turned and slipped away.

He might have called after her, but she did not hear it over the pounding of her heart and the pounding of the music. She might have felt someone touch her arm, but she was busy becoming lost in the crowd, pushing toward the door, seeking escape.

It was not until she was standing outside with the cool night air brushing over her face and the sound of traffic roaring in her ears that she realized she was on the verge of being sick on the street like a common drunk. She made her way shakily to a lamppost and hung on for dear life, swallowing back nausea and gasping for air, trying to still the violent pounding of her heart and to subdue the wracking shivers that swept her uncontrollably every fifteen seconds or so.

She did not know how long she stood there, gulping down a yellow-green sickness that was a blur of knife-edged emotions and searing memories, shuddering hot and cold and just letting it wash over her. She had been unprepared for this, that hellish party and the swift eruption of all that had meant sweetness and goodness and innocence in her life. She couldn't get it sorted out in her mind, the tangle of sunshine on her shoulders and the drone of honeybees, the garish laughter and the discordant music, kisses that tasted like honey and the warm scent of love and the dark blank eyes... evoking forbidden memories of strong, warm limbs and a body that had once been a part of hers, a man who had once filled her emptiness in a way that even now could not be forgotten—and the brief, cold stab of intense yearning that shot through her felt like the need to die. Dreams she thought she had forgotten, secret memories of what might have been, all she held precious and incorruptible had dissolved before her eyes in one brief head-on collision with the past, and it was more than her shattered psyche could take. She had looked into the dark, blank eyes of a stranger and all the neat ends of her life had begun to fray and un-ravel.... That man who had once held her heart in his strong delicate hands, that one man who had so pa-tiently taught her about loving and giving and living to the fullest... that very same man who was distant and hard and stoned and who looked at her with eyes as cold as ice.... She couldn't be expected to cope with it. She didn't have to.

But she did. She let it flow through her and over her and leave her weak and drained and then she reached to the very depths of her courage for the strength to stand up straight. Jessie just stood there for a long time, drinking in the night air, letting a slow peculiar calm seep through her. Through all the crises and pressures of her life Jessie had fortified herself by saying, "Well, that's not the worst that can happen to you." But this time she suspected it was the worst, and there was a very strange peace in having faced it and survived it. It was the worst; and it had happened at the worst time.

She noticed that the doorman was giving her peculiar looks, and she returned what she hoped was a reassuring smile as she moved to the curb. But she let two cabs pass before she realized rather vaguely that she needed to think about getting home. Still she stood there with headlights flashing in her eyes and a vague hollow feeling in the pit of her stomach and did not make the effort to hail a cab.

Of course she was overreacting to what was, after all, a very mild trauma, but that did not surprise her. She seemed to have increasingly little control over her actions or reactions these days. And it wasn't every day of a woman's life that she unexpectedly bumped into an old lover...her first love...her only love.... And here, of all places. Under such bizarre circumstances. That surely must be why even now she was finding it hard to believe that the whole episode was not just a product of an overworked mind on the verge of collapse, or perhaps the result of some hallucinogenic that had been slipped into her drink. That explanation was surely more feasible than the fact that Keith Michaelson had been at that party, blending into the thick tainted air of decadence and corruption, wearing a suede vest and red velvet pants and stoned out of his mind.

She heard the footsteps behind her, and she stiffened herself. Being prepared for it this time, it wasn't so bad when he stood beside her and said in a low voice, "I'll take you home."

She looked at him slowly. Her chest started to hurt and her heart began a slow, heavy jerking rhythm, but there was nothing she could do about that. He had pulled on a white gauze shirt and buttoned it to mid-chest but he had not found his shoes. Even in the uncertain light from the phosphorescent street lamps and the flitting headlights there was no trying to deny the fact that he was real, solid, and here. He still looked slightly dazed, but he seemed more in control of himself and the situation; there was determination about the harsh lines of his mouth, and tension radiated from the stiff arms and the hands that were bunched into the front-slit pockets of those ridiculous pants.

Jessie was proud of the steadiness to her tone as she inquired, "Are you sure you're in any condition to drive?"

"I'm sobering by the minute," he assured her grimly, and he stepped forward as a gleaming black Mercedes glided to the curb. She watched in absolute incredulity as he put his hand on the back-door handle and added, "But if it makes you feel better, I won't be driving."

She was too stunned to hesitate or protest as he opened the door and gestured her inside. She sank down into the rich wine leather interior and even had the presence of mind to give the driver her address—after Keith had settled beside her and looked at her inquiringly. They glided into the stream of traffic, and Jessie had vague thoughts about Alice Through the Looking Glass. It was only the sound of Keith's voice that kept her focussed, demanding the effort of concentration that kept her from following Alice's spinning and receding journey into Wonderland.

He said quietly, "You must have had some tussle with the devil on that street corner. You look about like I feel."

She looked at him. She was feeling more in control by the minute. The worst of the shock was over, and she was almost back to normal—considering the circumstances. She admitted, "It was a shock seeing you again...." Her voice was almost even, her breathing almost steady. "In that place... looking like... that."

He laughed, shortly and mirthlessly. "My mama always used to keep me in line by telling me to watch what I was doing because I could never tell who might be watching me. Tonight's the first time I wish I had listened to her." He looked at her, but she could see nothing of his face in the automobile's dim interior. Perhaps it was better that way. But there was a sober note in his voice as he added, "I guess... these weren't the best of circumstances under which to renew our acquaintance."

"Hardly." She took an almost steady breath. Conversation was easier now, almost natural. "I mean, really, Mr. Michaelson, a party like that—people like that—velvet pants? Whatever happened to the simple life?" Was that the note of bitterness in her voice? She had not intended it to be there.

He answered briefly, "It got complicated." And she thought she detected impatience in his voice as he went on, "It so happens that most of the people in that room had just finished putting in a twenty-hour day and were in a pretty bad way for some relaxation, so don't be so quick to jump to stereotypical conclusions, if you don't mind. We play hard, it's true, but we also work hard—" He broke off at her startled glance, and she thought she detected a trace of amusement in his eye as

he repeated firmly, "Yes, *work*. As for this get-up...."
Again he gestured vaguely toward his velvet clad legs.
"I told you, it's a joke. Some of the guys gave them to
me, and I thought it would be a kick to...." His voice
trailed off as he realized the triviality of the subject and
the futility of the explanation. The silence was uncomfortable, and he turned his face to look for a moment
straight ahead.

Now so many questions were racing through her
head that she could not get a firm grasp on any of them.
She watched in stunned silence and swirling confusion
as he reached down beneath the seat and began to pull
a pair of Gohills boots over his bare feet. Definitely
Gohills. And where else would a man keep a pair of
five-hundred-dollar boots except beneath the backseat
of his Mercedes? That Looking-Glass feeling was beginning to assail her again, and to forestall it she made
herself speak. Out of all the spinning questions and
tacky curiosities that were raging in her head, all she
could find to say was, "Are you living in New York
now?"

He got the last boot on and straightened up. She
caught his expression in the flash of a headlight, and
she knew at that moment he was thinking exactly what
she was: That this was the man who five years ago had
refused to come to this town, had had no part in her
fantasy.... There was a recognition of the irony in his
eyes, perhaps a twist of bittersweet sorrow on his lips,
and he answered, "No. L.A. I'm in only for a few days
because of Jackie. I have an office here, though."

She started to parrot the word *office,* but the car had
pulled to a stop in front of her building, and she simply
couldn't deal with it tonight. It was too much. Too
much too soon...she had to sort it all out. She had to

take time, and maybe it would all make some sort of twisted sense.

She waited until the driver opened her door and then she turned to Keith uncertainly. Yes, it was really him. After all these years, a face that was unrecognizable, eyes like glass, and a wall of time between them that nothing could breach, and she was too tired to try. She said, "Well, thanks for the lift...."

She was floundering over whether or not to suggest they get together, and her inclination was to say nothing, but he interrupted her harshly, "Don't be an ass, Jessie. I'm coming inside with you."

Then he was out of the car, and so was she. He did not touch her as they walked past the doorman and into the elevator.

As Jessie let Keith into her apartment there was another brief flare of that sense of unreality, as though this were all a jumbled-up and highly imaginative dream from which she would awake any moment now. And then, as crystal-globed lamps sprang to life and he stepped inside she felt a small twinge of nervousness, wondering what he would think of it, trying to make sense of the hurricane of events that had led to his being in her apartment, wondering what would happen now.

Jessie's apartment looked much more expensively furnished than it was. The apartment itself was almost beyond her means, but prestige meant a lot in her line of work, so she had taken the apartment and over the years, with her own good taste and Celia's decorating contacts had created an effect of chic elegance that did it justice but did not bankrupt her budget. The colors were silver gray and crystal white with touches of deep mauve and startling contrasts of fuchsia in unexpected places; original artwork adorned the walls, and small accent pieces scattered here and there lent an air of intriguing sophistication with just a touch of the avant-garde. Keith wandered about, curiously touching little things of interest, his eyes taking in every detail with an alertness she would not have thought he was capable of half an hour ago. She could not tell whether or not he approved.

She turned to hang her shawl in the closet, and when at last he spoke, the comment was neutral. "No need to ask how you've been doing. Obviously you've done very well. Nice view of the park."

She offered nervously, "Would you...like a drink, or something?"

He turned from the window, his face expressionless. "Yes. I'll get it." He moved to the bar and with his back to her inquired, "What would you like?"

"Nothing, thanks." She sank stiffly to a dove-gray divan and watched curiously as he poured a measure of Scotch into a tumbler, straight. Two strangers making polite conversation in meaningless phrases and stilted gestures...strangers.

He turned, a small smile on his lips that left his eyes blank, and he commented, "You stopped smoking."

"Yes." She watched him as he crossed the room and sat opposite her on the white brocade chair. The habit had faded away somewhere during a sun-drenched summer five years ago and she had never resumed. Surely he remembered that. But she only inquired pleasantly, "How could you tell?"

Once again he glanced about the apartment, and still she could tell nothing from his eyes. "No ashtrays, for one thing." He sipped his drink.

Stupid, meaningless conversation. "When did you start drinking Scotch?"

He lifted one shoulder disinterestedly, not returning his gaze to her. "A few years back. It's an acquired taste that more or less goes with the territory."

Territory. Now he had hit the crux of the matter, and she could not restrain herself any longer. "What are you doing here?" she demanded.

She thought he was being deliberately obtuse as he replied innocently, "I told you, Jackie—"

"No," she interrupted impatiently. "I mean, what are you doing here—with Jackie Damien, with Joey, with Gohills boots and a chauffeured Mercedes...."

For the first time there was a twinkle of mirth in his eyes. Only the humor seemed to be laced with cynicism, and it was not a very reassuring expression. He murmured, "You're awfully fashion-conscious, aren't you?" And then, watching her carefully, he replied with assumed nonchalance, "I am what is called a promoter. I manage musical talent. Flame is one of my clients. Jackie is another."

She stared at him. She had not known Keith Michaelson capable of a lie, but what did she know of this cool stranger? And why would he make up such a thing? It was just that of all the directions she thought he might have taken, this was not even in the running. She would have found it easier to believe had he just informed her that he held exclusive rights to the Upper East Side heroin market. Yes indeed, that would make far more sense.

She ventured, "I thought you had to be a lawyer to do that sort of thing."

He never took his eyes off her, scrutinizing her reaction, yet carefully maintaining that mask of distant amusement in his own eyes. "Not really." He shrugged. "You just have to be smart enough to know when to hire a good one. It helps if you know a little about the music business, but there's really very little skill involved."

So many questions. So many inconsistencies. Just when she thought the puzzle was solved more pieces turned up missing, and her head was spinning with the enormity of it. Keith Michaelson wore faded denims and three-dollar T-shirts and never bothered to concern himself with where his next meal was coming from. This jaded stranger drank Scotch and managed musical talent. Where did the two men meet—if at all? She had to ask, "Do you like it?"

He knew exactly what she was thinking. Perhaps he was wondering the same thing—what had happened to the man she had once known? And his eyes seemed to grow harder with each passing second as he answered evenly, "I like the money, the power. I like living in comfort. I like the freedom and all that comes with it. Surprised?"

She could not look at him any longer. She could not hold back the bleak emptiness that was sweeping her nor keep it from showing on her face. So much distance. They did not know each other anymore.

The silence dragged on and on, an uncomfortable, ringingly empty silence. She felt herself being sucked down into that vacuum, and she could envision herself becoming nothing more than a tiny speck of unanswered questions in the enormity of that gulf, her entire personality swallowed up by the emptiness that was encroaching upon her in relentless, powerful tides. It was with a last desperate effort to save herself that she made herself look up, painted the careful mask of indifference on her face, and inquired politely, "Do you ever hear from any of the old gang?"

He was watching her. All this time he had been watching her, and something of his own mask had slipped. Mingled with the curiosity on his face was a hint of sadness, and she knew his thoughts had been taking the same course as hers. Instinctively she hardened her heart against the first glimpse of familiarity she had seen all evening. Jessie could take indifference, she could deal with the distance, but don't let her start seeing in his face the things of him she had once loved, don't let her be reminded of the real man... don't make her face his emotions as well as her own.

He took a sip of his drink and replied, "Sure. I make it down to Nashville now and again—a couple of my acts record there. I keep up. What about you?"

She shook her head, and then she had to lower her eyes. A lifetime lay between that place and this.

And then he inquired abruptly, "What did you do with the cat?"

She looked up, startled, and for just a moment her face was a blank. Then, swiftly, with no warning whatsoever, it all came flooding over her—the carefree days, the contented nights, laughing eyes and strong arms.... The cat. The stupid cat. For just half a second it was difficult to breathe, and the pain that turned within her felt like the deliberate and methodical breaking of a heart. But she took hold of herself sternly, she would not give in to it. Her voice was only a little hoarse as she replied, "I—gave him to Anna...when I moved. It's cruel to keep an animal in New York."

He nodded, watching her soberly. With each passing moment more of the uncomfortable veneer that had shielded him was flaking away, and the man inside showed through. He was simple, frank, hiding little if anything, and she could not face that. She dropped her eyes again. The silence went on and on, and he simply sat there, watching her.

Then at last Keith spoke. "I suppose this is where I should tell you that you haven't changed a bit." His voice was somewhat gentler, though still underscored with a trace of irony and cynical amusement. She looked at him. She was surprised and disconcerted to see a softening in his eyes as they moved over her, slowly and assessively; yet sorrow mingled somehow with the wry twist of his lips as he looked at her face. "You look older," he admitted frankly. "Thinner, more sophisticated, and in some ways more beautiful. ..." His lips twisted in a way that was both amused and mockingly self-derisive. "Wiser than I ever wanted you to be ... and you're like a breath of springtime to me." he finished softly.

Said so simply, so honestly. It was like an echo from the past, and she could not deal with it. Great gulping spasms of sorrow shook her, and she wanted to cry but everything within her seemed to be dried up. She simply looked at him through the unbreachable distance that had grown between them and she could say nothing, do nothing, and eventually, feel nothing. It was the only way she knew how to cope. Stop the pain before it began.

He returned her gaze calmly for a long time. It was a sober look, timeless and unreadable. And then he said, "I guess we'd better talk about it. Are we supposed to be mad at each other?"

She let her mind wander back tentatively to a night five years ago, searching for the anger, the pain. Who had hurt the other more? Who had the right to be angry? Viewed from a distance it was hard to tell, it hardly seemed to matter. When she spoke her voice was quiet, her eyes bleak, "It was so long ago," she said.

"Yes," he agreed. He dropped his eyes to his near-empty glass, and he added, almost to himself, so quietly she had to strain to hear it over the sudden low hum of the air-conditioning unit, "I came back, you know. About a month later. You were already gone."

And that was too much. The pain twisted within her, the emptiness and the longing burning in her throat, the helplessness spreading through her stomach. She couldn't fight it any longer. She sat there and watched the long and empty years unroll before her eyes and wished desperately for the power to recapture even a small portion of what was lost to her...just one more smile from the man with eyes as clear as sunshine, just one more day of innocence, just one last glimpse of the child she once had been. But of course she could not recapture those moments. Time moved on, and neither of them were the people they used to be. She wanted to cry, but she could not do that either.

After a time he got up and went to the bar to replenish his drink. When he turned there was kindness on his face, a genuine interest in his eyes. "So," he inquired gently as he resumed his seat. "Tell me how you've been. Doing okay?"

The concern with which the question was asked tore at her heart. It made her think maybe it was possible after all to reach back in time and grasp something of what she had left behind.... Jessie looked at him and she wanted to say, No, Keith. I'm tired. I'm tired of selling human emotions with pretty lies and gilt packaging. I'm bone weary and I don't know how much longer I can cope and it scares me to death. I want to go home but I don't know where home is.... But she smiled, rather stiffly, and very falsely, and answered, "Okay."

He sipped his drink, watching her. "What are you doing?"

"Advertising. I'm the account executive for Greenway Baby Foods. You've probably seen the commercials."

He nodded. "Nice. Quite an achievement for a woman your age." Then, still very conversationally, "Television? Don't you miss your artwork?"

She did not answer. She didn't have to. Because he looked at her and he knew all the answers, all the bottled up emotions and all that was dying inside of her. He looked at her and the reach of his eyes was closer than a caress; for just a moment, it bridged the distance with understanding and took her back to what might have been. She suddenly wanted nothing more in the world than to have his arms around her, and in his eyes, for just a brief moment, she imagined that he wanted it too.

And then it was gone. He finished his drink in one gulp, stood, and said abruptly, "I've got to be going. Busy day tomorrow."

She stood more slowly behind him. It was definitely gone, that brief moment of wanting and tenderness in his eyes, if it had ever been there at all. The stranger was back, remote and in control, and Jessie was left with a bleak hollowness in the pit of her stomach that spread slowly outward and was almost paralyzing. Still, she managed to reply, "Yes. Me too."

At the door, he turned. His smile was polite, barely interested. "I'll be here a few more days. Maybe we could get together."

Her answering smile came with difficulty. "Sure." But she knew they wouldn't. There was simply no point. It was best to let it die a natural death, to put it back in the closet of dusty memories where it belonged and somehow move on....

He looked at her for another moment and something changed about his expression as his eyes went slowly over her face, resting for what seemed an interminable interval on her lips and then back to her eyes. She thought in that moment he was going to say something, and she thought that what he might have said would change everything, would somehow wipe away the emptiness and make everything all right.... But he didn't. He simply smiled at her, briefly and impersonally, one more time, turned, and left.

When he was gone, Jessie leaned against the door, resting her head against the cold wood and closing her eyes. She tried to cry, but she couldn't.

Chapter Eight

It took an enormous effort for Jessie to drag herself into the office the next morning, but she made certain none of it showed in her demeanor as she sailed through the reception area with her usual purposeful strides and automatic greetings. She looked smart, successful, and confident in the elegant camel-colored cape and matching skirt Celia had designed for her; the dark paisley-print silk shirt and matching scarf tied high under the collar gave just the right air of attractive femininity combined with competent business sense. She greeted her secretary, fended off her messages and reminders with a request for coffee, and went into her office, closing the door behind her. Duty compelled her to hang up her cape, put down her brief case, and to check her calendar, but that was as far as she got.

It would have been easy to blame this overpowering lethargy on Keith, but that was not it. Or maybe it was only a small part of it. Perhaps it was simply that since last night she was finally able to put a name to the strange malady that had been afflicting her for months; the nameless yearning that had been gnawing at her soul was gradually beginning to take shape. On this morning, like so many others, she did not seem to have the energy for doing anything but sitting at her desk and wondering what she was doing here, how she had gotten here, what had happened to the person she once was.... Like Lot's wife, she had made the mistake of looking back, and now she was in grave danger of suffering the same consequences.

And on this particular morning the uneasy void that filled her seemed to somehow revolve around days that were a warm butter yellow and nights sprinkled with stardust, daisies ankle-deep, and a man's husky laughter... and she wondered with a cool detachment how she could have turned her back on it all so easily. How could she have been so blind all this time to what was missing in her life? How could she have ever imagined that this was where she belonged? Yet she was trapped here in a cage of her own making, where nothing was real and nothing mattered, nothing touched her and somehow over the years she had grown to like it that way. The high-powered lure of Madison Avenue had formed a gilded shell around her heart, and until last night nothing had been able to penetrate it.... It frightened her a little to realize how close that shell was to cracking, yet at the same time she yearned for exposure. She wanted to be touched again, to care again, to let her heart reach for and find the things that were real and good and solid. That was what was missing in her life.

Her assistant came in with her usual brisk demand for a conference, and Jessie gave her the time, only half-attentive. Charlene was an ambitious little bitch, and Jessie did not trust her out of her sight. She wanted Jessie's job, Jessie's accounts, Jessie's future, and she made no secret of the fact. She intended to go straight to the top, and she did not care who she had to step over, kick out of the way, or sleep with to get there. Jessie watched her go with a vaguely amused smile and wondered whether she had ever been like that. Probably.... And the smile faded as she wondered what Charlene would think if she guessed that on this particular morning Jessie was more than inclined to simply give her her job, her accounts, and her future. The triumph simply wasn't worth the fight anymore.

Ray came in to find her staring aimlessly at the wall. He closed the door behind him and sat down, disguising the momentary concern in his eyes with a cheerful, "Well, well. You cut out on me early last night. Word was you got the hots for one of those freaked-out musician types. How was it, may I ask? Any good?"

Jessie said coolly, "Go to hell, Ray."

"That bad, hmm?" he mused, but she stared him down until he felt compelled to defend himself. "Just looking after your best interest, lovely, no criticism intended. Heaven knows, I'd be the last one to object to anyone you went to bed with, just as long as he kept you happy. You're turning into one of those frustrated she-dogs, dear heart; it's as obvious as hell, and it's wearing on everyone's nerves. Why don't you get yourself fixed up?"

Jessie leaned back in her chair and made a temple of her fingers over her chest, observing him with easy detachment. She knew there was no way out of this encounter and no way to sidetrack the conversation, so she would meet it with customary equanimity, experience having taught her well. "You are a disgusting little man," she replied evenly. "Is there something important on your mind, or did you just come to deliver your daily lecture on sexual hygiene?"

"As a matter of fact," he replied cheerfully, "there was just one little thing.... How would you like a shot at the Carlee Cosmetics account?"

Carlee Cosmetics. There was not a person in the agency who would not have killed for a chance at that account. Two years ago, a year ago even, Jessie would have been among them. Now, combined with her success on the Greenway account, this could have made her one of the top names in the business. But she only inquired with unreasoning apathy, "What happened to Davis?"

Ray shrugged. "He's drying up on us, going stale. We need fresh blood, and you—" he grinned at her magnanimously, pleased with his own generosity and anticipating her reaction "—are just the one to give it to us. The only one, as a matter of fact, by unanimous decision. Well?" he demanded when she made no response. "What do you say? Are you excited? Let's see a little jumping up and down, some clapping of hands, an impromptu display of childlike enthusiasm—even a hug or two. I've just given you the break of your career, baby!"

She looked at him expressionlessly. And she said slowly, "I'm not sure I want it."

His astonishment was abrupt and absolute. Ray stared at her as though she had just sprouted wings and was preparing to take a flying leap out the window. His expression suggested that a leap out the window might just be preferable to what she was contemplating doing to her career. And at last he blustered, his color rising, "What the hell do you mean—you don't think you want it? Do you have any idea what I just offered you? Did you even hear what I said? What has gotten into you?"

Jessie shrugged, gracefully and indifferently. "My schedule's pretty full.

"Screw your schedule! That's not it, and you know it. So you'll push the Greenway account over on Charlene, you've got it going now and she can handle it.... What the hell is this?" He was glaring at her. "Are you holding out for more money? That goes without saying. A percentage of the take? Yours. You don't have to play these stupid games, you know I've got no patience with them. You want a bigger office, more help, a prettier title, two weeks in Hawaii—hell, name it and it's yours. What are you trying to pull?"

Jessie smiled, slowly and rather sadly. "That's not it," she explained patiently. "I'm just not sure whether I want to take on another account right now. I appreciate the offer, but..." She trailed off.

Ray fixed her with that angry, intimidating stare for one more long moment, then looked away. He released a pent-up breath and ran his fingers through his thinning hair, and when he turned back to her there was dread mingled with the concern on his face. He said seriously, "All right, Jessie, let's have it. You've developed a serious attitude problem lately, and I think it's about time you let me in on it." He hesitated. "Are you on some kind of downer or something?"

She smiled when she realized the genuine worry that prompted the question. "No," she assured him. "Not my style."

"Been hitting the bottle a little more often than you should?" he suggested gently. "It's nothing to be ashamed of, you know, it happens to the best of us...."

For the first time in what seemed like ages, Jessie almost felt like laughing. "No, nothing like that."

He frowned. "Is it some sort of female thing that you'd rather not tell me about?"

And then Jessie did laugh. "Ray, you dear old-fashioned tyrant! I'm only thirty-one years old, and it's a little early for the Change, as any good medical book will tell you. Besides, it's sexist, not to mention dangerous, to assume every problem a woman has is hormonal. I could have you brought up on discrimination charges."

But he refused to be teased out of it. The frown lingered with the exasperation in his voice as he demanded, "Well, damn it, Jessie, what am I supposed to think? You said it yourself, you're thirty-one years old, and you're acting like a case of forty-five-year-old burnout. There's no reason for it. What is your problem?"

Her own mirth faded as she looked at him. She offered without much real interest at all, "Maybe some people just reach burnout faster than others."

He gave an impatient snort and jerked his face away. When he looked back at her his tone brooked no argument or evasion. "What the hell's the matter with you, Jessie?"

She sighed, dropping her hands on her desk in helpless resignation as she sat forward. She wished she could tell him. But how could she expect Ray to understand? What did he know about reaching for the stars and coming away with only a handful of dust, about grasping a dream and feeling it turn to cold clay in your fingers.... Still, she owed him an explanation. She said simply, "I am not a happy woman, Ray."

He got to his feet with a muffled exclamation of impatience. "Happy?" He turned on her in exasperated incredulity. "Good God, woman, what does it take? What the hell do you *want,* anyway? You sleep on damned satin sheets and wrap your pretty little body in rags that would make a fair down payment on a Cadillac. You've got an expense account that would make the Prince of Wales jealous, and if it's men you want I can name you half a dozen studs who are panting after you right now. You've got the most exciting city in the world at your feet and half the brains in this business running scared, and this is just the beginning. There's no limit to where you can go from here. What the hell do you want?"

In the ringing silence that followed his demand Jessie heard her own voice from far away, dull and almost querrelous, "I want—" To be young again. To feel again. To care again, to do something important with my life.... Maybe to make a meaningful statement on the condition of the world. I want to go home. "—I don't know, Ray," she said softly. "I just don't know."

"Baby..." His voice softened, he came over and laid an affectionate hand upon the back of her neck. "Honey, there's no reason for this. Of all the people in the world, you've got less reason than anyone to be depressed. Don't you know what you are, what you can be, in this business?" His voice brightened bracingly, sincerely. "You've got what it takes, sweetheart, don't you know that? Everything you touch turns to gold. We need that here; we need you, and we're not going to let you shoot yourself down the tubes for no reason, is that understood?"

Grateful for the effort if not the effect, Jessie tried to give Ray the courageous smile he expected. "Yes, sir."

"Good." He squeezed her shoulder bracingly and started for the door. It took very little to satisfy Ray; he was so confident of his own success he rarely waited to make sure of it. "Now, get your act together and let me see some life around here. I'll send the stats down on Carlee this afternoon."

Jessie knew it would be useless to object. And as she watched him go it occurred to her distantly that, while the Midas touch could certainly be a very useful asset, gold was an extremely unyielding substance from which to fashion a heart.

She took a client to lunch and had pink grapefruit with honey while he consumed an elaborate lobster dish and three martinis and insisted upon talking about everything else but the campaign. Her mind wandered, and he had made the proposition three times before she realized that he was suggesting they finish their conversation at his apartment. In a reckless streak she told him she would love to but her physician had advised her to abstain from intimacy until she finished her penicillin treatments, and he fell for it. She returned to the office wearily amused.

Waiting on her desk was the Carlee file and a basket of yellow daisies. Her heart began to thump and a girlish color flooded her cheeks as she went over to the flowers. The card read simply, "Dinner tonight?" and there was a telephone number.

She sat down behind her desk and took up the phone before her courage deserted her. She punched out the number with a shaking finger.

On the first ring she almost hung up. Dinner tonight? What was she thinking of? In the short time they had spent together last night she had been dragged through more emotional hell than anyone should be asked to endure. Why was she opening herself up for more of the same? Three rings, four.... She did not want to see him again, she did not want to be reminded of what she had lost and how he had changed.... Five rings. Six. He wasn't in. That was good. It was the best thing that could have—

"Gold Star Management, will you hold please?"

At first she was disoriented, thinking she had dialed the wrong number, but then she remembered he had said he had an office in town. Keith, with an office. An office in New York. This was really ridiculous. She sat there gripping the slim plastic handle with a soft-rock tune lulling in her ear, and she knew she should hang up. There was no point in it. What could they have to say to each other beyond the inanities they had exhausted last evening? She had no interest in this urbane man who sipped Scotch and cruised around town in a black Mercedes.... She did not know the president of Gold Star Management.

"Thank you for holding, may I help you?"

Jessie swallowed once, convulsively, but then she managed in her best professional voice, "Mr. Michaelson, please."

"I'll put you through to one of his associates."

Jessie opened her mouth to protest, but the soothing soft rock was humming in her ear again.

Her hand was growing sweaty on the telephone, and her heart was racing uncomfortably. Don't be stupid, Jessie, she told herself. It's over; you finished it last night. There's nothing for you here. He's different, you're different, and to keep dragging those differences into the light is only going to destroy what you had. You don't want to see him. You want to try to hold on to what's left of the memories.... But her eyes were drawn irresistibly back to the basket of daisies. She could almost feel the playful tickling of the flower under her chin. She could see a ramshackle cabin surrounded by a field of them. She could smell the sweet, sharp air and feel the dusty heat. She could close her eyes and—

"Leonard here. What can I do for you?"

Jessie took a breath. The voice on the other end was friendly, male, and young. She thought about hanging up. She said, "I'm trying to reach Mr. Michaelson. . . ."

He chuckled. "You and every other act in town. I'm afraid Mr. Michaelson isn't taking any calls today, but I'm sure I'll be able to help you. What's on your mind?"

He wasn't taking any calls. Well, that settled it. She was relieved. "Nothing," she answered. If her voice sounded unsteady she did not notice it. "It was personal. I'm sorry I bothered you."

Just as she was about to hang up the man on the other end gave a long, low whistle. "Hey, wait, lady, don't go away mad." Apparently he had read something into her tone she had not meant to be there. He sounded uncomfortable, reluctant. "Listen, I can put you through to his secretary, but don't blame me if he doesn't take the call. It's a madhouse around here today. Maybe you can leave a message."

"That's not—"

"Hold on."

The music again.

Damn it, she thought tightly, gripping the receiver. Hang up. You don't want to talk to him, you don't want to see him. . . . The man sent you flowers; you at least owe him a thank you. How long since anyone sent you flowers?

"Mr. Michaelson's office."

Jessie took a breath. "Is he in?"

A pause. "I'm sorry, Mr. Michaelson is unavailable

at the moment. May I transfer you to one of his associates?''

Damn. All right then, you called him. Simple courtesy. Thank you for the flowers but regretfully I am unable to accept your dinner invitation.... She said calmly, ''Would you just take a message please?''

''Certainly. The name?''

''Jessie McVey.''

A millisecond pause. ''Hold on, please.''

The interminable music again. Jessie swore out loud and almost banged the receiver down. And then a button was pushed, the music switched to a louder, harder rhythm and then ceased abruptly. Keith's voice, warm with pleasure, spoke into her ear. ''Jessie! I'm glad you called.''

Jessie became aware of her speeding heart abruptly. For a moment she couldn't speak, and then what came out was not at all what she had intended to say. ''I'm glad you could take my call.''

''Uh-oh.'' A hint of the familiar laughter in his voice beneath the apology. ''You didn't have any trouble getting through, did you?''

She loved the sound of his voice. Somehow it sounded different today. Somehow today she could imagine that the man on the other end had dancing cocoa eyes and shoulder-length hair and a silky beard. And somehow she found herself smiling. ''Your staff is very protective of you—in an off-beat sort of way.''

''Are you suggesting my employees could use an orientation course in telephone manners?''

His employees. How odd that sounded. ''Something like that.''

''Well, we're pretty laid-back here,'' he admitted, ''but I'm sorry you had trouble. I'll—''

"No, it's all right, really," she assured him quickly. She had almost forgotten the message she had resolved to leave. "I just didn't realize you were so busy."

"Actually, I am," he said before she could finish her sentence, "and that's why I'm glad you called when you did. It looks like I'm going to be tied up here longer than I expected, so I was wondering if you could meet me downtown tonight instead of having me pick you up. It will save confusion all around."

For a moment she did not know what to say. She had forgotten just how masterful he could be. Had he ever in the length of their relationship given her a chance to refuse even one of his invitations? "Well, I—"

"Let me give you the address. It's not far from your building. Got a pencil?"

She copied down the address he gave her, not knowing why. She had already made up her mind that it would be best not to see him; she really had no intention of going through with this.

"Do you think you can break away by six?"

"Yes, but—"

"Good. I shouldn't be tied up much longer than that, so you just come on over and we'll get an early start on the evening. And don't dress up."

"Keith, I—"

"I'm sorry, Jess, I have two other lines blinking at me and I'm not supposed to be taking any calls, so they must be important. I'll see you about six, okay?"

She must have responded in the affirmative, because the next thing she knew she was listening to a dead line. She sat there looking at the telephone receiver and thought in amazement that he had done it to her again. Some things, she supposed with a slow, rather silly smile, never changed....

Jessie could not stay in her office past five thirty. It was a fifteen minute walk to his building, and with every step Jessie was trying to think of reasons why she should dread this evening, convincing herself not to get her hopes up. But she did not feel dread. She felt as eager as a sixteen-year-old on her first date and excited for the first time in a long, long time.

But once inside the building she felt her first twinge of nervousness. What was she expecting from this evening, anyway? What did she have a right to expect except the obligatory dinner with an old friend? That was the only reason he had issued the invitation. He had sounded genuinely glad to hear from her this afternoon, but Keith was like that with everyone. He kept up with old friends.

And so she assured herself with a squaring of her shoulders as she searched the directory, what was wrong with that? They would share a few drinks and a quiet dinner and catch up on each other's lives.... People did it all the time.

The reception she received upon entering the Gold Star suite was quite different from the one she had gotten on the telephone that afternoon. The reception-ist greeted her with a bright smile and immediately left her desk to escort Jessie down a sunshine-yellow carpeted corridor with multicolored abstract murals on the walls to Keith's office. Jessie felt a twinge of guilt because she was sure Keith had followed up on her complaints about his employees' telephone manners, and she was certain of it by the effusive greeting his secretary gave her. Jessie was told immediately to go right in, Mr. Michaelson was expecting her, and she spared one amused look for the leggy young thing in miniskirt and striped legwarmers before turning to the private door that bore Keith's name in gold script.

For just a second she paused, victim again of that Wonderland feeling, and she wondered whether she should knock. The secretary smiled at her reassuringly, and Jessie scolded herself for her lack of composure. She had entree to the private offices of some of the most powerful men in this city; she would not be intimidated by one more gold-lettered door.

Outrageously loud hard rock music screamed at her from the quadraphonic speakers on the wall, blurring her impression of chrome and glass furnishings, midnight-black carpeting, and walls plastered with album covers and photographs. The lighting was indirect and tinted a very pale blue, lending an air of stark surrealism to the entire room. Keith was leaning back in a sculpted black leather chair, his boots propped up on an enormous desk littered with files and loose papers and a multitude of built-in electronic panels. He was wearing jeans and a green athletic jersey with the number 52 splashed on it in yellow letters, and a Stetson hat was pulled forward over his half-closed eyes. The long fingers that rested on his chest were keeping rhythm to the music, and he did not notice her entrance.

Jessie smiled. She did not know whether it was from amusement at the picture he made or sheer delight at seeing him, but she suddenly felt happy, relieved... and glad to be here. She stepped in front of the desk, leaned forward, and gave him a small wave to catch his attention.

The immediate warm pleasure that lit his face flooded through her like honey. He touched a button on the desk that plunged the room into silence as he sprang to his feet, exclaiming, "Jessie! Good for you, you're early." He swept off the hat and glided it toward a low-slung chair in the corner, grinning, "Pardon the disguise. It keeps people thinking I'm working when what I'm really doing is sleeping."

Jessie glanced about the room with amused skepticism. "Hard way to make a living," she commented.

"It's a rough job, all right," he admitted nonchalantly, and his eyes sparked as he came toward her, "but somebody has to do it." He stood before her, about two feet away, and unexpected delight tingled through her as the pleasure-lit eyes swept over her slowly. "You look gorgeous," he said. "But as usual—" he startled her by bringing his hand to the shoulder button of her cape "—you're overdressed."

"I came from the office," she reminded him, and she was taken aback by what the touch of his hand on her shoulder could do to her. It actually made her heart jerk, and she thought she felt a very faint blush starting. "What was so urgent that you couldn't call for me at my apartment like a gentleman?"

"Conference call." He swept the cape off and tossed it carelessly on his desk. "Fortunately it came through earlier than I expected, so I can at least be gentleman enough not to make you wait for your dinner." And as he spoke his fingers were deftly and efficiently undoing the scarf beneath her high collar; with a tug it joined the cape on the desk.

She caught her breath as he stepped back and looked at her thoughtfully, but she managed to joke weakly, "Look, Michaelson, maybe you can afford to be blasé about a three-hundred-dollar cape and a forty-dollar scarf, but I can't. Will you please stop throwing my things around?"

He grinned and clucked his tongue at her reproachfully. "It's vulgar to mention price tags, darlin'." And with swift decision his fingers fastened on the button at her collar.

Something weak and melting went through her, and she noticed a definite increase in the pace of her breathing. Maybe it was the sound of that old endearment—*darlin'*—in his sweet, unaffected drawl that took her back with a breathless rush to long-ago times, or maybe it was the feel of his warm, slim fingers against her skin. She only knew that the sudden sensations that coursed through her were so new they felt alien, yet so old they were unforgettable. He released the first button deftly, the second and the third, and the heat that swept slowly to her face was ridiculous, as was the sudden racing of her heart and the quickening of her breath. How many times had she been undressed by this man? There was no reason for the schoolgirlish excitement, the uncertainty and the brief flash of intense awareness, for all he did was smooth the pointed collar back over her shoulders, exposing a perfectly decent amount of chest; then he stepped back and looked at her assessingly.

Perhaps he looked at her a moment longer than was strictly necessary, but his eyes were hooded, and she could not read his expression. And when he looked up at her there was nothing there but a smile with the casual pronouncement, "You'll do." He turned and scooped up her cape and scarf with a flourish, his eyes twinkling as he presented them to her, "Your wardrobe, my lady. Next time wear jeans."

On his way out he advised his secretary to have his car brought around, and when they reached the street a sporty red Mazda was waiting for them. Somehow this was easier to resolve with the image of the Keith she thought she knew than a chauffeured Mercedes, and she inquired as she slid into soft white leather seat, "Is it yours?"

"Keep a car in New York City?" he scoffed, and closed her door. "What for?" He added as he got into the bucket seat beside her and started the ignition, "It's on loan for the evening."

"We could have taken a cab," she suggested.

He regarded her mildly. "To New Jersey?"

Jessie fastened her seat belt and said nothing. Somehow it all made perfectly wonderful sense that Keith Michaelson should have his pick of all the elegant restaurants and exclusive clubs in New York City and choose to dine in New Jersey.

Over glasses of Chianti in the softly lit booth of a small restaurant which, Keith assured her, served the best rigatoni outside of Italy or in, a strange, rather uncomfortable silence fell. It should have been the most natural thing in the world to be sitting in a place like this with him, it should have been like old times, but Jessie did not seem to be able to keep from reminding herself that it wasn't like old times at all. She could feel him watching her but she kept her eyes on the rosy liquid in her glass, afraid to return his gaze because she was uncertain what she would find there. There was a panic that accompanied the realization that, after all these years, they might not have anything to say to each other, they might not be able to find anything to talk about at all, and she had to break the silence with a quick inquiry. "How did you know where to send the flowers?"

There was a glimpse of something odd in his eyes as she glanced at him, but it faded away before she could understand it. He answered casually, "Contacts. New York is a big city with a lot of inner circles. It wasn't hard at all to find out everything I wanted to know about you.''

She laughed a trifle uncomfortably. ''That sounds ominous! What did you find out?''

He answered with disconcerting frankness and in a totally expressionless tone, ''Ray Jindrich.''

She caught her breath with a startled look and a soft, ''Oh!'' Maybe that was why he had been looking at her so oddly. She did not know quite how she felt about that, but she was flustered enough to try to avoid the issue by teasing, ''You shouldn't make shallow judgments, Michaelson, especially since the things you were doing with that blonde last night are illegal in some states.''

He winced even as a relaxed twinkle came into his eye. ''You're never going to let me live that down, are you? God help me if I ever make another move without looking over my shoulder first. Just remember,'' he pointed out on a slightly more serious note, ''it could have been you who was caught in an indiscreet moment instead of me, and then the tables would have been turned, wouldn't they?''

And how would he have felt, she wondered, if he had discovered her glassy-eyed and half undressed in the arms of some male sophisticate at an uninhibited Manhattan party? Perhaps, it occurred to her slowly, the same way he had felt when he found out about Ray Jindrich. She said quietly, ''Don't believe everything you hear in this town, Keith. Ray is my boss and sometimes a pretty good friend. It's only his reputation that makes people believe otherwise.'' She smiled at him. ''Okay?''

If there was relief in his face, it was disguised by the flickering candlelight. He returned her smile and lifted his glass to her before sipping from it. The awkwardness that had been between them began to slip away.

She watched the shadows play on his smooth, angular face and catch in the reflective lights of his eyes, and she could not help remembering the first time she had seen him, never guessing that she would fall in love with the long-haired, bearded man who came to her door one rainy February morning.... Seeing him now was a lot like the first time. The face was different, the body older, the conditions vastly altered, but still there was something of that first encounter, the strangeness, the uncertainty, a lingering expectation on a faraway level....

He caught her staring, and she apologized with a small shake of her head. "Sorry. I just can't get used to it."

The relaxed smile in his eyes told her he knew exactly what she meant, even as he inquired, "What?"

She looked at him frankly. "Your being rich."

He gave a small, startled sound that might have been choked laughter, and the brief spark in his eyes was both amused and tolerant. Then he shrugged and took another sip of his wine. "What's rich? Your average blue-collar worker brings home just enough to feed and shelter his family, and he has to work like hell to do it. You give a man an annual income of $300,000 and half of it goes to Uncle Sam, the other half goes up his nose. Nobody ever has enough."

That was a very callous but stingingly accurate way to put it. Jessie tried hard to read the unspoken message in that statement, as she inquired carefully, "And do you fall into that category?"

His eyes were frankly laughing now. "That's a very mercenary-sounding question, little darlin'. Wishing you hadn't turned down my proposal all those years ago?''

Swift color tinged her cheeks with a sudden sting of unexpected pain, and she hid both swiftly by lowering her eyes and sipping her wine. In a moment she managed casually, "But you must admit, Keith, this is all a little...surprising, to say the least. You're the one who always used to be so contemptuous of material success, talking about the false glitter and the rat race and—and—shark-bait...." She almost choked on the words because they had such bitter significance for her now. He had known, even back then, what she was only now beginning to admit to herself. He had seen so clearly how empty the dream she chased would be.... Yet it turned out the advice he had given her with such prophetic clarity so long ago was hollow, deceptive—he had not even followed it himself.

There was a note of exasperation to his voice as he returned, "For heaven's sake, Jessie, I never meant to give you the impression I was a complete idiot. I never said I would turn my back on money if it fell into my lap, and success is only a matter of perspective. Knowing how to handle it is more important than achieving it.''

"Fell into your lap, eh?" There was a bitter twist to the smile she had meant to be teasing. "That makes you sound rather...lazy.''

He seemed to consider that thoughtfully. "Not lazy," he decided after a moment. "Just a man with his priorities straight.''

She regarded him steadily over her wineglass. "What are your priorities, Keith?''

He did not appear to resent her interrogation. It was almost as though he had expected it. "I like my work,'' he answered her. "The hours are crazy and the pace is hell sometimes, but there's satisfaction in it, and I have an escape valve for the pressures. I don't let it keep me from the important things in life."

Yes, she had seen his use of that escape valve last night. And she wondered what the important things in his life were these days. She was certain they had nothing to do with fishing in a still mountain lake amidst the drone of insects and a field awash with yellow daisies.

Somehow she lacked the strength to pursue the conversation, and she was grateful when the waitress placed two steaming plates of fragrant rigatoni before them. The food was delicious, but Jessie did not have much of an appetite. She complimented him on his choice of restaurants and he mentioned idly that he had been to Italy a couple of years ago. They talked about that for a while. After a time, though, the conversation became desultory because the only things Jessie could think of to say began with *Remember when?* She refused to do that. She let the silence fall.

Long after the waitress had removed Keith's plate, Jessie continued to push the food around on hers because she could feel him watching her and she wanted to avoid meeting that gaze. A low aching tension built within her, and at last anything became preferable to the heavy silence. She took up her wineglass and met his eyes bravely.

She did not know what she expected to find there. Accusation, disappointment, the cold distance.... Certainly not the gentle warmth, softness, and something vaguely resembling tenderness that made her feel as though he were looking through her, beyond her, and into some region she was completely ignorant of...for what could he see in her to put that look of quiet appreciation on his face?

"I like the color of your hair," he said. "Sun kissed."

That flustered her. That brought back from nowhere a husky drifting voice, "You've got gold in your hair...and stars in your eyes." The stars had faded from the eyes of the woman who sat across from him now, and the gold was just an illusion.

She took a quick sip of her wine and replied flippantly, "I wish I could take credit for it. All compliments and or complaints are to be directed in writing to my hairdresser, who gives me a ten-percent commission for advertising."

The smile in his eyes faded slowly into warm curiosity, a sort of lazy interest. She grew uncomfortable under that assessive, gently thoughtful gaze, and she had to shift her eyes. And then he said quietly, the words rolling off his tongue in that beautifully familiar, effortlessly sensuous drawl, "What's troubling you, Jessie Dee McVey?"

She could not hide the swift surprise, and then the uneasiness, in her eyes. Of course, as perceptive as ever, he would not have been blind to the tension, nor would he be lulled into ignoring it. It was useless to try to deny it. But she was confused. "I'm not sure...." Her hands tightened about the stem of her glass; she lowered her eyes to its red depths. "I know what you mean."

"Don't be offended, darlin'," he encouraged gently, "but I've seen eyes like yours glittering at me from dark street corners and shady alleyways—hard and world-weary, disillusioned and confused and, beyond it all, scared to death. It doesn't look right on your face.

It's more than just the two of us running into each other like this after all these years—though maybe that's a part of it. What I've been seeing in your eyes since last night took a long time to build, and I had to know what happened to put that look there. Tell me.''

It was a long time before she could speak. She swallowed several times on nothing and tried to find the right words, but they wouldn't come. *Tell me.* How long had she waited to hear those words.... Talk to me, lady. Tell me.... Demanding honesty, promising understanding. Tell him. She wanted so badly to tell him.... But the best she could do was a small smile and a light shrug and a skimming glance across his eyes as she answered, ''I'm not sure I know the answer myself. Nothing dramatic, I guess. Midlife crisis, maybe. I'm thirty-one years old, and I'm wishing I had something to show for it.''

He acknowledged her effort with patience and acceptance, and if he recognized the missing truths behind her explanation he did not criticize. ''You're a talented lady, and you're getting the recognition you deserve,'' he said. ''You're at the top of a fast-paced world, and you're shining bright. Isn't that what you wanted?''

She couldn't answer. She couldn't expect him to understand, not this man who lived in the glittering world that was slowly destroying her and who enjoyed it; who, in fact, seemed to thrive on it.... What was it he once said, about her being unable to handle pressure? Maybe that was the difference between them. She didn't know. She only knew that he wouldn't understand. Not anymore.

Her smile was very weak and her voice a little shaky as she said, ''You always had all the answers, didn't you? You're always in such perfect control—of yourself, your environment...." She softened what might have been taken as a criticism with another wan smile. "Must be nice."

He regarded her seriously, his slender fingers resting lightly about the curve of his wineglass and tracing an absent pattern over the smooth surface. He said, "I don't know about that. A man's control is limited by the choices he makes. As for having all the answers...." He dropped his eyes and finished off the wine in his glass. "I lost you, didn't I?"

Swift, sharp pain clutched at her with that matter-of-fact statement, she started to shake her head in slow protest. No, she thought, you didn't lose me.... She did not know how she would make her voice work but she could not let it pass. "That's not true," she said quietly, hoarsely. She stared at her glass, watching the slowly tightening death grip her fingers formed around the stem. "There was so much.... You taught me so much...."

"Sure." His voice was calm, expressionless. His face was blank. "I taught you how to play, I taught you how to fish...I taught you how to make love. I taught you how to choose. And, eventually, I taught you how to leave me. One thing I've learned, Jess, in my years as a professional manager, is there is a limit to how far you can control other people. You do the best you can, but there's a point when you have to let go, and it's up to them.... And then you spend the rest of your life wishing you'd done it differently." His tone was bleak with the last, his expression enigmatic. And then it was gone. He said abruptly, "Hell, let's get out of here. I'm getting maudlin."

At the car he said, "I need to stop by Joey's place before I take you home, if you don't mind. They're leaving on a three-week tour tomorrow, and there are some things I need to check out with them before they go. Besides," he added with a grin as he opened her door, "I think Joey wants to apologize to you for the way things turned out last night. He didn't mean to send us both into shock, and the way you flew out of that room last night made him think the next we'd hear from you would be on the critical list of some hospital emergency room."

Jessie felt numb during the drive back to the city, and he did not talk much. Half-formed emotions and uncertain thoughts moved sluggishly in a convoluted pattern through her head, twining and interlacing and turning back on themselves. Perhaps tonight she had expected to find some answers, but in fact she was more confused than ever.

Joey's penthouse apartment was the scene of an impromptu jam session, where the other band members, sound men, and road crew were in high spirits, pumping out the adrenaline for tomorrow's tour. At first Jessie felt an almost instinctive shrinking away, for the scene was so much like one of the night before—like so many nights before—but Keith's hand was firm on her back, and then she was in the midst of it. And it wasn't like last night at all. When the other band members crowded around her, greeting her and joking with her and trying to outdo one another with displays of acuity of memory, Jessie had the strangest feeling that no time at all had passed since they last met. They were the same four boys who had once crowded around a small table in a smoky bar, natural, unaffected, completely at ease in their success. Jessie could not help remembering Keith's concern on that very same faraway night that his ambitious friends would be swallowed up by success—apparently he had been wrong. What else had he been wrong about?

Jessie was given a drink and deposited in a chair away from the center of activity, where Keith's voice rose and fell and intermingled in laughter with that of the other men and the occasional twang of guitar strings or roll of drums. There were papers to be signed, last-minute reminders, a schedule check. Jessie sat back and sipped her drink, surprised at how comfortable she felt here, waiting for the uneasiness and the sense of claustrophobia to come. It never did.

She looked up with a smile when Joey sat on the arm of her chair, but the young man looked unhappy. He said without prelude, "Listen, I'm sorry if I blew anything last night. I didn't mean to freak you out. I thought you two would be glad to see each other."

Glad to see each other? It disturbed her to realize she still did not know the answer to that. She smiled. "It's okay. I'm sorry I left without saying good-bye."

Joey did not seem reassured. "It's just that—back in Tennessee, you know—it would have taken a blind man not to see that you two had something pretty heavy going on. You were all he talked about. And then after you broke up—well, that was a bad scene, too, but I never realized that after all these years. . . ." He trailed off, looking disconsolate.

It occurred to Jessie how lucky Keith was to have such a caring friend. But then, it was impossible not to care for Keith when he gave his own friendship so abundantly and so sincerely. . . . She said, "It's all right, really. I am glad I got to see you all, and—" her smile was genuine, encouraging "—that you're all doing so well,"

Joey brightened. "Yeah, that's something, isn't it? I

always knew it was out there somewhere, but of course we never would have made it without Keith.''

Something within Jessie tightened in alertness. She sipped her drink and said cautiously, "Oh?"

"Sure," responded Joey easily. "I mean, he got us our first label and everything—unofficially, of course—but it was more than that. We would have gone under that first year if he hadn't been there, for damn sure.''

"You were his first clients?" Jessie felt like an undercover reporter, and it wasn't something she was proud of, but she could not go on under this burden of curiosity.

He laughed. "You could say that. I mean, it's a long story. After our first hit we thought we were so damn smart, you know, thought we had it made. We went through a couple of managers, and they were eating us alive, but Keith was always there to untangle our messes and get us back on our feet, so we finally figured, hell, why are we paying these other jerks for what Keith is doing for free, and he became our manager.''

"I see." Jessie took another sip of her drink. "So you really gave him his start."

Again Joey laughed. "Not exactly. I mean, it was the System that made his name in the music business, and we had to practically twist his arm to—"

Jessie was confused. "System?"

For a moment Joey looked incredulous, then he excused her ignorance with a dismissing shrug. "I guess if you're not in the business you wouldn't know. It's a kind of keyboard—hell, there's no way to explain it to you if you've never seen it. It's the biggest thing since the Moog. Everyone uses it in concert now; made him a fortune, too. Anyway, I felt kind of bad for a while about talking him into taking us on, because he was all wrapped up in this sound-design business, and we were a full time job...." His shrug and his grin were abashed. "I guess I should really feel bad about it now because it's all gotten so out of hand. See, Keith's trouble is he doesn't know how to say no. Pretty soon some of the hottest names in the business were beating down his door and he couldn't turn them away. But," he defended himself philosophically, "if you look at it in a large way, it's got to be for the best. I mean, it's damn near impossible to find a guy you can trust these days, and all the people Keith has helped get started or kept from going under.... The thing is," he explained, and a slight frown creased his brow as he tried to put his meaning into words, "everybody's out to get you in this business, and that's no lie, from your own producer right down to the damn music critics. Other managers, all they want to do is wring you dry. They'll set up a schedule designed to burn you out and then throw you out in the spotlight and say 'go for it'—making sure, of course, that they've got favorable mention in your will first. But Keith, he's looking out for *you,* all the way—even it it means he's losing money, even if *we're* losing money sometimes,—the thing is he's got your best interest right up front. He'll hold your hand when you get scared, you know? It sounds stupid, but that's important in the kind of life we lead. A case in point: Jackie Damien. You know he hit the skids a couple of years back, came damn close to doing himself in." Now a troubled light crossed his eyes, as though he did not like to be reminded of this graphic example of an occupational hazard. "When his record sales started slipping, he got the jitters, started hitting the hard life in a bad way—going to concerts so messed up he couldn't remember the lyrics to his own songs or

not showing up at all, wasting studio time, finally ending in an O.D. Well, after that nobody in the business
would touch him. But all he really needed was to be
working, you know? And even though Keith said he
wasn't taking on anybody else, he's nursed him through
this new album, I mean day and night, smooth-talked his
way into a couple of big promoter's hearts, given him a
new start. When it comes to that, do you have any idea
how many times over the years Flame has come this
close to breaking up? Over stupid things—'' And then
he broke off with an abashed grin. ''Hell, I'm talking too
much again.''

''You always talk too much, Joey.'' Keith laid a
friendly hand on Joey's shoulder and looked down at
Jessie. ''Are you ready to go, Jess?''

Jessie said good-bye to the band and wished them luck
on the tour, and she thought she understood something
of what had happened to Keith, what events had led up
to the reunion with a stranger at a wild, midtown party.
In the car she said thoughtfully, ''It suits you, what
you're doing now. I never would have imagined it before, but somehow it seems almost—inevitable.''

He grinned in the passing shadows of other vehicles.
''I'm glad you approve. Sounds like Joey remembered
his lines just like we rehearsed them.''

She laughed. ''Is that why you took me there tonight?''

Keith shrugged, and she could see the mischievous
sparkle in his eye beneath the sudden glare of a headlight. ''He owed me one. I knew it must have been a
culture shock for you last night,'' he added more seriously. ''The music business has a bad reputation, and
I'll admit most of it is earned. You were ripe to jump to
all sorts of judgmental conclusions about me and the

way I choose to lead my life. I hoped that being with the band tonight under slightly different circumstances would remind you that we're all still people—not saints or demons, just people.''

Jessie was silent for a moment. Then she said hesitantly, ''What about me? Were you shocked at the way you found me?''

''No,'' he said simply, and she did not know whether to be reassured or disappointed.

Keith walked her to her door and followed her inside without hesitation or invitation—just as he had done in the old days. When Jessie turned from hanging her cape in the closet she found Keith had wandered over to her desk, where he was examining her sketch pad with its assortment of political cartoons. It was so much like the first time that her heart caught and began to ache. ''You've kept in practice,'' he complimented her. ''These are fantastic.''

Jessie felt a warm, satisfied blush begin to tingle in her cheeks. She had not realized until that moment how starved she was for appreciation—for his appreciation. It shone in her eyes and was reflected by a lustrous softening of his. They looked at each other in a moment of unspoken communication that she wished would go on forever, but some inane instinct for self-preservation prompted her to inquire rather casually, ''Would you like a drink?''

''No.'' He came over to her, the same look of tenderness and quiet understanding in his eyes, a gentle smile tracing the pattern of his smooth lips. ''I know it's early, but—'' he touched the tip of his finger very lightly against the corner of her eye ''—I've never seen anyone who looks more in need of a good night's sleep than you do. I'll say good night.''

Jessie's heart was racing in a delayed reaction as his finger moved away. She would not have believed that so simple a touch could do that to her. She was not aware that her eyes were searching his anxiously, and she could not account for the breathlessness to her tone as she replied lightly "I'm not at all sure that was a compliment!"

"I'm not at all sure it was meant to be," he answered, and his eyes, very sober, never left hers.

Suddenly she knew she did not want him to leave. It was an intense knowledge, as desperate as it was fierce, and she said quickly, "Will I—will I see you again?"

His hands came up slowly and curved around her upper arms. His expression did not change. It was surely meant as nothing more than a friendly gesture; there was no reason for the sudden lurch of awareness that began in Jessie's stomach and spread inexorably to her chest. His fingers were warm against the silk sleeves of her blouse, and she felt the flesh prickle underneath. She looked up at him uncertainly, hoping, needing, wishing, praying that none of it showed in her eyes....

"Good night, Jessie," he said softly, and he kissed her.

She was almost certain he had planned no more than a friendly good-night kiss, because almost the moment his lips brushed hers he started to move away. She could feel the half-second's uncertainty in his indrawn breath and the tightening of his hands on her arms. Then his lips moved on hers, tentatively at first, and the shock of the act began to give way to the wonder of discovery and the straining floodgate of sensation.

Jessie's reaction was immediate and unpreventable.

She lost her breath, and her head spun, and swift, shaky heat surged through her—but perhaps that was just from shock. Surprised instincts flamed to life from the depths of her confusion, sending her heart into an instant slamming rhythm and her nerves into a hotly charged center of response.... She did not understand it, she could not control it. She only knew that she was swirling and receding into weakness, yielding to the steadily increasing tightening of his muscles and the hardening of his mouth on hers—more than yielding, pushing herself into it, grasping for it desperately, deepening his swiftly kindling passion with the unexpected depth of her own. She did not know what she was reaching for, what she was straining toward...a ghost of the past, a promise of the future. And dimly, very far away, a part of her was pulsing with ecstatic wonder, the thought so small it was hardly recognizable.... I love him. *I still love him.* All these years a part of her heart had been sealed away, waiting for him to open it, protecting its most treasured secret. She loved him. It hadn't changed.

But of course that was impossible. It wasn't the same. The man who was burning his way into her senses and turning her blood to fire was different from the gentle lover she once had known. The hands that dragged slowly upward to press against her face were hot and rock hard with barely controlled power; there was a ruthlessness to the way he forced her mouth open to receive the invasion of his tongue, and her response was frighteningly overwhelming, more intense than it had ever been. She clung to this stranger and received him and wanted more of him, yet all the while a low desperation was building within her that felt like the acid taste of tears.

"Oh Jessie," he whispered against her neck. His breath was hot and unsteady, and the words came to her through the jerky pulse of her own thundering heartbeat. "All night I've wanted this—to touch you, to feel you.... Will you—" The hard pressure of his fingers against her face dragged her mouth urgently back to his.

She thought in one glorious, swirling moment, Yes, I will...forever.... But the sound that bubbled up from her chest was a choked protest, and she broke away.

He caught her arm swiftly as she started to turn, and he gathered her to him in an embrace that was deliberately gentler, reassuring, and apologetic. And she could do nothing but let him hold her, feeling the jerk of his heart against her chest and the heat of his face against her cheek, wanting him to go on holding her but knowing it couldn't last.... "Darlin', I'm sorry. I didn't mean to be so rough—it's just that I've wanted you so badly for so long.... Stop, it's okay...." His husky voice soothed her mind as his stroking hands upon her back gradually calmed the shaking but nothing could ease the gnawing pain and the raging confusion that was growing inside her. When she felt the warm, delicate fingers on her face again and his lips upon her cheek she knew how easy it would be to succumb to this, to let herself believe it was possible, to dwell forever in this fool's paradise.... She gathered the last of her strength and moved away.

Jessie walked three steps away from him, clutching her arms at the elbows, keeping her back to him, and then she could go no farther. The imprint of his fingers was still on her face, and her mouth was bruised from his, and the raw ache deep within her echoed unfulfilled desire. She felt shredded and tattered, hurting all over. She thought if only she could cry it might be better, but tears were locked away deep in the core of her and she could not release them.

It was a long time before he spoke. When he did it was a quiet demand, simple and toneless. "Why?"

"For God's sake, Keith," she said tightly, "this is not a scene from an old movie!" With an enormous effort, she turned to face him. "We can't just pick up where we left off five years ago and start over!"

His eyes were blank, his face very hard. But his voice was even as he replied, "Where we left off is a lousy place for anyone to start over from. That was not what I had in mind."

Her control was breaking into fine, brittle pieces. "What did you have in mind, then?" she cried. "A quick tumble for old time's sake? A one-night souvenir of your trip to New York? What?"

The swift, hot emotion that darkened his eyes frightened her. She took an instinctive step backward as he exploded.

"Damn you, Jessie!" Further expletives were lost in the sharp hiss of his indrawn breath, and the dangerous flame in his eyes was hidden by the abrupt motion that dragged his fingers through his hair. When he next spoke his tone was tightly controlled, but rage and disappointment still smouldered in his eyes. "I can't believe this," he said quietly. "Do you think I'm a complete imbecile? Do you think I don't know what's been going on in your head? It's the same old status thing—five years ago it was New York girl meets unemployed dropout, and now it's what? Successful advertising exec meets parasitic rock-star promoter? *What,* damn you!"

She shook her head violently, her eyes widening and

her cheeks paling with instinctive horror as she choked out, "No, Keith, it's not—"

"And stop cringing from me," he snapped. "I'm not going to hit you, though God knows why I don't. It's the only thing I haven't tried to knock some sense into your head."

She saw the muscles of his arms bunch with the tightening of his fists that seemed to lend authenticity to his threat, but all he did was jam his fists impotently into his pockets. The anger in his eyes tore at her heart, plunging her into turmoil and helplessness. Why now? Why did he have to come back into her life now when everything was such a mess and she was hanging by a thread, when she was confused and beaten and grasping at straws.... Why did she have to meet him again now, just when she needed him most?

His eyes burned through her with dark intensity as he demanded lowly, "Jess, when are you going to open up that gilded heart of yours and see that there's a woman living inside? Is it such a frightening thing to do—to find out who you really are and what you really want, to let yourself respond to the real things in your life?..." And he broke off abruptly, as though suddenly realizing the futility of trying to get through to her, and there was a harshness in the way he turned his head, as though he could no longer bear to look at her.

"No." The word was a broken whisper. If only he could understand, she didn't *know* who she was or what she wanted anymore, and she was slowly suffocating under the pressure of trying to find out. And the only person to whom she had ever been able to open her heart was him.... How desperately she wanted it to be that way again.

Her fingers dug into her arms and her eyes willed

him to look back at her, pleading with him to understand. "Keith, don't you see—all this time—we're different people! You've changed, I've changed . . . I don't
know you anymore!"

His eyes were a cold shield that barely hid impatience. "Circumstances change, Jessie," he returned
shortly, "conditions alter, and appearances may be different, but people don't change. I'm the same man you
didn't quite trust enough to share your life with five
years ago, and you haven't changed. Back then you
were hiding behind a bad marriage and a fear of commitment; who knows what you're hiding behind today." He dropped his eyes, and the weariness and the
defeat in his voice tore at her soul. "I'm not even sure I
want to know."

Was he the same? she wondered bleakly from far
within the depths of desperation, or had the power of
success and the passage of time gilded his heart as well
as hers, stripping away the love that had once dwelt
there, leaving him empty. . . .

As he turned to leave her she was afraid she would
never know.

At the door he stopped, and her heart began a frantic
racing again as she thought he would come back to her.
If he had come back to her nothing would have mattered except that he was hers, in this time, in this place,
for one more night.

She heard the soft release of his breath, she saw the
tense muscles across his back forcefully relax. But he
did not turn to her. His voice sounded very tired, and
quiet, and he said, "Hell, I didn't mean for this to happen." A brief silence was filled with tightening hope on
her part, weary self-reproach on his. Still he did not
look at her. "I thought I was smart enough not to make

the same mistake again. I didn't mean to push you."
Another short breath, and his shoulders squared. She
thought surely he would turn, and come back to her.
She ached for him to do so. But all he did was turn the
door handle, hesitating for just another moment before
he walked through. And then he said quickly, without
looking at her, "Look...if you ever need a friend...
you call me, okay?"

If he had waited one more moment, she would have
called him. Jessie thought she would never need a
friend more than she did right then. But then Keith was
gone, and she was alone.

Chapter Nine

Addison Sheppard, president of Greenway Corporation, shifted uncomfortably and could not quite meet Jessie's cold, totally expressionless gaze. A yellow-red color began to seep out of his tight collar, and he defended himself with belligerence. "It happens all the time. No operation is perfectly foolproof, there's always a margin of error, there's no reason for the FDA to jump down our throats like this. If it had been anybody else—"

"We've got to be prepared for a full-scale war, Jessie," Ray put in grimly. "The media is going to come down on this with all barrels open. Greenway has been a household word for over thirty years, a scandal like this—"

"A scandal like this could ruin me," interrupted Sheppard tersely. "An institution—a national landmark—wiped out...." He snapped his fingers briefly. "Just like that. And why? Just because a few contaminated jars slipped through our inspection? You ask any of our competitors how often it's happened to them. And because it's Greenway, they're acting like we've destroyed a public trust! They're determined to crucify us, and for what? How many products are recalled every year, Ms McVey, let me ask you that!'' His voice was rising, his flabby hands tightening on the soft leather padding of his chair, his color becoming dangerous. ''Do you know? Well, I know! And what happens to them—they suffer a minor setback, that's all, they continue production and recover their losses in a matter of months. But not us. They're determined to destroy us over this thing.''

''Really, Mr. Sheppard,'' Jessie said smoothly, ''I hardly see cause for hysterics on anyone's part.'' Her voice was very composed, her legs crossed gracefully and her hands resting casually folded in her lap. But her eyes were glittering, and the icy quality of her voice caused both men to tense suspiciously. ''I mean, as you said, it was only a few jars of a contaminated product, and how many illnesses—fifteen, twenty? No fatalities, yet, am I right? Certainly people are overreacting. Just because a three-month-old infant lies helpless and suffering in a hospital room with a machine breathing for him and tubes feeding him—hell, that's no reason for anybody to get upset, is it?''

The sharp intake of breath that echoed her speech was like a sudden sharp flare of electric current; it left both men too shocked to speak for a second. It was, fortunately, Ray who recovered himself first. ''Good point, Jessie,'' he said hurriedly. ''We can't afford to ignore the emotional impact on the public where children are involved. We have to understand the psychological dynamics involved....''

His voice faded from Jessie's ear as she thought about the two years of her life she had dedicated to this campaign. She saw the soft-sell television spots she had designed, the sixty-second daytime TV ''A Talk with Dr. Lester'' commercials, cleverly designed as public service information spots. The frank, attractive brochures filled with questions and answers about baby care that had been distributed to pediatricians and obstetricians all over the country. Two years of her life had been spent teaching the public that Greenway was a name you could trust, the final authority on baby care, the only good and honest thing in a world filled with deception. They had even had to employ a full-time pediatrician and a staff of nurses to answer telephone calls from mothers who were concerned about everything from diaper rash to colic, and who turned to Greenway before they did their own pediatrician. Two years of her life had been devoted, waking and sleeping, to this corporation. Two years of her life directed at persuading the public to buy poisoned baby food.

Ray was saying, "I know this may sound drastic, but if this thing goes the way I think it will—the way I'm afraid it will—we should seriously consider repackaging and relabeling...."

And it all made a perfectly logical, very predictable sort of sense. A deep, long-awaited calm settled over her as everything fell into place at once. Conditions change, circumstances change, but the only thing that really matters is what is inside the package. Eventually the glitter will begin to fade, like gold-plated leaf beneath the weight of time, and one is forced to take a long hard look at what lies beneath.

And rarely, very rarely, is one lucky enough to discover that the prize protected by all the layers of gilt is more valuable than gold.

"What do you think, Jessie?" The attention of both men was riveted on her; anxiety was in Ray's eyes, suspicion in Sheppard's.

Jessie smiled and got slowly and gracefully to her feet. The very calmness of her movement seemed to disturb the two men; the quiet confidence in her voice sounded eerie against the atmosphere of highly-charged emotions and hovering catastrophe. She said, "Obviously, the agency does have some obligation in this matter. We are the ones, after all, who insinuated Greenway into the confidence of the American public, and I think our next course of action is clear." There was a cautious relaxation in the eyes of Addison Sheppard that was quickly destroyed by her next words. "We must apologize," she pronounced calmly. "We have violated a public trust, and we have to take the responsibility. As for what I think of a man who would poison baby food..." She turned vaguely sorrowful eyes upon the man who was stuttering and twitching in incoherent incredulity, her voice was very quiet. "You don't really want to know."

She turned and left the office.

Jessie did not notice the odd look her secretary gave her as she returned to her own office. She did not know that for the first time in many years her eyes were clear, her step easy and purposeful, her smile genuine. She only wondered with a sort of peaceful amazement as she closed the door to her elegant, comfortably furnished office why it had taken so long. Five years of her life spent in pursuit of an empty dream, keeping her away from the only thing she had ever really wanted....

Her hand was steady as she picked up the telephone and punched out the number. She did not know what she was going to say to him, she had no speech prepared. She only knew that her heart was overflowing and he was the reason why....

"Gold Star Management."

Her voice was very calm. "This is Jessie McVey calling for Mr. Michaelson."

There was a slight pause. "I'm sorry, Ms McVey, he's not in."

A tingle of uneasiness rippled at her determination when she realized he might not want to talk to her. She could hardly blame him.... But it didn't matter. This one last time she had a firm hold on all that was important in her life, the one thing that really mattered, and she *would* talk to him. He had to know....

She inquired, "When do you expect him?"

"I'm afraid I don't know."

Jessie dug quickly for the name of the young man who had seemed so sympathetic the last time she called. She was not giving up. "Will you transfer me to Mr. Leonard please?"

When the crisp, friendly voice answered the phone, she identified herself and asked again for Keith. She was certain this man would at least tell her whether or not Keith was trying to avoid her, and if so, that he could be trusted to deliver a message.

"Sorry," was the answer, "he left New York early this morning." There was a pause and a shuffling of papers. "He didn't leave any messages...."

Jessie was not certain whether her short breath was from relief or disappointment. Perhaps it was only business that had called him away unexpectedly.... "Is he in Los Angeles?"

"Nooo..." There was amusement mingled with reluctance and perhaps a faint trace of embarrassment in his voice. "To tell you the truth, he didn't exactly tell any of us where he was going.... He should be checking in with one of the offices in a few days, though. You want to leave a message?"

The disappointment that crept through Jessie was cold and debilitating. Was it possible that he could just walk out of her life and become lost in the jungle again? No, she wouldn't let that happen. Somehow, someday, she would find him again, and when she did, no amount of time nor altered circumstances would keep them apart. But there simply wasn't much she could do about it now. "No," she said quietly. "I won't be here in a few days. Thank you for your help...."

A short breath. "Listen, it's hard to say, but he might be in Tennessee. He usually goes there when he gets like this...."

Something within Jessie quickened, like the sudden bright flare of sunshine through a dusty windowpane. "Nashville?" she said urgently, her heart speeding.

"No, it's someplace in the mountains, that's all I know. He goes there to get away from it all, you know? But it won't do you any good, because nobody can reach him down there, there's not even a telephone—"

"Thank you!" Jessie whispered, and she dropped the receiver back into the cradle. She sat there for a long moment, and it was as though the clear wash of sunshine had entered her body, her mind, her heart, and left them purged with its pulsing radiance. It was like stepping out of the shadows and looking into untroubled skies for the first time in her life, and for a moment the beauty of it was so dazzling she only wanted to sit there and soak it in. But the promise of the future was too compelling, and she had to move.

She was cleaning out her desk when Ray Jindrich burst into her office. There were only a few things she wanted to salvage from this part of her life—the sketch pad that she kept around for cartoon doodlings, a crystal candy dish Celia had given her one Christmas, a single blossom from the basket on her desk, which she snapped off and tucked into the buttonhole of her jacket.

Ray roared, "What the hell do you think you're doing? Do you realize what just happened up there? What has gotten into you?"

"Very simple, Ray." Jessie took her keys from her purse and laid them on the desk. "I want out. No," she smiled at him, as gently as she could. "I *am* out."

For just a second he was nonplussed. Clearly he could not bring himself to believe her, despite the strange calmness in her eyes that left no doubt she was, indeed, serious. "If I had any sense," he expostulated, "I'd be kicking your butt out the door! What the hell is this little display of dramatics, anyway? Do you know you almost lost us the biggest account we have—and got us threatened with a lawsuit as well? Fortunately," he grumbled, some of his fury dissolving into bluster beneath the unnerving complacency of her gaze, "I was able to smooth things over with Sheppard, so there's no reason for dramatic exits. Now put down your damn purse and get back behind that desk where you belong. We've got some serious strategy to plan."

She said quietly, "No, Ray." And she moved past him.

He whirled incredulously. "Jessie, you can't be serious! You wouldn't walk out on me now—we need you to pull us out of this thing! You can't just—"

Jessie stopped; she looked back at him thoughtfully but only vaguely concerned. She said, "Let me suggest that you give Charlene a shot at this, you might be surprised." And her smile was a little vague. "She's got what it takes to go far in this business."

"Wait a minute." Residual anger had faded into sharp concern and something almost like horror as he touched her arm. "Jessie, calm down, just think about what you're doing. Look, okay—" he dragged his hand roughly through his hair, trying to calm his tone "—you've been working too hard lately, I can see that. Maybe you're going through some kind of professional crisis, but that's okay, that will pass. Take a couple of weeks off. We can't really do anything until the furor dies down anyway, and you can go somewhere to re-group—the islands, lots of sun and rum, you'll see, all you need is a little vacation. . . ."

She shook her head firmly. "No, Ray, I need a per-manent vacation." Her voice gentled as she looked at him, trying to make him understand. "Ray, don't you see, I don't belong here anymore. . . ." The softening of her voice made it seem as though the next words were spoken entirely to herself. "I never really did."

"Jessie." The urgency in his voice forcefully turned to gentleness as he restrained her. "As a friend, okay? I'm talking to you as a friend. If you walk out on us now, you'll never work in this business again. You're too talented to do that to your life; you have too much invested in this career to just throw it all away. For God's sake, what will you do?"

She returned his troubled gaze with clear, calm self-confidence. "I'm a pretty good political cartoonist," she said. "I've got a lot to say that people need to hear. I'm going to give it a shot."

His incredulity turned to horror. "Good God, wom-an, do you have any idea what that market's like? You'll starve!"

Her smile was tender and came from very far away. "There are worse things," she said.

"Jessie!" The desperation in his voice made her pause at the door. "At least—tell me what you're going to do. Where are you going?"

There was only a moment of the softening silence between them before she opened the door. "Home," she said simply, and she closed the door behind her.

Jessie's plane arrived in Knoxville at eight o'clock the next morning. She rented a car, and it did not occur to her that he might not still be there, that she might be wrong altogether about his destination.... It didn't even occur to her that she might not remember the way. None of that really seemed important. She only knew that she was going back where she belonged, following the dictates of a heart that had been too long silenced.

She knew there was a very real possibility that he might not want to see her. As she concentrated her attention upon keeping the little car upon the winding mountain trails she tried not to lose her courage. She knew she had done everything within her power to destroy his love over the years; she had no right to ask for a second chance or even forgiveness. She knew that there was probably no place for her in his life now, but she owed it to herself, and to what they once had been, to tell him, to explain to him...to try.

Jessie's heart stopped as she came upon the clearing, the dilapidated little cabin with its peeling shingles and its field of daisies nodding in the warm morning breeze. It started beating again as she saw a mud-splattered blue Blazer parked behind it. Still, she could have been wrong; it could be someone else using the cabin.... And then the door opened, and he came out.

He was wearing low-slung jeans and a checked cotton

shirt, which he had not buttoned. His hair was tousled and his face shadowed with a stubble of beard; it occurred to Jessie that, as it was only a little after ten, the sound of her car might have woken him up. He had come here to rest, after all; he probably did not want to see her.... Her heart was a tight, barely pulsing knot in her chest as she got out of the car and slowly crossed the rickety footbridge.

Whatever emotion might have been in his face had been brought under control by the time she reached him. There was only cautious curiosity there, a sort of hesitant disbelief as he looked at her, and he said simply, "Hello."

She smiled, tightly and nervously. The morning sun warmed the helmet of her hair, and a sudden breeze scattered a dusting of dandelion seeds before her face. She said rather weakly, "Surprise."

Keith lifted an eyebrow; the glare of the sun in his eyes made them impossible to read. "That's an understatement. I thought I was the only one in the world who knew how to find this place."

Again, she smiled nervously. "Actually, I didn't have any trouble at all. No wrong turns." For perhaps the first time in her life. "Funny the things you remember, isn't it?"

"Yes," he agreed quietly, and the morning stillness rang with the unspoken truths behind that statement. Jessie could feel the nervous racing of her pulse, she tried to keep her breathing calm and steady. She wondered if he had any idea how badly she wanted to step into his arms, to rest her head against the silky warmth of his bare chest.... She wondered what he was thinking.

She looked around her quickly, but the brightness

she had intended to inject into her voice came out as wistfulness instead. "It hasn't changed a bit," she said.

"Some things never do." Again the words faded into an echoing silence, which was broken only by the background trilling of katydids and the scuffle of small animals, the breeze that swept across the buoyant heads of daisies and the rhythmic lapping of the green-blue lake against the shore. Jessie felt herself melting beneath the intensity of a gaze she could not read, yearning and anticipation swelling within her and focusing on the need to hold him, to feel him against her, to tell him with her hands and her lips and her body what was bursting within her heart....

He said abruptly, "I bought this place as soon as I could." His gaze left her and wandered over the landscape. "The lake, the surrounding acreage...a man needs a place to call home, you know?"

"Yes," she whispered. "I know."

"I was going to build a house here...." He looked back at her, and she knew his mind was not on his words. "Never seemed to have the time...."

The breeze dragged a wisp of hair over her eyes; she pushed it back. She could not delay any longer. She must pull together all her courage and face him with her mistakes and inadequacies, her regrets and her sorrow; she must be prepared to discover rejection and contend with emptiness.... She said, "Keith, I'm sorry to intrude on you like this." She spoke quickly, urgently. "I know you came here to be alone and—and you probably don't want to see me again." She determinedly kept her voice steady. "But you said—that last night, you said if I ever needed a friend..."

"It's okay." His reassurance was swift, his tone

gentle. He stepped forward and the warmth of his hand rested lightly upon her shoulder. "Let's talk."

Let's talk. What beautiful, enduring words, words that tugged at the strings of her soul and drew her outward to him.... How desperately she had needed to hear them from him today.

He led her toward the lake; she sat down upon the stubbly grass, and he lowered his lean form beside her, sitting close but not touching her. He looped his arms about his upraised knees and gazed out over the lake, encouraging her with his silence to take her time. And Jessie needed time. How did one put into words what could only be spoken by the heart? Yet he waited, quietly, patiently, and she had to try.

She drew her legs up before her Indian-style and absently plucked a daisy, removing the petals one by one as she spoke. He loves me, he loves me not.... She could not look at him. "A long time ago," she said, straining to keep her voice steady as her eyes were focused on the slowly diminishing petals of the flower, "you asked me what I would do with the stars if I had them. I didn't understand you then, or perhaps I did and I just didn't want to admit it. I was reaching so hard for the things that I thought were important in life that I couldn't see I was throwing away real happiness with both hands.... You were right about the glitter, Keith. I guess I knew that the minute I set foot in New York, but I spent five years trying to avoid admitting it to myself, and in the process nearly destroyed my life and all that I valued." She took a shaky breath and pulled off another petal. "It was a close call, but I finally got my priorities straight and—and I've left."

That was it. That was all there was to say—or almost

all. And in the silence that followed Jessie felt a bleak despair bubbling up through the center of her as she thought, he doesn't care. Why should he care? What difference does it make to him what I've decided to do with my life when his own has taken him in such a drastically different direction?....

"So," he said after a moment, "what are you going to do?"

Was that polite interest in his voice, or perhaps something more?... She took another steadying breath and replied, "Look for a simpler life. Do the things that are really important to me, that give me satisfaction. I thought...I'd try to break into the cartoon market. I know it's a long shot, but it doesn't really matter if I'm successful—materially, I mean. What matters is that I will be doing the thing I do best, something that has a value that can't be measured in dollars...something that's important. And..." Her closing statement sounded almost lame. Still, she had left the most important things unsaid. "I'm going to move back down here. I always liked Tennessee."

A fat honeybee landed indolently on Jessie's dismembered flower; she brushed it away and determinedly pulled off another petal. Only the thundering of her heart filled up the silence. She had to go on. Her whole body was trembling as though from a cold draft, and her voice was tight and shaky, but she had to tell him. She had to try, this one last time. "Keith, I—I know it's too late for us, we can't go back in time... t-too much has happened between us, and we can't pick up where we left off.... I—I didn't come here to fling myself at you or to—to play on your sympathy or anything." Her muscles ached with the effort to keep them from shuddering, and her throat was so tight the words were choking there. "I—just wanted to let you know—to tell you that you'll always be a part of me... that nothing can change and no one will take away... that I'll always love you...."

"What?"

The abruptness of the exclamation sent her startled gaze flying to his. In his eyes she saw an expression sharp with intensity and dark with shock, and the pain that flooded her was more acute than any she had ever known. For a moment the colors and the brightness blurred together in one burning wash and a single hot tear rolled down her cheek. He was angry and she did not blame him, but she had to say it: "I know I have no right to say that," she choked, "I don't expect you to believe me—but it's true, I never stopped loving you—"

"Lady," he said quietly, "why the hell did you wait so long to tell me?" His face was harsh and his eyes were dark with a barely contained emotion that burned in their depths like a kindling fire as he went on roughly, "You never said it. Do you have any idea what kind of hell I went through all these years, knowing how I felt about you but not knowing what was going on inside you? Why..." His voice softened as he heard the muffled catch of her sob. "Why didn't you tell me before?"

Jessie could only shake her head wordlessly, and a single tear splashed on the hand that cupped the flower and glistened there. She should have said it sooner; there were so many things she should have said and done sooner, but now it was too late....

His hand came slowly forward to cover hers; he plucked off the last petal. "He loves you," he said quietly.

Her breath froze in her body as she looked at him, a moment arrested in wonder and cautious disbelief. The blood stopped flowing through her veins and the tears drained away into nothing, for it was there in his eyes—the wanting and the tenderness, the steady adoration, the clear, unadulterated truth. And he said gently, "What do you think *forever* means?"

She was in his arms, broad muscles straining against her breasts and pounding the rhythm of his heart into hers, his warmth engulfing her and his unshaven face scratchy against her cheek. She tasted the sundrenched flesh of his neck intermingled with the salt of her tears, and his voice was husky and breathless in her ear. "I fell in love with you that first night you took me in from the storm, and I knew it wasn't the kind of feeling that would go away because I didn't even care if you loved me back.... I just wanted to be with you and make you happy—it's what I still want. Even when you were gone...through all these years, there was an emptiness there that nothing and no one could fill, because it was reserved for you, waiting for you.... Darlin'." Tenderly his lips moved to brush against her wet face. "Why the tears? It's over now, we're together and nothing will ever separate us again...."

She tightened her arms about him, pressing herself into him, helpless against the gulping sobs, the great cleansing power of tears too long locked inside. "No, let me cry," she whispered brokenly into his neck. "It feels so good to cry."

They were lying in the grass when at last her tears had spent themselves and left her feeling weary and renewed. Her head was resting against the silky warmth of his chest where his shirt bared it, and his arms were about her waist; the morning sun fell over them like a hot blanket. The scent of clover was in her nostrils, and her field of vision was awash with yellow daisies. She could have stayed like that forever, listening to the steady thump of his heart and the faraway drone of insects, but there was one more thing she had to know. Her hand tightened upon his chest, her fingers gathering a swatch of crisp dark hair, and there was a note of uncertainty to her voice as she inquired, "Keith... when you left New York... were you trying to get away from me? Did you... ever plan to see me again?"

The muscles of his chest rippled as he bent his lips to her hair. "Walk away from you the moment I'd found you?" he returned incredulously. "Darlin', you know me better than that—I'm too fond of controlling other people's destinies to turn my back on a challenge." There was a sober note to his voice as he lay back down and added, "When I first saw you again there was no doubt in my mind about letting you just walk away. How could there have been? I thought I could ease you back into trusting me again, gradually let you grow comfortable with me and maybe even teach you to care for me a little...." The tightening of his arm upon her waist soothed away her instinctive protest. "But that night in your apartment I realized I didn't have as much control as I thought I did over my own emotions; I didn't have the patience for a long courtship. I was afraid of scaring you off again; I had to back away and try to cool down. But no, love, I had no intention of giving up... I never would have."

She raised her face to his, and the kiss she gave him was as warm as sunshine and as pure as childhood. But within moments the kiss deepened with the flare of passion too long ignored, the kindling flame that each of them alone had the power to ignite in the other. The flood of heat that weakened Jessie's limbs made the day seem chilly in comparison; the delight of discovery shone with dazzling colors behind her closed eyes and made all of nature's abundance pale in comparison. His hands roamed restlessly over her body as the urgency of her kisses played over his face—the stubbly lashes, the coarse cheek, the smooth brow, and the sweep of his nose, and his breath was hot and unsteady against her mouth as he whispered, "Darlin', I feel control slipping again...." His lips brushed the corner of her eye, moved to nibble at her earlobe, spurring her own erratic breathing. "And if I don't make love to you within the next three minutes I can't be responsible for the consequences...."

Her hands moved over his arms to circle his shoulders, gathering and kneading the taut muscles there. She arched her neck to receive the slow, warm movement of his lips, and she murmured huskily, "Why wait that long?" Her eyes shone and sparkled with the clarity of the mountain lake, the surety of the future.

"Two reasons." His lips moved upward again, over the curve of her jaw, her pointed chin, to stop with a swift breath upon the open invitation of her mouth. "First." A warm touch upon the corner of her lips. "I'm so greedy for you I'm not willing to share even a small part of my feast with our little friends of the insect persuasion, and secondly..." His arms tightened about her, slowly he drew her to her feet. "I need to talk to you."

She stood there in the firm circle of his arms, every part of her body touching his or brushing against him, quivering with joy and anticipation and bathed in a contentment like none she had ever known. "So talk," she whispered, and touched her lips to his chin.

She felt a slight quivering in his own muscles as he drew her close one more time; she heard the unsteadiness of his breath against her ear. Then he loosened his hold so that he could look down at her. The deep light in his eyes drew her, and the tenderness of his curving smile caressed her, seeming to demand that her fingers come up to touch it. She loved every angle and plane of that face, the coarse scratchiness that brushed against her fingers and the sweet softness of his lips, the dark swoop of the brow and the clearwater eyes beneath. She whispered, "Three minutes and counting."

There was a sober tone to his voice, though the light in his eyes did not fade as he said, "Jessie, I know you've had a rough time of it, and I want to do everything in my power to ease the hurt you've suffered these past years, to help heal the scars...." How like him to concern himself only with her needs, never thinking of the pain she had caused him. She had never loved him more. It would take a lifetime to tell him how much she loved him. "Darlin', I lead a fast-paced life," he told her gently. "I have people depending on me and commitments to keep, and I know that on the surface that sounds like everything you're trying to escape from, but it's the life I've chosen, just as you, now, are choosing your own way. Things are not as frantic as they used to be; most of my people are on their feet now and I'm able to spend more time with sound design, which keeps me home more...."

She stilled his words with one finger laid lightly across his lips. "It doesn't matter, Keith." Once before she had let circumstances keep them apart. Now the roles were reversed: He was the one who held power and success and she sought the quiet life, but the important thing was that each of them was comfortable with their choices, and surface considerations would no longer blind her to the value of the only true and perfect thing she had ever had in her life. She said softly, "Two minutes."

The softening of his smile wrapped around her like a warm glow. Yet still there was a touch of uncertainty in his tone as he said, "This may come under the heading of an Indecent Proposition... but I'm not glued to Los Angeles, you know. I told you I was planning to build a house here, and if I do—and keeping in mind that the last time I asked you to marry me you ran away—will you live with me?"

"That is a very indecent proposition," she told him. Her eyes never left his face; they were sure, clear, unreserved. "I've had enough of those to last a lifetime. Can't you do any better?"

The moment was frozen in his indrawn breath, the anxious searching in his eyes. He said huskily, "How do you feel about a large-scale public commitment with all the trappings of permanence and white lace?"

"How do you feel about the words 'Till death do us part'?" she whispered, and she leaned toward him.

"I love them," he murmured just before his mouth covered hers, and there was only the sound of their mingled breaths for a long, long time.

"One minute," she murmured at last, her hands buried in the silky depths of his hair, her parted lips taking in deep gulps of the warm, masculine fragrance of his neck.

"Thirty seconds," was his somewhat breathless reply, and he bent to scoop her into his arms.

The warm morning sun moved to an afternoon glow, spilling over rumpled sheets and silhouetting the languorous dance of moving forms in the exquisite ballet of love, lying at last like flakes of gold upon shimmering bodies wrapped in adoration, gleaming in her tousled hair and from the drowsy depths of his eyes.

"I think I could learn to like this," she murmured, inching even closer with a tightening of her arm about his chest.

"You'd better." His fingers threaded through her hair, a light caught in the depths of his eyes as he watched the shimmering pattern it made across the pillow. "I have a feeling it's going to last for a long, long time."

"Forever," she whispered, and turned to draw him down to her again.

"No." His voice was like honey, his touch the power that turned the day to gold. Slowly he closed her eyes with a lingering kiss. And his answer was, "Longer."

Yours FREE, with a home subscription to

HARLEQUIN SUPERROMANCE T.M.

Now you never have to miss reading the newest **HARLEQUIN SUPERROMANCES**... because they'll be delivered right to your door.

Start with your **FREE** LOVE BEYOND DESIRE. You'll be enthralled by this powerful love story...from the moment Robin meets the dark, handsome Carlos and finds herself involved in the jealousies, bitterness and secret passions of the Lopez family. Where her own forbidden love threatens to shatter her life.

Your **FREE** LOVE BEYOND DESIRE is only the beginning. A subscription to **HARLEQUIN SUPERROMANCE** lets you look forward to a long love affair. Month after month, you'll receive four love stories of heroic dimension. Novels that will involve you in spellbinding intrigue, forbidden love and fiery passions.

You'll begin this series of sensuous, exciting contemporary novels...written by some of the top romance novelists of the day...with four every month.

And this big value...each novel, almost 400 pages of compelling reading...is yours for only $2.50 a book. Hours of entertainment every month for so little. Far less than a first-run movie or pay-TV. Newly published novels, with beautifully illustrated covers, filled with page after page of delicious escape into a world of romantic love...delivered right to your home.

Begin a long love affair with

HARLEQUIN SUPERROMANCE. ™

Accept LOVE BEYOND DESIRE **FREE**.

Complete and mail the coupon below today!

- -

FREE! Mail to: Harlequin Reader Service

In the U.S.
2504 West Southern Avenue
Tempe, AZ 85282

In Canada
P.O. Box 2800, Postal Station "A"
5170 Yonge St., Willowdale, Ont. M2N 5T5

YES, please send me FREE and without any obligation my
HARLEQUIN SUPERROMANCE novel, LOVE BEYOND DESIRE. If you do
not hear from me after I have examined my FREE book, please send me
the 4 new **HARLEQUIN SUPERROMANCE** books every month as soon
as they come off the press. I understand that I will be billed only $2.50 for
each book (total $10.00). There are no shipping and handling or any
other hidden charges. There is no minimum number of books that I have
to purchase. In fact, I may cancel this arrangement at any time.
LOVE BEYOND DESIRE is mine to keep as a FREE gift, even if I do not
buy any additional books. 134 BPS KANC

NAME _____ (Please Print)

ADDRESS _____ APT. NO. _____

CITY _____

STATE/PROV. _____ ZIP/POSTAL CODE _____

SIGNATURE (If under 18, parent or guardian must sign.)

SUP-SUB-22

This offer is limited to one order per household and not valid to present
subscribers. Prices subject to change without notice.
Offer expires October 31, 1984

BOOK MATE PLUS®

The perfect companion for all larger books! Use it to hold open cookbooks... or while reading in bed or tub. Books stay open flat, or prop upright on an easellike base... pages turn without removing see-through strap. And pockets for notes and pads let it double as a handy portfolio!

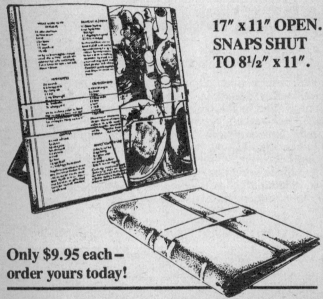

17″ x 11″ OPEN. SNAPS SHUT TO 8½″ x 11″.

Only $9.95 each — order yours today!

Available now. Send your name, address, and zip or postal code, along with a check or money order for just $9.95, plus 75¢ for postage and handling, for a total of $10.70 (New York & Arizona residents add appropriate sales tax) payable to Harlequin Reader Service to:

Harlequin Reader Service

In U.S.
P.O. Box 52040
Phoenix, AZ 85072-9988

In Canada
649 Ontario Street
Stratford, Ont. N5A 6W2